CH00793903

IF I LOVED YOU

Regency Rogues: Redemption, Book 2

Rebecca Ruger

Published by Rebecca Ruger, 2020.

Chapter One

Emma Ainsley picked up the tray laden with mugs of ale and cautiously made her way through the crowded taproom of the King's Arms Inn. A deluge of rain had driven many a traveler inside this night. While she might be happy with the extra money she would make in tips, she'd rather have been left to her usual duties as the inn's chambermaid. But that same rain had prevented the regular girl, Alice, from getting in tonight and Mr. Smythe, the proprietor, had tapped Emma to fill in. She'd done so before, but rarely and never with so heavy a crowd. Mr. Smythe had sensed her reticence and assured her that he'd let no man put a hand to her. Alice, with her saucy ways and flame red hair, happily allowed these infractions to garner more tips.

Feeling somewhat assured that at least one of Mr. Smythe's eyes was on her at most times, Emma now delivered three mugs to a table of rough looking sailors, taking up their coin without meeting their eyes, and then two more tankards were set upon another table, this one settled by two nabobs, who didn't bother to meet Emma's eye.

The last tankard on her tray belonged to the elderly gentleman at the back of the taproom. He was kindly and had spoken politely when Emma had asked what he wished. Dressed as he was in fine clothes with a perfectly set cravat, Emma knew he was quality. Perhaps even minus such rich garments she'd have known; this man held himself aloof, had a superiority about him that only money could beget. Carefully, Emma set the mug before the man, thinking that he reminded her of her own father, though that dear man had been gone now more than ten years.

"Here you are, miss," the man said and pressed a generous amount into her hand.

"Thank you, sir," she said and met his eye. Friendly blue eyes they were, though tired looking, sad even. "The rain brought you in?"

He nodded, sipping from the mug. "Carriage stuck in the puddles up the road," he told her when he'd swallowed. "Getting on to midnight so I imagine I'll be here all night."

"Mama Smythe puts out a good and hearty breakfast, sir. Come morning, with your belly full, you'll be glad you had to stay."

The man glanced up again at Emma and smiled at her attempt to console him.

"Now what's a fresh face, young thing like you doing working here with all these ruffians?" His voice was raspy, as if he were actually older than he appeared.

"I don't normally work the taproom, sir," Emma answered. "But the rains kept the usual girl away, so they pulled me from the chambers."

"They should have left you there, girl," the man said with a shake of his head. "Tell your man behind the bar to watch those ones over there." He lifted his tankard and his eyes to a four top nearer to the bar. Emma considered the four men, all young and dressed as farmers—but not local, for she'd never seen them before. They'd bothered her not at all as of yet, so she didn't know what had caused this man to be suspicious of them. "Sure enough, they do appear uninteresting, eh?" This man asked of her now.

Emma shrugged her shoulders, thinking that indeed they did. "If you need something else, my name is Emma," she offered then, though it was certainly not her practice to give up her name. She left the gentleman then and glanced around the crowded room, gauging who might need another round. As everyone seemed settled for a little while at least, Emma approached Mr. Smythe and asked of him if she might take a few minutes to check in upstairs.

As was ever the case, Mr. Smythe—though fair and honest as an employer—gave her a long-suffering sigh and a shake of his head. "I'll give ye two minutes, girl. Too much fretting, ye do, for one so young."

"Thank you," Emma said, leaving her tray at the end of the bar to race up the back stairs to the rooms she herself kept at the end of the hall. True, it was not the ideal circumstance for her, but she'd little choices when it came to dwellings that she could afford. She drew a key from her apron pocket and slid it into the lock, opening the door slowly as not to waken Bethany. Tiptoeing in the darkness, as she'd not ever dare to leave candles burning, Emma made her way to the crib at the far corner of the room. She peeked over the rails and breathed easier when she saw that Bethany was sleeping as soundly as she ever did.

The baby—Emma still thought of her as a baby, though she was nearly two years old now—was on her stomach with her legs drawn up underneath her, her fine blonde hair, curly and delicate, covering most of her face. There was something to be said about a child in slumber, Emma thought, recalling that this very peacefully sleeping and angelic appearing little girl had certainly put Emma through her paces today. She was at an age where trouble seemed to follow her everywhere and only this morning Emma had wakened to find the child sitting next to her upon the narrow mattress she occupied, having climbed from the crib for the first time.

As much as Emma enjoyed watching Bethany grow and change and become more and more her own little person, sometimes this child certainly did frighten her with her fearlessness.

But she loved her so. Bethany was the beginning and end of Emma's family, as they had only each other, and Emma had vowed that this child would never live a day and not know she was loved. Softly, she smoothed her hand over the little girl's back and then left the room as quietly as she had entered, locking the door once more behind her.

Returned once more to the taproom, Emma again made rounds with her tray, taking orders and delivering drinks. She did notice—as the elderly gentleman in the rear had warned—that the four farmers near the bar seemed to become louder and more unpleasant as the night progressed. But she was happy to observe that their increasing nastiness was not directed at her, but only amongst themselves. As she approached them for perhaps the sixth or seventh time with a full tray of tankards, she was aware that an argument had erupted between two of those men. It had begun with only verbal slurs being slung, but as Emma set their order upon the tall table, the two arguing men did stand, thrusting their chests at each other.

Emma had lived here at the King's Arms long enough to know when a fight was brewing and made haste to leave the drinks, take the coin, and get away. This scrum escalated faster than others, however, despite Mr. Smythe's shouted warnings from behind the bar that he would tolerate none of this, and the entire foursome were throwing punches before Emma could completely get away. Using her tray more as a shield, a grimace tightening her face at the heightened level of noise and action, Emma tried to duck away from the skirmish and reach the safety of the bar. She was peripherally aware that others around had come to their feet and that the huge form of Mr. Smythe was closing in.

But Emma, with the tray partially blocking her view, had not moved quick enough to remove herself from harm's way, and when the fists began to jab seriously, she caught someone's badly thrown punch to the side of her head. Stunned and dazed from the force of the blow, she went down hard, falling to her knees, the tray dropped from her hands. She slapped her palms against the floor just in time to keep herself from falling further onto her face, but this was poor timing as well, for those long and thin fingers were crunched under the heavy boot of one of the stumbling combatants.

At this she cried out, knowing immediately that something had broken within her hand, the sickening sound of a cracking bone heard even above the ruckus of the melee. Cradling her hand against her chest, she tried to scooch away just as two strong hands grabbed her under her arms from behind and lifted her completely and swiftly away from the fray.

When she was lifted up onto a stool, far removed from danger, she turned to find the elderly gentleman behind her. Standing now, he was taller than she might have guessed, his shoulders broad and square despite his age. Still stunned, Emma only sat there as he carefully took her injured hand into his much larger ones to examine the damage. She moaned at even this soft touch, the pain nearly unbearable, but did not pull her hand away. She watched as he separated her index finger from the others, noticing the instant redness and swelling about the digit.

"'Tis broke, all right," he observed, not having to raise his deep voice much. By now, Mr. Smythe, with the help of some local patrons, had removed the offending party from the premises. The gentleman lifted his graying head just as Mr. Smythe strode to them. "Have you a doctor nearby?"

Looking very concerned, Mr. Smythe cringed a bit as he spied Emma's wounded finger but shook his head in answer to the question. "Not one around save ol' Doc Beck," he said and then chewed his lip thoughtfully. "This time o' night though, he's usually gone too far into 'is cups to be of any use to anyone."

The gentleman looked none too pleased by this sorry statement and turned again to consider Emma's finger. "Perhaps if my carriage were freed by now, I could send for my own physician—or better yet, drive you there myself," he said, gaining Emma's gaze now.

"Oh, I couldn't leave, sir," she refused immediately. "Perhaps just a bit of ice and— "

"Child," the gentleman interrupted, "ice will not set the break. This needs immediate attention." He turned again to Mr. Smythe, his polite manner thus far evaporating. "You, sir, oughtn't to have this child working in such a fashion—no matter the circumstances," he finished angrily when the proprietor looked as if he might defend himself. "She is too small and fine for such a seedy chore as serving the taproom."

"Sir," Emma cut in, unwilling to see Mr. Smythe scolded when he had always been so fair and tolerant, "you shouldn't find fault with Mr. Smythe. The rains here are to blame—and those men who fought—that is all."

But the gentleman shook his head, not at all in agreement but perhaps unwilling to pursue this when he was concerned more for her broken finger. The condition of his birth and up-bringing, and indeed, his present position in life were then un-mistakably apparent as he began to issue orders in such a tone that it was obvious he had never been gainsaid.

"Send a man to fetch my coachman from up the north road," he instructed the attentive proprietor. "He'll be found with the three-wheeled carriage. Tell him to fetch immediately Doctor McNair—rouse him from his bed, if need be—and convey him here posthaste." He withdrew several notes from his pocket and handed them to Mr. Smythe. "Here, this should get it done quickly enough." He then removed his attention from Mr. Smythe, considering the task under way, and focused again on Emma. He had set her hand carefully onto her lap and now placed a hand at her shoulder, which drew her gaze again to his. "Where do you reside, child?"

Emma lifted her good hand to point toward the ceiling. "I have a room abovestairs."

"Then let us get you there to await the doctor." With that said, he made to scoop her up in his arms but Emma was quick to protest. She jumped off the stool and proclaimed herself fit to walk, though spared a moment to wonder if this elderly man, de-spite his still strapping appearance, could have actually borne her up the stairs in his arms.

Gingerly holding her hand, she began to leave the taproom, aware—only somewhat nervously—that this very solicitous man was following her.

"Have you family about?" The gentleman asked as they reached the door to Emma's room.

Opening the door, listening for any sign that Bethany was awake, Emma answered, "I only have Bethany." She held the door that the man might follow her inside, deciding cautiously to keep the door wide open, and then indicated the crib at the far corner of the small room. She watched his eyes widen before he moved nearer to the baby's bed to glance down with something close to wonder at the sleeping tot.

"You've a child," he said, turning to Emma to consider her, "and yet you don't seem much more than a child yourself."

She detected something in his tone but could not say if this were censure or surprise. She normally did not explain her situation to strangers, but there was about this kind man an air that invited her to make clear her circumstance. "Bethany is my sister's child—Gretchen died giving birth to her. We haven't other family, our parents having been gone now for nearly ten years, so 'tis only Bethany and I that remain."

This news seemed to take him aback. "And the child's father?" He asked expectantly but seemed not shocked by her response.

Emma shrugged to indicate she hadn't a clue whom that man might be and watched the man nod in acceptance of this. After a moment, in which time he passed a cursory glance around the meager accommodations, the man said, "Seems not an ideal place to raise a child."

As her finger began to throb in earnest, Emma again cradled her left hand to her bosom. She knew he spoke truth, in fact had considered this often herself, but she hadn't yet figured out a way to advance her circumstance. And, too, the Smythes and the King's Arms Inn was truly the only family and home she could ever recall. The Smythes were good to her and expected little more in return than a hard day's work; and they adored the baby and were helpful and tolerant in all regards to Bethany's care.

In response then to his voiced concern, Emma said wishfully, "I would hope one day to have quarters of my own, perhaps a little house for just the two of us, or rooms taken in an establishment that might see less...um, traffic and such. But for right now, this suits us fine." When his thoughtful eyes remained on her fixedly for another moment, Emma said nervously, "You needn't stay, sir. It is very kind of you to send for your own doctor but he might be a while yet. I'd hate to keep you from your own bed."

"Emma, girl, 'tis no trouble to me. I'd rather wait and be assured that your finger is set properly."

She guessed he might have said as much. "Please sit, then," she offered, and joined him at the small table where Bethany and she often took their meals. "I—I don't even know your name and you have done such a kindness for me. I have some monies saved—I will repay what you've put out to fetch the doctor and—"

But he waved a hand in refusal of this. "My girl, I am Benedict, the Earl of Lindsey, though I insist you call me Michael, and your monies should be saved for your plans for you and that beautiful child."

Emma nearly gasped at such informality—the very idea of addressing a lord by his given name seemed so preposterous—but he chuckled over this, his dark gray eyes seeming to lighten.

"I've reached an age, Emma, where titles and wealth seem to have little meaning if you've not the character to back them. What makes me so remarkable a person that you must address me as 'my lord'? Nothing, I say, but what society deems my illustrious birth." He spared a moment to gauge her reaction, but Emma sat mutely and he continued. "And wealth—what of it?

Why should I not visit some helpfulness upon you? Clearly I can afford to summon a doctor with coin, and you cannot. It seems a small thing to do to assist you when already I can attest that you are a good and charitable person. So satisfy an old man's need to do good finally and let it be."

Emma thought him charming, his tone level and agreeable and not at all preachy. She didn't like the idea still of accepting his money but thought somehow that he seemed to need to do this and then could only think to say, "You are not old."

He laughed outright at this but was prevented from commenting upon her remark as Mr. Smythe appeared then in the open doorway and announced to Emma that the man who entered behind him was Doctor McNair. Mr. Smythe delivered this news while keeping a watchful and suspicious eye on the earl.

Lord Benedict stood and greeted the doctor, who set his black bag upon the table where Emma sat. The earl explained what had happened and instructed the doctor, who seemed very professional and not at all what Emma was used to in the country doctors she knew, that he wanted the finger set properly that she might have no lasting or damaging effects from shoddiness.

Doctor McNair gave no indication that he was insulted by the earl's near-insinuation that any of his previous efforts might have ever been less than satisfactory. He went to work immediately, examining the injured finger over the top of his wire-rimmed spectacles.

This small activity within the room must have woken Bethany, for the child at that moment sat up in her crib and began to cry. Occupied as she was with the doctor—and wondering, too, how she might even lift the child presently—Emma called out in a cooing voice that all was well, hoping the baby might immediately go back to sleep. But these strangers in her room, and tapers lit to afford the doctor better lighting, pulled the toddler into complete wakefulness and in another minute, Bethany was standing up in the crib to survey the scene.

Lord Lindsey surprised Emma yet again, this time by striding over to the crib and picking up Bethany into his arms, seemingly unconcerned with baby drool and a possibly wet nappy spoiling his fine garb. Emma watched expectantly, waiting for the inevitable strangeness to grab hold of Bethany and bring about another cry. Yet the earl's tone had taken on a sing-song quality while he soothed her and bounced a bit and Bethany made no sound of protest at all. In fact, she appeared rather taken with this stranger as her fingers delved sleepily but curiously into the earl's finely knotted cravat.

"I think she likes me," the earl said then with a childish zeal and increased his efforts to entertain Bethany, who began to giggle at the rising tempo of his bounce.

Emma considered the earl's delight in her child and thought straight away that this man must be lonely. She didn't know how she reached this conclusion, having known him for so short a space of time, but she knew it to be true.

While the doctor set her finger into a small but well-crafted splint, Emma continued to watch the dancing pair and she knew somehow right then that they would be seeing more of this man, the earl.

Chapter Two

"One more bite," Emma cajoled, trying to get Bethany to finish her breakfast. They occupied a table in the empty dining room, the hour being so early and the inn being nearly vacant, that Mrs. Smythe had invited them then to dine here instead of in their cramped and small room. While Bethany carelessly chewed her eggs and porridge, Emma considered the hand holding the baby's spoon. The splint remained, the doctor having directed her to keep it on for at least three weeks; but the swelling had lessened, and the pain had definitely receded. She thought she might suffer no lasting impairment after all, as she was quite heartened by this small improvement after only one week.

Bethany babbled and chewed, her hands occupied by small wooden toys—a crudely carved pair of horses—made for her by Langdon, the shy young lad who tended the stables and yard. In another few minutes, when she had finished eating, Emma imagined she might be able to take her out of doors, as her duties for today would likely be small, with only two rooms let presently.

Emma lifted her head as the main dining room door opened, thinking that if guests were now coming down to breakfast, she would need to take herself and Bethany out of this room. When she saw instead the figure of the Earl of Lindsey step into the room, she knew she was only slightly surprised by this; she'd as much as expected him.

"Good morning, my lord," she greeted him warmly, as without his aid that night last week, her finger might indeed be in poorer condition.

"Good day to you as well, Emma," the earl said with a pleasant smile. He approached the table, his bearing tall and sure. "I thought I had given you leave to call me Michael."

"You had," she admitted with a smile, "but I've not reconciled in my head yet that this is at all appropriate. Please sit—have you broken your fast?"

The earl took the chair next to Bethany. "I have, thank you. And how are you, young miss?" He asked of Bethany, his voice rising an octave while he tousled her blonde hair.

Bethany babbled happily now to the earl, apparently recalling him though she had spent only one short—and sleepy—instance with him. The baby watched curiously as the earl took up one of her horses and pretended that it galloped about the table, landing with a high jump upon Bethany's arm. This sent her into fits of giggles, and she shoved the other piece at him that he might do the same.

"I hope that I expressed my thanks well enough last week, my lord," Emma said while he continued to amuse Bethany.

"Michael," he corrected, seemingly automatically. "And you did—endlessly. How is the finger, by the way?"

Emma lifted the digit for his perusal. "Much better already though it still pains me to bend it even slightly. But I've two more weeks with this very annoying splint."

He nodded at this and then met her eyes, and she thought, in the light of early morning, the gray was nearly blue, actually. "What brings you back to our little inn, my lord?" She asked with a pointed grin at the earl, still uneasy referring to so fine a person by his given name.

He smiled in return, shaking his head at her stubbornness. "I was curious as to your recovery." This answer seemed only half the truth and so Emma was not surprised when he added, "I dislike the idea of your arrangement here—you and the baby living and working in a common inn where incidents such as have befallen you might be a regular circumstance."

"You are very kind to consider our state of affairs so thoughtfully and with such concern," Emma allowed. She had never encountered a member of the elite who had shown such interest—let alone, care—in her very existence. "But you should know that it is unlikely I will see the inside of the taproom again. Mama Smythe was quite distressed when she'd heard of the incident and," Emma informed him with a small smile, "gave Mr. Smythe quite a time of it, as if it were his fault."

"But it was," the earl contended firmly and with little charity for Mr. Smythe, "though I came here not to castigate the man." Again, he trotted the figure of the horse over Bethany's arm, smiling delightedly at her thrill. "I came here to offer you a better position."

Emma promptly stiffened, her eyes suddenly wary. Instantly, her sister Gretchen's circumstance, her very hopes surrounding so many interested males, came to mind. She'd not have thought of this kind man—

The earl held up a hand to stop the unpleasant direction of her thoughts. "No, my girl, I offer nothing nefarious—only a betterment for you and Bethany." Upon gleaning that Emma remained cautious, nearly ready for outrage, he clarified further, "I only thought to put you up in a small house—no, no, dear, not for those purposes. You had mentioned that was a hope of yours, to have your own home. Expecting nothing in return but perhaps a friendship, I would like to give you that."

Emma was stunned. Still guarded about his true intent, but more shocked than anything. "Why would you want to do that?" She asked what was foremost in her mind.

"Because it would please me to do so," he said with a shrug, as if it were that simple. "Because, my girl, it unsettles me to consider what might further befall you, and one day this beautiful child, should you remain here. Sure, the Smythes would try their best to prevent any misdeed from happening, but you—I think you have no idea how your type of...innocence draws such attention, truth be told. I think you haven't any idea that one day a man or men will not be able to resist the very temptation you present. I'm shocking you, I know. But, Emma, I sat at that table in the taproom and I watched as they ogled you. Their fear of your Mr. Smythe will only protect you so far. One day, someone will risk Smythe's wrath and you will be hurt."

He was frightening her. In truth, Emma rarely stepped foot inside the bar that she was able to count these occasions on only one hand since the beginning of this year. She had an inkling of what he inferred but hadn't any real idea of the complete calamity that might become of it. "My lord, I appreciate that you are anxious over my circumstance here, but I insist that I am in no danger, truly."

"You are naïve if you believe that."

"I've spent half my life here," she told him, trying to dissuade him from this notion of impending catastrophe. "In all those years—while Gretchen lived, and since—I've not encountered any more trouble than I might find at any residence or position."

The earl shook his head sadly. "It seems to me, my dear, that you've only been fortunate, but that this luck cannot continue. I only wish to circumvent the possibilities."

Emma placed her hand over his, sitting on the tabletop. "I don't know a more generous soul than you—to offer this when you know me not at all. I truly do thank you for your thoughts and your desire to help us. But I must still refuse, as I never intend to rely upon another for my very well-being."

Michael Benedict seemed not so much angry at this, as he did resigned to her obstinate insistence upon self-reliance. Almost as an afterthought, he added softly, meaningfully, "You know, my dear, what happened to your sister is also a possible consequence—if you weren't careful."

Emma responded to this very thoughtfully. "I mourn my sister daily, my lord. But I have never looked upon Bethany as a misfortune or a misdeed. She was simply meant to be."

The dining room door opened again and this time it did admit several guests of the inn and Emma was then forced to excuse herself and Bethany, bidding a polite goodbye to the earl.

Only two days after that, the earl returned to the inn, this time inviting Emma and Bethany out for a drive in his fine carriage. The day was sunny and mild for early May and the earl confessed to Emma—when she hesitated while considering his invitation—that his Landau carriage, with its removable top, was new and he was quite proud to show it off a bit.

Emma, believing this to be a falsehood, supposing that the earl hadn't a self-important or conceited bone in his body, accepted anyway as Bethany looked once again as if she had taken quite nicely to this man. And so Mama Smythe gave her leave to depart for the afternoon and the earl bundled Emma and Bethany into his vehicle, sitting across from them on the very comfortable leather seats. They headed into Lambeth, where on Saturdays, there was always the open market in the square, and the earl was delighted to usher Emma and Bethany about, carrying Bethany himself most of the time. Dismissing Emma's admonitions, the earl purchased a baby doll for Bethany from an overpriced vendor, the figure's head and body being made of porcelain and the clothes of greater cloth than her new owner. He bought them lemon ices to enjoy and laughed when Bethany finished hers so quickly she began to eye Emma's.

They were three hours gone to Lambeth that day, and Emma had to admit she hadn't ever in her life partaken of so frivolous an afternoon, nor had she ever enjoyed herself more, and so she said as much to the earl when they'd taken again to the carriage and made to return to the inn.

"My dear," he said in his always friendly tone, "cease with your 'thank yous' and such. It gives me pleasure, as I enjoy greatly the company of you ladies." On this return trip, Bethany had wanted to sit with the earl, and he held her securely in his lap while she remained enthralled over her pretty doll.

Over the next few weeks, and then months, Emma saw more and more of the earl. He was always solicitous, always engaging, and never improper. After a while, it did occur to her that Michael Benedict really was just a lovely person who hadn't much companionship. He'd told her he had only one son as family, his wife having passed four years ago, and that his son's business concerns and seat in parliament kept them apart more often than not. He spoke effusively and with a fatherly pride when talking of Zachary, his son, telling Emma that Zachary was much like him, but she thought there was not a person in all this world who might resemble Lord Lindsey in kindness or goodness.

Michael and Emma had their first—and only—intense argument after almost four months of visiting when she inquired of Mr. Smythe who the new man might be, now employed by the inn. He seemed to have no other occupation but to guard the taproom, only on rare occasions having to prove his usefulness by having to remove an unruly patron or such. Aside from that, he appeared otherwise unoccupied, standing at the door to the taproom, which met with the open space where the front hall and registry desk were located.

Mr. Smythe harrumphed at Emma's question, confusing her until he enlightened her that this man was not particularly an employee of the inn, but rather hired by "that earl of yours". Frowning over this bit of news, it didn't take Emma long then to consider the man's true purpose and the reasoning behind it. She had to wait three days to be visited by the earl again to let him know that she did not care at all for this circumstance, that she was perfectly capable of taking care of herself, and that it was insulting to Mr. Smythe to imply that he certainly could not. She told him all of this when he entered the inn, the two of them standing in front of the registry desk in the front room.

Michael Benedict did not refute the man's purpose, nor his part in his presence. In fact, the earl looked for a moment rather sheepish when he admitted, "My girl, I also tried to hire a nanny for the baby, that when you work you needn't drag her room to room with you, and that you might have a little more freedom in your life."

With her hands on her hips, exposing her outrage, Emma could only stare at the earl, as if he'd grown another head.

At her inability to speak, her amazement being that great, the earl continued, "Your Mr. Smythe, however, is a stubborn and proud man though I think I'll wear him down yet. I'll be interviewing prospective nannies at the end of the week."

Further aghast, Emma felt an instant and harsh anger. "My lord, I must resist—I *will* resist. Enough is enough. I cannot let you do this."

Untroubled by her upset, and firm in his own stance, the earl asked, "Can you give me one very good reason why I should not?"

"The greatest reason," Emma replied without hesitation, "is that I *like* having her with me. If I didn't have Bethany with me while I tended the rooms, I'd see her not much at all."

For all the thought the earl apparently put into the betterment of their lives, he obviously had not considered this simple reasoning. But he was ever rational and open-minded, and it was easy for him to concede. "In truth I hadn't contemplated this. I only thought to help you."

Emma relaxed her rigid stance and softened her tone. "And I thank you, Michael. I truly do." To appease him somewhat, and because she considered him after all these months her friend, she did occasionally make use of his name as he wished. Yet, their friendship did not give him leave to run her life. "Might we reach a compromise, my lord?" At his raised brow, she suggested, "I promise if I have a need, I will come to you. And you will promise that you will not guess at my needs and act before consulting me."

"Fair enough, Emma dear." He gave her then that smile that she'd grown to love, the sheepish one which appeared wholly out of place on this seasoned and respectable gentleman, when he said, "Of course, this would all be so much easier if you just let me have my way."

Emma made a face at him, "Funny, my lord, I was thinking the exact same thing."

The earl grinned and then Mama Smythe was heard at the top of the stairs and only brief seconds later, she was coming down, bearing Bethany, fresh from her nap, in her arms. The older woman laughed happily at Bethany's excitement over the earl's presence and handed the child over to him when she'd reached the ground floor.

"She sure enough takes to you, milord," Mama Smythe observed, having not her husband's distrust of the earl. She put Bethany's doll into the earl's hand as well, as Bethany was once again taken with the buttons upon his surcote.

"I'll be getting to the back parlor in a moment," Emma told Mama Smythe. "I see the Throckmortons have finally vacated it."

Mama Smythe waved a pudgy hand. "No worry, dear. It's early yet. I'm off to bake the bread. Good day, milord."

"Good day to you, Mistress," the earl returned. Bethany had grown tired of his buttons and began to reach for Emma. The earl kissed her round and pink cheek and pushed her into Emma's waiting arms. "Go to Mama."

"Mama," Bethany repeated instantly, as she often did these days.

Emma stared, first at Bethany, then at Michael, her jaw nearly dropped. She should correct the child immediately but hadn't thought of this situation before now. "Maybe Auntie," she suggested, looking to Michael for confirmation.

He only shook his head. "Mama will do."

"But I'm not—"

"But you are, my girl," Michael insisted. "In her little life—all her life—you are the only mother she will know. Let it be."

Wracked with indecision, Emma felt a tear escape. The profound effect that one simple word had on her was startlingly strong and she hugged Bethany tightly to her. Michael chuckled over her high emotions and kissed Emma's forehead. "Let it be, my girl," he insisted again, and Emma hadn't the will or the desire to gainsay this.

Chapter Three

Zachary Benedict tipped up his tankard, finishing the remaining ale within. He'd sat here at the King's Arms Inn for the past hour, watching with ever-increasing anger as the tart with the red hair served up more than simply food and drink. He thought of his father and his well-mannered lifestyle, his attention to decorum, his very fastidious nature, and wondered how the hell he'd ever wound up consorting with the likes of this chit.

Glancing around yet again, happily taking his eyes from the young woman, Zach took in the whole of the establishment. The inn was orderly and well-kept, decidedly cleaner than many an inn he'd seen in his life, so it rather surprised him that it employed so base a creature as this girl.

Emma Ainsley, Zachary thought with a sneer, observing the girl again as she allowed a patron to lay a hand on her bottom.

The old man must have indeed been lonely in his last years, if this were the company he'd kept. Shaking his head, Zach wondered to what extent his father's lows had actually reached; if he had begun to take common serving wenches as mistresses, what other madness might he have practiced.

Since the day more than a week ago when he'd been informed of his sire's sudden death, Zach's world had been turned upside-down. He been close with his father, having all his life looked up to the man, who had—to his previous knowledge—never so much as walked on the wrong side of the street. True, Zach's own enterprises of the past few years had kept them apart more often than not, but this only added to his grief when he'd received the awful news. But his sadness was then compounded by confusion and a bit of anger when he'd been read the will and learned of this Emma Ainsley, and the tidy monthly stipend she'd been afforded by his father. Zach's interest was only further piqued when he learned of the hired man set to work at the same establishment as this woman.

To look at the chit, he'd not have guessed her to be worth the monies put to her, but Zach had to conclude that his father certainly thought her wares pleasing enough, if he'd bothered to include her in his will only two months ago, and include her generously indeed.

Distastefully, he inclined his head to summon the wench once again to him, bound to get on with this business, however offensive it might be. Ambling his way with a practiced sway to her ample hips only fueled further Zach's already pounding irritation. As she neared, Zach again wondered at his father's tastes, for this woman was clearly one who'd seen more years than likely she'd admit to, not all of them kind, and whose brazen manner with any and all left a distinctly sour taste in his mouth.

When she stood directly before him, her tray pushed with strategic ambition into one hip while her hand clasped the other, she offered him a flirtatious and hopeful smile, just as she had every time she'd approached him today. "What can I do for you, fine sir?" She asked, aiming for a seductive tone, which proved completely off-putting to Zach.

"You are acquainted with Earl Lindsey?" He asked, his tone informing her that he wasn't here to seek companionship.

"I might be," she answered saucily, but with suspicion. "Who's asking?"

"When was the last time you saw him?" He wanted to know. Zach needed to know how recently this tawdry affair had taken place, for certainly it had a lasting effect on his father.

The wench frowned a bit now, not prettily. "I still want to know who's asking."

"The present Earl of Lindsey is asking," Zach answered curtly. "Now answer the question."

Sensing now that she'd get no offers from this gent, the wench sighed audibly, looking irritated herself. The false sultriness disappeared from her voice. "I ain't seen him in months. And I only seen him a few times anyway. He was all about Emma, only wanted her."

Startled, Zach frowned sharply at the server. "You are not Emma Ainsley?"

"Nothing to confuse between me and the princess," she said with ill-concealed hostility.

"Where can I find Emma Ainsley?" He wanted to know then.

But she only shrugged her shoulders and made to depart. Wishing to smack her, but needful of her help, Zach grabbed her by the arm and thrust several coins into her free hand. "Fetch her now."

He watched the red-haired wretch consider denying him, her eyes contemplating the coins in her hand. She might have liked to toss them in his face but with a small huff, pulled her arm from his grasp and left the taproom.

Zach blew out a frustrated breath and set to wait for the real Emma Ainsley to appear. Twining his long fingers around the empty tankard before him, he contemplated his growing fury, and wondered if Emma Ainsley was cut from the same cloth as the red-haired woman. Keeping his eyes trained on the door through which the woman had disappeared, he was soon rewarded with her reappearance. But no one had followed her, and Zach's frown darkened yet again.

In the next instant, however, the frown vanished completely when a woman—a girl, really—walked into the taproom. Stunned by this unexpected turn, Zachary Benedict sat a little straighter upon his seat as he studied whom he supposed now was the actual Emma Ainsley.

The tart gave her no direction that Zach could see so that Miss Ainsley was left to search the taproom for whoever might have summoned her.

Zach's next breath emerged rather quickly, and it came to him quite suddenly that his father had indeed not lost his mind. If this in fact were Emma Ainsley, he blamed his father not at all for forgoing his well-heeled position in life to take up with her. In all his thirty odd years, Zach could not ever remember being deprived of breath upon first sight.

Until now.

Emma Ainsley's eyes moved about the room, having started at the side opposite from where Zach sat, affording him several long seconds to appreciate her allure. Beautiful was too tame a word to apply to such a beguiling face and form. She stood perhaps a few inches over five feet, her build slender, yet curved in all the right places. Long gleaming tresses of perfect mahogany were tied in a neat ribbon at her nape, falling then to her hips, while a few stray tendrils escaped to frame a face over which the angels must certainly sigh. She was too far away to discern the exact color of her eyes, but they must be blue, he decided—only blue would do justice to those eyes, large and round and tilted so charmingly up at the corners, set upon skin perfectly creamy and smooth, just a hint of color from regularly seeing the sun, he guessed. Her nose was small and delicate, and below, her parted lips bowed generously enough to surely tempt a saint.

In the next instant, her eyes did settle upon him, and Zachary determined that Emma Ainsley was just about as enchanting a creature as he had ever seen. As he was watching her and did not look away when her eyes landed upon him, she wisely guessed that it was he who had called her, and began to walk toward him. Something inside him twisted and roiled as she moved, as at least half a dozen hungry eyes followed her with frank appreciation. This, however, recalled the reason for this meeting, and Zachary was miserably reminded of exactly what she was. Strangely, this seemed to lessen her appeal not at all.

But something in his visage must have changed with these thoughts, for her steps faltered—almost imperceptibly—and her ethereal features took on an anxious mien. In a moment, she stood beside his table, her hands worrying the skirt of her apron, which covered a simple and well-worn gown of gray.

"I am Emma Ainsley," she informed him, her voice soft and slow, nearly exotic the lilt of her tone.

"I am Lindsey," was all he said, scrutinizing with great intent her face at this introduction. He knew immediately when this clicked in her head, for her lips parted again, her beautiful eyes widening with distress. Slender fingers flew to her mouth to stifle a cry as her eyes watered immediately.

"What—where is...?" She couldn't seem to form a complete thought, and if Zachary didn't know better, he'd have imagined that her grief was genuine as she realized that if he were the earl, it could only mean that his father was deceased.

"My father died on the 19th," he said simply, nearly brusquely, disliking this feigned anguish of hers.

With a small squeak at the harsh slant he applied to his tone, Emma Ainsley slumped into the stool opposite Zach, covering her face in her hands, crying with such trueness he nearly thought her sincere. She tried noticeably to control her sobs, taking huge breaths to stave them off, but they continued to come. She did not cry loudly, as to attract attention, but with seeming true pain, keening softly. After a moment, in which time Zach's discomfort had grown powerfully, she lifted red and wet eyes to him.

"What happened? He was not unwell," she protested, waving her hand in agitation. "I saw him a fortnight ago—was there an accident?"

Zach shook his head, beginning to believe that her sorrow might be genuine indeed. "No, he was not unwell," he answered vaguely, his mind moving ahead, for if this torment before him were real, he needed then to know the exact extent of the relationship between this lovely woman-child and his father. "He, ah..." he said, making an effort then to bring himself back to the question at hand, "he suffered a stroke, that is all. He was gone almost instantly."

This evoked a fresh wave of tears and Zachary began to feel decidedly uncomfortable, as he knew not what to do to console the poor girl. As they—her vocal sorrow, that is—were beginning to draw undue attention, Zach touched his hand to hers to garner her attention, as she had covered her face again. She startled and jumped at his touch and looked sharply at him.

"Perhaps there is a private room we might use to conclude our business," he suggested, raising a brow expectantly, "and where you might...grieve without so many watchful eyes upon you."

Surveying the room then as if it hadn't occurred to her that many eyes indeed did watch her—perhaps often and fixedly, even when she wasn't beset by grief—she nodded quickly and stood, facing Zach once again. "Um, I have rooms abovestairs," she said, pointing imprecisely toward the door from whence she'd come. Something seemed to strike her then, some thought made her tilt her head curiously at him. "Had you... other business with me other than... bearing this news?" she asked and then sniffled more.

Taken aback as he was by the sight of those haunting eyes, Zach did not answer immediately, but considered as he also stood from his stool, that she tried just now with this query, to dismiss him.

"Yes, I have business with you, Miss Ainsley," he said coolly.

She nodded tensely and led the way from the taproom, ignoring the watchful and frowning eye of the beefy man behind the bar. Zach met the proprietor's stare straight on, in such a foul mood as to nearly want to provoke something here. But the man, having curled his lip to advance his own opinion of Zachary, continued only to apply a damp towel to the inside of the used tankards and otherwise intrude not at all.

Zach followed her down a dim corridor and up a flight of narrow stairs at the end of the building, pretending that he was not at all entranced by the smooth sway of her hips, nor the length of her dark hair floating down her back. Upon the second floor, she opened the last door and stood holding its handle while her hand invited him inside.

A middle aged woman, with a harsh country look of long years of sun-up to sundown work, sat in a chair within the room. She may have been dozing but jumped a bit as light spilled into the room.

"What is it, girl?' She asked, rising and going to Miss Ainsley, giving a quick matronly frown to Zachary.

"Oh, Mrs. Smythe, the earl... he's gone," the younger woman cried. Mrs. Smythe looked equally upset and hugged the girl long enough to cause Zachary discomfort, impatience perhaps, standing in the doorway.

He took in the whole of the room in one glance, the lone narrow cot in one corner of the room, the pretty lace curtains hanging from the one small window, the neatness of these chambers despite its cramped appearance, and even the warmth they seemed to emanate. But his brow furrowed, forgetting all of this, when his eyes settled upon a pine crib, crudely made, in another corner. Zach's brow lifted as he realized the crib was occupied.

Sitting up within that piece of furniture, while two chubby hands held tightly onto the side rail, a cherubic blonde baby began to bounce her bottom upon the firm mattress at the sight of Emma. "Mama! Mama!" The child cried happily.

"Thank you, Mistress, for looking after her," Emma Ainsley said rather absently but dismissively as she went to the child. Mrs. Smythe bobbed her head a bit, her own eyes glistening with tears and left the room, giving one more hard glare to Zach and making a point of pushing the door even wider open.

Glancing nervously at Zach, Emma went directly to the child, scooping her up and out of the crib. "You should be sleeping, darling," she said softly, kissing the girl's pink cheeks, seeming not at all put out that the child was indeed awake. But upon gathering the baby to her bosom, another bout of tears consumed her, and she kept her back to Zach while she cried heartily into the baby's hair.

Zach witnessed this scene with something akin to horrified shock. While the child looked nothing like his father, seemed in fact to resemble her mother quite favorably, aside from the very blonde hair, Zach had to imagine that this was indeed...his sister.

He erased all expression from his face as Emma turned to him again, while the child clung to her neck. He discarded the idea that Emma Ainsley appeared entirely too young and too...innocent to have borne a child—for the evidence stood not ten feet from him—and finally understood the stipulations in his father's will. The monthly stipend had been created to care for his father's child, not simply the mother.

"Please, have a seat," Emma offered, indicating the small cloth covered table and two slat-backed chairs which were pushed snugly against the wall at the end of the cot.

Feeling as if the wind had been knocked out of him, Zachary certainly thought he *should* sit right now and pulled out the closest chair, depositing himself upon it.

"Who is this?" He asked, wondering why—embarrassment not being a plausible excuse—his father hadn't informed him that he had a sibling.

"This is Bethany," Emma told him in a teary voice, taking up the opposite chair, pulling a very expensive looking doll upon the table top nearer to the child, whom she settled nicely in her lap. The little girl, however, seemed as curious about Zach's presence as he was about her very existence. "Bethany, say 'good day' to Lord Lindsey."

"Good day," said the baby, though it sounded more like 'goody'. And then she giggled and gave her full attention to her doll, whose dress, it seemed, might have cost more than the plain frock that Emma herself donned.

"I am sorry for your loss, my lord," Emma finally said, but her eyes did not meet his. "Your father spoke often of you." She struggled with these words, and Zach thought she might begin to cry again, but she did not. Eventually, she did raise her watery eyes to his, and he was amazed anew at the bright blue of those orbs, and the pain reflected there presently.

"Thank you," he acknowledged, and found himself so disturbed by this woman and these circumstances, and the presence of this child that he thought to get right to the crux of his visit. "I came today, having been read my father's will only yesterday. I was not aware of your existence until only then." Without further preamble, he informed her, "My father made provisions for you in his will, added only recently, and you will thus be given a monthly allowance. I assume his intent was that these monies be used for the care of...Bethany." Admittedly, at this moment, he was a bit surprised to find no spark of interest in her eyes at this news, no lightening of those sad features upon hearing of her good fortune. Purposefully, he named the monthly sum she was to be granted, expecting now for certain to witness some selfish jubilation, some twisted grin that might have said, *Ah, I swindled the old man after all*, but there was no evidence of this either.

"I don't understand," she said instead.

Perturbed by her lack of telling response, Zach said tersely, "Miss Ainsley, my father changed his will to include you—apparently you made quite an impression upon him—and changed it so benevolently toward you that you needn't remain here in this hovel if you preferred not to, and you needn't slave belowstairs for little more than a swat on your rump and too little coin. I am only surprised that my father allowed you to remain here while he lived."

She waved this aside, seemingly still affected by the very fact of the earl's death, and said vaguely, "He...he tried often to persuade me to find other accommodations—your father was exceedingly kind and generous when he needn't have been—but it wasn't his responsibility to take on the burden of Bethany and me."

Growing angrier by the moment, her continued pretense at innocence draining him, Zach bit out sharply, "I beg to differ, Miss Ainsley. Many mistakes my father might have made—pardon me for saying you might have been his greatest—but he was a man of honor and he knew his obligation and thus, it *was* his duty to see to your care, and that of the child."

Now it was her turn to frown heavily at this, but she also appeared a bit shaken by his rough tone and pointedly unkind words. The child in her lap had refocused her attention on Zach as he'd spoken so callously, and now he met with two pairs of equally blue eyes, both wary and unnerved.

Emma Ainsley stood, settling the child again at her trim hip, and squared her shoulders as she said to Zach, "Lord Lindsey, I am sorry for the loss of your father and I do thank you for bringing me this news when it is quite apparent you'd rather be anywhere else." She walked to the door with clear intent, holding the handle firmly. "I did not ask anything of your father, and I do not need it. Bethany and I do just fine by ourselves. Good day, my lord." And she waited expectantly, her breath coming in short and shallow huffs.

Zach stood and strode purposefully toward her. "This is not something you may refuse, Miss Ainsley. I will not allow the child to continue to live here." He gestured angrily to the sparse room as a whole, and again his tone was brusque. After all, who was this chit to refuse these monies? Was she holding out for more? "If you think—"

Her hand, lifted to silence him as no man had ever dared, did indeed quiet him.

"I think, *my lord*," she began with mocking emphasis, "that your father was twice the man you are—for you are not more than an overbearing brute without a speck of his kindheartedness. The money is yours. I refuse it. Good day."

"So be it," he allowed contemptuously. With only one last look at the baby, he stalked from the room, hearing the door slam behind him when he was barely passed through it.

Zach Benedict seethed the entire ride home to his estate in Cheltenham, which he had made his permanent residence upon his sire's death, giving up his bachelor pad in Mayfair for now. No doubt the chit had gotten under his skin, but he didn't know if he were angrier at her refusal of the allowance and her dislike of him, or because she was reasonably off-limits because she had been his father's mistress. Yet one thing he did know, the very picture of Miss Emma Ainsley, in all her proud glory as she'd effectively kicked him out, would stay with him for a very long time. There had been rare occasions in his life when he did envy his father, despite the fact that he loved him truly, but of a certainty this was one of them.

Chapter Four

Emma sat upon the grass at a safe distance from the King's Arms Inn, Bethany cradled in her lap, and stared with something akin to horror at the smoldering frame of her home, or what remained of it since the fire had decimated the entire place only last night. Her throat was raw and dry from crying, her cheeks and hands sooty from her initial attempts to douse the fire which had begun innocently enough in the kitchens as a small grease fire within the hearth. Sadly, she glanced sideways at Mama Smythe, who felt herself responsible for this misfortune, as it was she who'd set the bacon too close to the flame, the pan filled with perhaps too much of the fatty meat. Mama Smythe, too, sat in the grass near to the stables, her cheeks stained as well with tears and ash, crying still while her husband tried to soothe her.

But there was little any might say to the Smythes or Alice or Emma or Langdon, the stable hand. Their home was gone, their very livelihood burned to the ground so that only the back stairs and one front wall of the establishment remained standing. In fact, though the fire had burned itself out, assisted by a light drizzle which had begun near dawn, the rubble still did smoke and smolder.

The few patrons of the establishment had since removed themselves, the taproom's local customers gone to their nearby beds, thinking the incident unfortunate but happy they'd not been harmed; and those who'd taken rooms had fetched their carriages and teams and put themselves back upon the road, likely searching for the next posting inn to accommodate them. This left only the six residents of the King's Arms Inn sitting miserably in the yard.

Emma once again tucked Bethany's curious head into the crook of her neck, trying in vain to keep the child from becoming too damp from the continued drizzle. While she was infinitely thankful that she'd had no difficulty removing Bethany from the quickly burning building, she was faced now with a new predicament, as everything in the world she possessed had gone up in smoke with the entire inn; they had, literally, nothing but the clothes on their backs and Bethany's precious doll from Michael.

In the next few minutes, while the Smythes and their employees remained dazed and disoriented, the annoying drizzle became a serious rain and Mr. Smythe suggested gruffly in a hoarse voice that they at least move themselves into the relatively dry stables. They stood as a group, Emma hoisting up Bethany, Mr. Smythe lifting a sobbing-anew Mama Smythe to her feet, while Langdon trudged off with slumped shoulders and Alice spared one last unhappy glance at the King's Arms. They slopped through the increasing mud of the yard toward the stables just as the sound of an approaching carriage came to them. As one unit, they stopped to stare at the coming shiny carriage, thinking it a hopeful traveler, one whom they'd likely direct to the Feathers Tavern of Lambeth. When it drew up sharply and very near to them, however, and the door opened before the driver might have been of assistance, the carriage revealed a person not unknown to a few of the residents of the former Kings Arms Inn.

Emma inhaled quickly, her surprise great as the new Lord Lindsey stepped hastily from the vehicle, his very gray eyes instantly upon her. He covered the short distance between them in only a few long strides, seemingly unconcerned with the others present. A large and firm hand found her upper arm. "You are unharmed?" he asked in his deep voice, it being unnecessary to inquire of what had transpired, as the still-smoldering remnants told the story. His piercing gaze raked over both Emma and Bethany.

Emma could only nod, stunned at his presence, having thought when he'd left the inn more than a fortnight ago that she'd not see him ever again. Whatever was he doing here? She wondered. She'd made her position, at that time, perfectly clear.

He lifted his eyes from hers, though his hand remained lightly upon her arm, and found the frowning gaze of Mr. Smythe. "Was anyone injured?" At the proprietor's negative response, Lord Lindsey returned his steely gaze to Emma. "Come on, then," he said, and it was apparent that he'd learned much from his sire and expected automatic compliance—despite Emma's previous refusal of him and his rudely put overture.

Emma did not move, shaking her head in confusion. His hand fell from her arm, the warmth it had brought absent then as well. "Come where?" she wanted to know.

He frowned, as if this should be obvious. "I shall take you to Benedict House."

"Why?" Her own frown mirrored his. Why did he behave, as he had previously, as if he were now accountable for her? She knew him not at all, aside from the few snippets she heard from his gentle father, yet he acted as if he'd some right to a say in her life.

"Why?" He repeated, his tone echoing the one he'd employed at their first meeting. "Because you've nowhere to go," he said, as if he spoke to a simpleton, indicating with a pointing hand the ruins of her home. "Because you haven't monies, I imagine; because I suspect this man hasn't a plan for you." He threw his thumb over his shoulder to rudely identify Mr. Smythe as 'this man'. "And because it is raining." He was nearly yelling now, his voice carrying unfavorably over these witnesses.

Raining it might be—Emma felt the chill of the dampness to her core, was aware that her hair was plastered horribly to her forehead, and that her gown clung with growing discomfort to her cold body—but she'd be damned before she accepted the questionable hospitality of this man.

Sheer outrage at his high-handedness made Emma bristle. Shifting a watchful Bethany to her free hip, she leveled this man with her meanest glare. "I've informed you already, my lord," she started, "I am under no obligation to you and likewise, you are not to me. This was my home and these people are my family. So here I will stay." Having pronounced this, she marched regally to the stables, exhaling nervously, knowing many eyes were upon her at this unprecedented outburst, but feeling the heat of only one particular gaze. She continued stalking away, thankful when she detected movement behind her, assuming her housemates had begun to follow. Just as she reached the stables and lifted her hand to pull open the sliding door that had been closed last night, a hand clamped down bruisingly over her arm once again. She was whirled around, and abruptly tightened her hold on Bethany as she crashed into Lord Lindsey's chest.

"You little fool!" He growled. "Haven't you the sense God gave a goat to know when to swallow your pride and accept charity?"

A swift thought raced through her mind just then—this man likely wouldn't know a gentle tone or kind word if he were smacked upside the head with it. He was absolutely nothing like his dear father.

Emma opened her mouth to protest his callousness once again but Mama Smythe's voice came to her before she could speak.

"Girl, you ought to go with him," her friend said sadly, much to her chagrin.

The innkeeper's husband added, his voice without emotion, "I haven't a plan for us—for me and the missus—let alone do I know how to help you and Alice and Langdon."

Emma turned to stare with a gaping mouth at Mr. Smythe before swinging her eyes back to the missus. "Go on, girl. For Bethany, you must."

A quick glance at Alice proved that she was filled only with her usual steaming animosity towards Emma and Langdon's visage, as ever, was unreadable.

"I'll not stand in the rain all day while you determine that you haven't any options," Lord Lindsey informed her, and Emma wondered if he'd ever exercised a tone that was not curt or arrogant. She pinned him with a fleeting hot glare, her anger increased when she realized that he seemed, unlike the rest of them, untouched by the rain. His perfectly tailored clothes appeared to wilt not at all; his black as night hair chose not to hold any moisture and thus the thick locks only curled a bit more, but otherwise seemed unaffected; and even his shiny Hessian boots, Emma saw, were troubled not at all by the mud puddling in the yard.

"Go now, love," Mama Smythe persisted with a small sob when Emma looked as if she'd refuse yet again.

More tears came now as Emma recognized that indeed she hadn't any other choice. She had Bethany to think of—she couldn't very well house the child in the stables indefinitely. With a wave of fresh tears, she strode to the Smythe and hugged them fiercely. She couldn't speak, broken as she was now at the thought of leaving the only home and family she'd known for the past nine years. Mama Smythe took up Bethany in her arms, crying more raggedly at the thought of losing the child, and squeezed the baby tightly, cooing fretfully to her.

Alice surprised Emma then by offering her own embrace, and more so when she whispered in her ear, "He'll take good care o' you. Just don't allow him liberties." With this cryptic warning, Alice removed herself and walked to the stables.

Young Langdon stepped forward to say his goodbye, extending his hand shyly. But Emma had ever retained a soft spot for the stuttering lad and drew him into an embrace that he finally melted into. "Take care of yourself, Langdon," she cried to him.

"I-I-I will, Miss Emma." And the lad blushed furiously and stepped back just as Mama Smythe returned Bethany to Emma.

She faced the Smythes again. "But you'll send for me when you...have figured out what might be done, where we might go? We'll all be together again?"

They nodded, though without conviction which alarmed Emma. With one last hug, the Smythe's and Langdon retreated into the stables, leaving Emma to watch them walk away. She stared at the empty and open door for several seconds, crying and wanting so badly to dash inside with her friends.

"Come," Lord Benedict called from behind her, his tone finally softer.

Emma turned and drew a deep breath, clinging to Bethany as she walked then to where he held open the carriage door. She hesitated only a moment before stepping inside and taking up one side of the vehicle, holding Bethany on her lap. She watched as Lord Benedict folded his enormous frame into the seat opposite her and rapped his knuckles against the roof that the driver might depart. When his dark eyes then met hers, she removed her gaze jerkily, finding greater interest in the scene outside the window, watching as the picture of what remained of the King's Arms faded from view.

She allowed only one more tear to slide down her cheek, her fearfulness at the coming unknown causing her great distress. This was eased not at all as the cold man across from her made no attempt at conversation and thus the nearly hour-long drive to Benedict House was made in near perfect silence—broken only occasionally by Bethany's babbling.

Emma maintained a painfully stiff posture, allowing her eyes to find his person only when she was sure his attention was engaged out the window. Peripherally, she was aware that several times, his detached gaze had settled curiously upon Bethany, but still he said nothing. She felt, too, those few instances when those dark gray eyes shifted to include her—she realized the heat of that gaze to her toes.

Shivering a bit, she tried to regard the man sitting across from her without being noticed. She was honest enough to admit she'd thought him incredibly handsome upon the occasion of their first meeting—that is, until he spoke. But it was hard to overlook that rich and dark hair, naturally set into lazy waves, which fell onto his forehead in such a way a girl might be tempted to risk his sharp gaze just to move those locks aside; and one could not disregard the powerful figure of the man, for he was taller and broader than most, and seemed to have no need of the padded surcotes so heavily favored amongst the elite; and then there were those eyes—deep and penetrating, bright with passions that surely drove the man, and undoubtedly able to consume her, if he dared.

In a moment of weakness, she might even admit to herself that the picture of his lips, the hard set of those generous lines, had plagued her for several days after his first coming. She'd imagined them softened by a smile, a small smile of wonder mayhap directed at her, and had felt a weakness in her knees just considering this unlikelihood. One last quick glance at the hard contour of his jaw, set to arrogant disregard, and Emma was able to shake herself completely free of these useless—indeed, dangerous—musings and fret instead over her coming future.

Emma's first look at Benedict House proved just as unnerving as she'd suspected it might. Located just north of Southwark, the manse sat deep in a wide valley, the light stone façade of the three-story home bright against the green trees and lawn of the well-manicured property. A large and wonderfully maintained drive wended its way around a man-made pond which sat in front of the house. With a tremendous amount of awe, Emma took no pains to hide her expression as she glanced out the carriage window as they pulled in front of a set of huge, polished wooden doors at the top of a wide expanse of steps.

This time when the carriage stopped, Lord Lindsey did await the service of the footman who came without delay from the house to pull open the door and place a small step upon the ground for their use. The earl exited first, then surprised Emma by reaching into the vehicle for her hand as she struggled only a bit with a now sleeping Bethany.

"Thank you," she murmured quietly as her feet touched the ground. She glanced upward, following the clean lines of the blonde colored stone, taking note of the enormous windows and imagining that there must be fifty rooms inside this home. But the earl afforded her no prolonged opportunity to appreciate his home, his hand still upon the back of her arm guiding her inside the place, where he was greeted with a near reverent bow by an aging but precise butler.

"Thurman," the earl addressed his man at the door, "fetch Mrs. Conklin, as Miss Ainsley and the child will need to be shown rooms and have baths readied."

"Yes, my lord," intoned the butler, and closed the door beside them to see to this task, not forgetting himself at all to even pass more than a cursory glance over Emma and Bethany's rumpled and soot-ridden appearance. As the old man disappeared down a nearby hall, Emma took a moment to take in her sumptuous surroundings.

The foyer in which she stood was three stories tall, flanked by a double set of stairs sporting a dark red carpet over the expensive Italian marble of the floor of the hall. Portraits, larger and taller than Emma herself, graced the walls on either side of the stairs, invoking earls and family from decades and centuries ago. The walls upon which they hung were papered in delicate shades of robin's egg blue, having about it a small and scrolling floral pattern in subtle tones. Directly above her head, suspended from several gleaming chains perhaps thirty feet long was a chandelier of sparkling beaded glass and ivory hued candles. There were, all about this ground floor, doors of shiny dark wood, opening to rooms surely as opulent as this foyer, Emma imagined.

She brought her overwhelmed gaze back to the earl, who seemed to be watching her intently—expectantly—with those unsettling gray eyes.

She might have said something then—anything at all to alleviate this general upset he caused her with those severe glances of his—but was saved this endeavor by the immediate arrival of a graying and plump woman, who bore down upon them from further down the hall, wringing her hands hastily upon her not unclean apron.

"Mrs. Conklin," said the earl to the woman, who was obviously the housekeeper, "this is Miss Ainsley, and the child is Bethany. They will require rooms for an extended stay and baths and a meal immediately."

The round little woman bobbed her head dutifully and sized up Emma and Bethany in one sweeping but not unpleasant glance. "This way, then, Miss," she said, and turned already to ascend the left staircase.

"Shall I carry the child for you?" The earl inquired of Emma, his first true attempt at solicitude, she thought. But she refused him with a small shake of her head, possessively snuggling Bethany against her, and took off quickly to follow where the housekeeper had led. She trudged wearily up the stairs, and once upon the second floor where the woman turned down a long corridor, paid little attention to such evident luxury about her until she was brought to a room near the end of the hall.

In all her young life, Emma thought she'd never seen so pretty a bedchamber as this. She was accustomed to cramped spaces and low-slung ceilings and rustic and sparse furniture. She had never seen such extravagance as these tall walls and painted and papered ceilings; she had never beheld a room where the windows were taller even than herself, or where the furnishings were nearly twice the size of her. Upon one wall, nestled between two heavily draped windows, sat a four-poster bed tall enough that a small and necessary stool rested near one side. It was covered with a beautifully embroidered coverlet in soft shades of pale yellow and blue and more fluffy pillows than Emma would ever have need of in her entire lifetime. There was a huge wardrobe, the wood embellished with intricate carvings, matching perfectly another piece, this one an armoire, which sat opposite the bed. In one corner of the room was an oversized dressing table, painted gaily with flowers and ribbons, and in another corner a writing table, complete with embossed stationery and an inkwell and quill, was positioned adjacent to more windows, that one might view the gardens below at the north side of the house.

Moving around the room upon the thick and plush Aubusson carpet, Mrs. Conklin opened one of several doors, and showed a small anterior room, equipped with a pretty covered cot and stool. Another door was opened and revealed a dressing room, decorated in similar shades of yellow and blue and having mirrors on two entire walls, and the last door showed another full bedchamber, this one having a huge crib and rocking chair.

"'Tis the nursery," Mrs. Conklin informed her in a friendly tone and then asked of Emma if she were awaiting the delivery of her trunks.

Reminded again of her sorry circumstances, Emma shook her head. "We were only last night burned out of our home," she told the housekeeper. "We have nothing."

Mrs. Conklin seemed unperturbed by this news. "Likely of no concern, Miss. His lordship will see to dressing ye, no doubt. 'Tis lucky ye are that ye escaped intact."

"Lucky, indeed," Emma agreed. "I think I'll put Bethany in the bed here—I don't want her to awaken afraid, as this will all be unfamiliar to her."

"A good idea, Miss," Mrs. Conklin said with a nod and she moved to pull back the heavy counterpane of the four-poster bed.

Emma carefully laid Bethany upon the very middle of the bed, thinking she'd like nothing better than to climb in beside her right now, but imagined that a bath was a more pressing need. She mentioned this to the housekeeper, who was motherly enough to tuck the linens up and around Bethany, who stirred not at all.

"A bath is just what ye need, Miss. Give me a few minutes to boil the water and have the footmen set up the tub in the dressing room."

"Thank you, Mrs. Conklin," said Emma and she closed the door behind the woman as she left the room. Glancing once again about the lovely room with awed appreciation, Emma then stripped herself down to her shift, removing her apron and gown, and serviceable boots and stockings, too. Unable then to resist further the lure of the inviting bed, she thought only to rest herself for a moment while she awaited her bath and so climbed in beside Bethany and laid her head upon the sweet-smelling goose down pillows.

Chapter Five

When Emma opened her eyes, it was immediately obvious that evening had come. Startled, she sat up quickly, unable to believe she'd slept so long and soundly. She turned to find Bethany and was distressed to discover that the space beside her was empty. Jumping from the high perched bed, she dashed about the room, calling for the child. Her panic began to increase when there proved not a trace at all of Bethany, in any of the small attached chambers. Frantic after only a minute, she yanked open the tall, painted door and called again Bethany's name out into the long corridor. Forgetting then her inappropriate attire when there was no response, she forged ahead and ran down the hall in her bare feet, thinking to summon help in the search. Just as she gained the top of the stairs, the lord of the manor appeared at the bottom, holding a giggling Bethany in his strong arms.

Relief was instant, her hand covering her chest in the hopes of slowing her racing heart. The pair below glanced up then, realizing Emma's presence at that moment.

And that's when she realized that she remained clothed in only her shift, for the dark eyes of the earl scanned her heatedly from head to toe. Heat suffused her, touching every spot his eyes did. Lamely, backing up a step as he began to advance up the stairs, she explained, "I—I couldn't find Bethany. I didn't think...I just ran out...." This last trailed off as he reached now the landing, his gaze finally meeting her eyes, though Emma had quite a time trying to keep her own gaze focused, wishing only for the floor to open and consume her.

Dear Bethany saved her further embarrassment—indeed, further blazing scrutiny—when she reached out cheerily from the earl's arms, crying, "Mama!" Emma took her from the earl, startling slightly when those powerful hands of his touched briefly the skin of her bare arms.

"I heard her waken a while ago," he told Emma, seeming disinclined to remove himself from their presence just now. "I did knock, but when there was no response, I assumed that you might still be asleep—Mrs. Conklin had told me you'd 'dropped like the dead'—and I thought to remove Bethany before she wakened you."

It was awkward, tasted funny on her tongue even, but Emma did tender a grudging, "Thank you."

The earl waved this off, and ruffled Bethany's riotous curls as he said, "Anna and Meredith, two maids here with children of their own, gave her a bath and found this garb for her," the earl said, indicating the baby's new clothes. "We were getting to know one another."

Bethany was a very inquisitive child—at times downright mischievous—which begged the question, "She didn't cause any trouble, did she?" Emma could just picture those pudgy little hands upending costly antiques or treasured family heirlooms. She nearly cringed, awaiting his reply.

He surprised her by giving a short laugh, seemingly amused by Emma's worst expectations. "She was fine—no trouble at all. We even visited the stables and found her a grand little pony that she might ride one day."

Emma thought now not the time to point out to the earl that one day—when Bethany reached an age to actually ride a pony—they would likely have been long gone from Benedict House. Gone, indeed, from the earl's life altogether.

With nothing else to say to this man who unnerved her so, Emma then excused herself, and took Bethany farther down the hall to their rooms. She cringed still, imagining the dark eyes of the earl following every step of her barely clad form. *Dear Lord in Heaven!*

He would send a bath up to her now, he called from where she'd left him. Emma acknowledged this only with a nod turned vaguely his way before shutting herself and Bethany behind the closed door of her chamber.

Once there, closeted in rooms that were entirely too opulent to suit her, Emma set Bethany down upon the soft carpet and let her explore merrily her new surroundings. This allowed Emma to again marvel at the insistence of the earl that they come here to Benedict House. True, she and his father had been friendly, the old earl being made of a fine and virtuous essence, but she knew from Michael Benedict himself that he'd not seen his son in months and hence, was possibly not aware of their friendship. She missed Michael terribly—truth be told, at times unable to imagine him gone completely from this world.

But Emma considered the new earl as unlike his father as the sky was the grass. So why, Emma wanted to know, did he feel it necessary to offer her and Bethany this benevolence? Had Michael Benedict included in his last testament some profound wish that she be housed here, that monies be made available to her that Bethany should know a better life? Michael had offered as much to Emma, and repeatedly. She had politely but firmly refused him, inferring that she and Bethany simply weren't his concern. She'd loved that about him, however, that he cared for her and Bethany and thought to do this simply because he could. But Emma was ever a proud girl, and she'd never taken a snippet of charity in her life. To be sure, she'd been tempted, for Bethany's sake; but always she had refused, her pride being a greater thing than her need.

Yet here she was now, homeless and without a farthing, induced to rely upon the curious charity of Michael Benedict's son, who displayed not an inkling of curiosity as of yet over the very fact that his father had—in essence—taken monies from him to share with her. He'd asked not one question about the relationship she'd had with Michael. Perhaps, she imagined with little effort extended to afford him generosity, he was so taken with his business of being arrogant and overbearing, he hadn't additional wherewithal to consider things such as this.

Shaking her head now at such uncharitable thoughts, she watched as Bethany made to climb up the front of the huge wardrobe and moved to distract the child with some activity less dangerous. She was considering her limited options in this regard, glancing around a room wholly unsuitable for an active two-year old, when a knock sounded at the door. Emma called for entrance and saw Mrs. Conklin enter, bidding her a cheery hello and advising her that she would be directing several footmen with the set up of her bath in the next room. The housekeeper promised to send a maid to help her with this chore but Emma declined—much to the amused horror of the older woman—as she'd not once in her life required assistance for so simple a chore as bathing. She did ask, however, if there might be some articles of clothing to be had—perhaps there was a maid of similar proportions, she suggested—as her gown was likely beyond repair, the soot and smoke of last night's fire having wreaked heavy damage.

Again, Mrs. Conklin appeared entirely outraged at such a simple suggestion, her little button eyes nearly bursting from her face. "Oh, my dear, no," the housekeeper rushed out. "His lordship sent 'round to the village this afternoon, while ye slept, and procured some garments for ye—yer not to be wearing a servant's togs."

This woman's agitation over this circumstance only raised more questions in Emma's mind. With another shake of her head, her confusion presently being a powerful thing, Emma waited silently then while her bath was fully prepared but did accept Mrs. Conklin's offer to see to Bethany while she disappeared into the dressing room. Bethany, being a child used to attention from many, went happily along with Mrs. Conklin, who cooed delightedly at such a pretty baby.

Emma actually luxuriated in the large copper tub filled with steaming and scented water. Never before had she not been forced to hurry through her bath, because Alice needed the use of it, or because Bethany needed her care, or because she was needed at work. She washed her hair with a vanilla spiced bar and her body with the softest cloth imaginable, even as she promised herself she would not—should not—become accustomed to such extravagances. When the chore of the bathing was done, she was loath to give up such a fine position and rested her head on the pillowed back of the tub, closing her eyes in wonder at this magnificence.

Soon enough, however, the water did cool, forcing her out of the copper and into a dry and fluffy sheet of cotton. She squeezed out as much water as she could from her long hair but knew this would take hours to dry. She left the dressing room, wondering how she would ever manage to empty the water, supposing it would take her many pails and many trips to and from the tub to see to it.

Upon the bed, laid out prettily for her inspection, was a clean and pretty gown of pale blue. Carefully, she fingered the material with a cautious hand, considering the fine muslin a perfect weight for a cooler spring evening. The cut was modest, perhaps intended for a younger girl than she, the bodice being shirred, and the skirt falling straight from just below the breast line. Next to these lay undergarments; a clean shift of pure white; a straight hemmed petticoat with an eyelet stitching; and stockings much lighter and silkier than anything Emma had ever known.

A bit of girlish excitement swept over her. Oh, to be sure, she'd not be at Benedict House long enough to get used to such fine things as this, but she was thrilled to have the chance to don so pretty and well-made a gown. Wringing her hair out once again, lest the wetness ruin the gown, she dressed herself quickly and considered her reflection in the tall cheval glass near the armoire.

She thought she appeared not herself at all, being so accustomed as she was to heavier and darker clothing than this. She lifted her wet hair, carelessly pushing it up as if secured atop her head and considered the view, tilting her head this way and that. She saw her stocking-ed toes peeking out from beneath the hem of the frock and wondered what had become of her sturdy boots—they would do no justice to this pretty ensemble, but they were all she had. In this gown, she appeared taller and leaner than she'd thought of herself, but considered that the straight cut achieved this, her former attire usually being gathered at the waist and flounced from there. She studied the tight-fitting shirred bodice and the high cut of the scoop neckline and again determined this piece had originally been produced for someone much younger than she—but tall, apparently.

The door to her chamber opened then and Emma whirled around, dropping the mass of her hair as Mrs. Conklin had returned. In her hand she carried a pair of ladies' slippers, these being a muted silver tone, the tops embroidered with a scrolling pattern of blue thread.

"These should do ye fine, Miss," Mrs. Conklin predicted, gesturing for Emma to sit at the dressing table stool.

"Where is Bethany?" Emma wanted to know, trying not to sound alarmed.

"Ooh, that little cherub," Mrs. Conklin prattled. "Off with his lordship again, while they wait on ye."

"His lordship waits for me?" Emma asked, her fingers thumping her chest.

"Dinner was held for ye, Miss," the housekeeper explained succinctly. "Now SueEllen should be—ah, here she is." Right on cue, a maid, younger even than Emma entered the chamber, her head bobbing nervously. "SueEllen will tend yer hair, set it nicely for ye and then she'll show ye to the parlor where his lordship keeps the baby."

"Thank you, Mrs. Conklin," Emma intoned, appreciative of the woman's efforts on her behalf—though she thought them largely unnecessary—but more wary now of her dinner appointment with the earl. Why, it was almost as if she were being treated not at all as a servant, but as a ... lady.

Zachary Benedict lounged haphazardly upon the thick carpet of the formal parlor, unconcerned that he likely rumpled the evening wear Emery, his valet, had painstakingly readied for him. He watched with growing amusement —and admittedly, with a growing fondness—as his baby sister giggled and repeated her efforts to climb over his prone form. She must think him some mountain to ascend, though he thought she particularly liked the descent, when he assisted a bit, turning his body so that her hands found the floor on the other side of him and she tumbled head over heels off him. She would scramble unevenly to her feet then, her limited vocabulary allowing only for a call of, "Again!" Naturally, when she turned those magnificent blue eyes and that scant-tooth grin upon him, Zach was at pains to resist. 'One more time' had been several occasions ago.

If his peers, those starchy-collared bluebloods he met with in parliament, could see him now, they'd like as not question his very—well, maturity, if nothing else.

In the middle of Bethany's latest tumble, he heard the door to the parlor open, and the unmistakable sound of a quickly drawn-in breath. Bethany righted herself once more, clapping her hands with enthusiasm, unaware that her mother watched from the doorway.

"Again!" Bethany insisted.

"Good heavens, no!" Emma called out sharply, striding across the room to the pair on the floor. "Bethany, love," she scolded gently, "you mustn't...wrestle with his lordship."

Zachary laughed out loud, partly amused by Emma's horrified mien, and partly because Bethany screwed her face up with such distaste over her mother's reaction. She might not completely understand her mother's admonition, but she understood the gist of it—she was not to be doing what she had been doing.

Zach pulled himself easily to his feet, sweeping Bethany along with him in one smooth motion, swinging her out and above him while she giggled yet more until he settled her neatly at his chest. But she was ever her mother's daughter and reached almost immediately to be taken by Emma. Zach then gave his full attention to his sister's mother. Her changed appearance had not initially gone unnoticed by him, but his perspective from the floor had not been this engaging.

Dressed as a lady, Emma Ainsley assuredly rivaled any of the fancy misses of the *ton*. More intriguing, perhaps, for her complete lack of artifice. She was a natural—an incomparable, the *ton* would say. Beauty such as this was not bestowed with any kind of regularity, not that Zach had ever seen. She was fresh and lovely and had about her a vitality to her features that was vastly appealing, and Zach once again thought he understood his father's absorption with this girl.

At Zach's prolonged perusal, and his attended silence, she grew uncomfortable and shifted a bit on her slippered feet.

"My lord, someone seems to have misunderstood something—somewhere," she said nervously. "I have been given rooms upon the second floor and they appear to be family apartments. And Mrs. Conklin delivered this frivolous piece," she went on, holding out the very flattering gown she wore, "and I'd not spend a moment upon my knees in this thing; the fabric would shred in no time at all."

An electric jolt went through Zach at her words, a tormenting and provoking picture forming in his mind, until she spoiled the craved image by adding innocently, "I haven't a clue how work should be accomplished in this, my lord. I cannot scrub and dust and such, wearing such fine things as this."

Shaking himself mentally, blinking twice to assist in the purging of that image of her upon her knees, Zach drew a deep breath and thought to clarify to her, "Miss Ainsley, the only misunderstanding seems to be your own. You've been brought to Benedict House, as my father had wanted, to ascend to this life as it is naturally Bethany's due." He considered her a continually perplexing miss—all that she desired, and swindled from his father was within her grasp, yet she balked at every turn. Did she not fear that overplaying her game of innocence might come back to bite her? What fun it might be to acquiesce to what she pretended to want; he might shrug and tell her that yes, a mistake had been made and naturally her rooms were to be below stairs and her workload would be heavy. How might she react to that?

But for now, it was Emma's turn to appear nonplused. Absently, she straightened the hem of Bethany's gown over her arm. "Bethany's due? My lord, if I might ask, exactly what did Michael's—excuse me, your father's—will declare?"

"All that I have previously mentioned," Zach explained, having a hearty dislike of discussing finances and trivialities with her. He would have continued, just to have this business out of the way, but Thurman arrived to announce that dinner was served, and Mrs. Conklin was fast on his heels, announcing that she would see to Bethany while they dined, scooping the child out of the girl's arms and trotting off through the door still held by Thurman.

Zach watched Emma's jaw tighten and suspected that she hadn't a great fondness for the ease in which the child was repeatedly removed from her. He imagined that at the inn, Bethany was rarely out of Emma's sight, and rarer still, he guessed, were the instances when her care was seen to by someone else. He watched her cross her arms over her bosom, as if she didn't know what to do with them if she weren't holding her baby.

Lightly, he touched his hand to her arm to guide her into the dining room. He'd instructed his staff that they would make use of the smaller of the two dining rooms this evening, the larger being occupied by a table that comfortably sat forty guests, which would prove awkward as there was only the two of them.

The small dining room—the Paneled Room, his mother had always called it for the rich and dark paneled walls—sat at the rear of the house, overlooking the vast rose gardens for which the Benedicts were known. Inside, Zach pulled out the chair at the foot of the table and watched as Emma uneasily sat herself within it. He moved to the other end of the table—this one sat only twelve and was thus more informal—and took his seat there, nodding to Thurman that he should begin to serve.

Sensing that she remained perplexed by his father's desires, Zachary explained the terms and desires in a straightforward manner. "Miss Ainsley, it apparently was my father's wish that his child not be raised at the King's Arms Inn. Possibly, the inn is less unsavory than most, but it remains that—" he stopped and gave her a questioning glance for she had begun to stare at him, her eyes widened to alarming proportions, as if he'd announced the sun might never rise again. Briefly, she closed her eyes, her frown now heavy upon her brow and then those blue orbs appeared again, and she directed a pointed stare again at him.

"Please repeat that, my lord," she said in a carefully neutral tone.

Zach lifted a hand, silently asking what had stunned her so, but did as she desired. "I've stated that it seems obvious that my father desired that his child not be—"

"Please stop."

Now Zach frowned, at her flagrant disrespect, and at her puzzlement. Wherein came the difficulty? It seemed a simple enough theory to him.

"Bethany is not your father's child," she told him finally.

If it could ever be said that the new Earl of Lindsey had ever been dazed and bewildered, it should be said now. He made three attempts to ask a question, and three times his lips clamped shut on his stumbling words. Finally, a simple "What?" emerged clearly.

"I don't know how you might have come to that conclusion, my lord," she said, her voice growing anxious with unease. "Had your father intimated such... in some regard?"

Zach could only shake his head blandly in the negative, his gaze on her but his eyes unseeing. It wasn't possible, was it? He'd just assumed the baby was his sister. No, he hadn't specifically inquired if this were true, because—well, he supposed the obvious overtook him.

He was brought back to attention when her slender hand clamped nervously over her mouth momentarily, her eyes widening with a sudden realization. "Oh, my. You brought me here—you brought Bethany here!—only because you thought she was—oh." She stood abruptly, unbalancing the chair for a split second, while her features took on an embarrassed and hot flush. "Dear Lord, how mortifying," she mumbled, fleeing the table with a careless, "Excuse me," but not before Zachary caught sight of the brightness of tears in her eyes.

Chapter Six

It took him a moment, but Zachary did lose eventually the foggy haze of uncertainty that had enveloped him. Thrusting himself from his chair, he followed Emma out of the Paneled Room, but found her not at all in the corridor, nor even midway up the stairs. She must have run, he thought. Tears and fear could often chase a person quickly from one place to the next. Zach took the stairs three at a time and strode purposefully down the second floor, rapping loudly upon the door to Emma's chambers. He waited then, breathing heavily, and not from the exertion of his chase.

Foremost in his mind was, *how will I make her stay now?* If she wouldn't even admit to him that Bethany was his father's child, what inducement could he level at her to keep her here? He didn't think he had misread the innuendoes of his father's will; he didn't know why she lied about Bethany's parentage, but he did know that something inside him did not want Emma Ainsley gone from Benedict House. He thought, while he rapped again when no one answered, that his desire to keep her here was kindled not half so much by her very real allure, but more so by that haunted, ethereal look about her that made a man want to protect her.

"Miss Ainsley!" He called when there remained no answer to his knock. Eschewing propriety, he pushed open the door and found her standing once again in only her shift, the discarded gown and stockings and slippers chaotically littering the carpeted floor. She appeared fretful, and then further unnerved when she realized his presence.

"Whoa," he said soothingly, but steadily as he strode across the room to her. "Slow down."

"I am here under false pretenses," she prattled. "I shouldn't have come—I shouldn't have accepted your aid. I thought you knew.... I never imagined you considered that your father—oh, it doesn't matter. We shall be gone shortly. I've asked Mrs. Conklin—"

He took her arms firmly in his grasp, giving her a small shake. "You needn't run off, Miss Ainsley." Zach used a gentling tone, concerned over this very real anguish. She tried to pull from his hold but he held tight. "Regardless of who Bethany is or isn't," he said, thinking it not the time to investigate her lies, "my father's will still provides for you and her. You are welcome here. Miss Ainsley, do you hear me?"

"Yes, my lord, you are speaking very loudly," she said, but seemed to have an inability to meet his eyes.

"Wherever would you be going dressed as you are, anyway?" he thought to ask.

She shook her head fretfully, still held by him. "Mrs. Conklin was to bring me something less... fine. I would pay you back. I wasn't stealing. But I would also need a few changes of clothes for Bethany and something warm to bundle her in."

"Enough. You are going nowhere. Might I remind you—you haven't anywhere to go." He bent his head, trying to engage her eyes. She remained resistant.

"I—we—cannot stay here." Tears threatened again, pooling around the blue of her eyes.

"Miss Ainsley, tell me why you won't admit that your daughter was sired by my father. Do you expect a wealth of anger from me?"

This did bring her eyes to his. The blue was troubled and dark and desperate. "My lord, Bethany is not even my child, and I only met your father less than a year ago."

Zachary remained skeptical. Truth be told, his skepticism increased with this bold statement. "Then explain to me why my father thought it necessary to include a provision in his will to care for her."

"I don't know. I was shocked to learn of it from you. He tried many times to give me aid, and I refused—"

"Holding out for more?" He asked bitingly, unable to resist.

Emma did now shake him off, hugging her arms about her and moving away from him. "Think what you will. It matters not to me."

"Make me understand!" This, furiously, wanting so much for her to give him some plausible reason to trust her, to believe her. Inside, somewhere deep where male pride lived, he wanted her to prove to him that she had not been his father's mistress, even as he deemed this impossible.

"My lord, pardon my seeming ingratitude," she said with such frostiness, he wondered that she was the same person who'd bravely held back tears only moments before, "but I owe you nothing. My relationship with your father was our business. What he did for me was his decision. And none of it—then or now—should be of concern to you."

"Those are now my coins afforded monthly to you, so I beg to differ," he contradicted sharply.

"Which I have repeatedly refused. Consider yourself freed of the burden." She turned away from him with this, but was spared further verbal assault when Mrs. Conklin entered, appearing jumpy and ill at ease. She carried several dark garments in her hands and gave a questioning, worried glance to Zachary. At his answering stiff nod, the housekeeper mutely laid the garments on the end of the bed and trotted off quickly, pulling the door closed behind her after only one more nervous peek at Emma.

Zach stood stiff and still while she sorted through the apparel, choosing what appeared to be one of his housemaid's plain black gowns and then disappearing into the dressing room. Indecisive—but resolved that she must remain here—he worked his hands through his hair and waited for her to reappear. When she did in a very short amount of time, she was clad in that black, unadorned gown and once more wore her own heavy but serviceable shoes.

"Dare I ask what you are planning?" He tried, albeit unsuccessfully, to keep the irritation out of his voice.

"To be away from here, that is all," she answered shortly and did not bother to spare him a glance as she walked purposefully to the door.

"Wait," he called, heaving a frustrated sigh, but she did not and Zach then moved quickly, reaching the door just as she made to pull it open. His palm flattened on the thick wood and slammed it closed. "Wait," he demanded, this time sharply. "Think about what you are doing—where might you go? How might you support Bethany?"

She didn't turn around, but only bowed her head, one of her hands still on the door knob, the other flattened against the wood below his. He saw only the silken tresses, piled so artfully atop her head, saw the exposed creamy skin at her nape, and the despairing slump of her small shoulders. "Let me be," she pleaded softly.

Zach shook his head slowly, but she did not see this. He should, he knew. He should let her go, exorcise her from his home and mind. "I cannot," he admitted gruffly. "No less than before. If what you say is true, then I must know what it is about you that so captivated my father that he deemed it necessary to care for you as he did."

She spun around quickly at this, suddenly alarmed then to find herself so close to him, for their faces were only inches apart. "Can you not imagine that he simply pitied me, and that is all? I did not invite his pity. I did not encourage it, but possibly that is all there was to it. He was kind to me, and I enjoyed his company. At times, I thought him a lonely soul who might have actually looked forward to the time he spent with Bethany and me. He was...my friend." She'd started out slowly, stumbling, but her voice grew in steadiness as she proclaimed this likely truth. "And I miss him so," she said with a cry.

Zachary heard her words—her response did register—but his eyes and several other senses were keenly attuned to just her lips. He watched the fullness of them move around her words, saw her tongue snake out to wet them, and knew he could only guess at their taste and texture. Unless he dared....

Without further thought to the conflict his actions might cause, he simply lowered his head and touched his lips to hers. Softly, he glided his mouth over hers, taking in her startled stiffness and indeed, the very soft heat of her mouth. He dared further, shifting his body to be nearer, resting one hand at that naked nape, drawing her closer. He felt a moan—half resistance, half unpracticed desire—escape her. Seizing upon this indecision, he pressed his lips fully unto hers just as his body leaned entirely against her. She gasped at this head-to-toe contact and

Zach took advantage of this as well, grazing his tongue along the seam of her lips and then satisfyingly within, touching his tongue to hers, dancing around it as he had only previously dreamed.

He felt the weight of her rounded breasts pressed against his chest, and then the evaporation of that stiffness of her form. For the smallest space of a second, she melted into him, and his body responded with a soaring desire. But this surrender lasted only a heartbeat and in the next instant she was pushing her hands between them and against his hard chest.

"No."

That was all she said. Firm and determined, she gave a final push, and moved herself away from being trapped at the door.

Breathing heavily, hand rubbing his jaw, Zach followed her agitated progress around the room. She wasn't particularly going anywhere, only seemed to be brewing something within.

Finally, she faced him again, her countenance raw, anxious, while he stared once more at her mouth. *Made for kissing. Jesus.*

"Is that why you insist I remain, my lord?" Her voice was ragged and low, a wealth of pain told there. "You think that you might just pick up where you believe your father left off?"

His gaze swung sharply to hers, his jaw tightened, but he said nothing immediately. He deserved that. Barely discernibly, he shook his head, pursing his lips with consideration, his eyes meeting hers squarely. He shouldn't have kissed her, he knew that much, and the hurt in her voice made him doubly sorry that he had. He hadn't a proper defense for that kiss, other than that it was possible to justify it in his own head since he'd been the one beleaguered with thoughts of little else since first meeting Emma

Ainsley. Wisely, Zach withheld this information, believing it not likely to appease her.

There had little occasion in his life when he'd been called upon to tender an apology; and less occasions, truth be known, that he'd considered the recipient worthy of his inconvenience. This, he knew, was different—Emma Ainsley might possibly be as innocent as she put forth. Surely, her eyes abetted her claim of purity, and if he gave this deliberation a fair trial, her untutored response to his kiss had corroborated this assertion as well.

"My apologies," he said stiffly. She gave no indication that she had even heard him, just stood there, arms distrustfully crossed over her breasts, ostensibly waiting for ... more. "You should not imagine that I insist you stay for only that. I do so because I know you haven't anywhere to go, and in all honesty, I am not entirely convinced that Bethany is not my sister. I just haven't reconciled in my head why you might be lying about this."

"But I am not," she argued miserably, and it was obvious she thought she'd never persuade him otherwise.

"I suppose your role in Bethany's birth can be easily proven or disproven," Zach suggested crudely. "Unless, of course, there have been others."

This seemed not to garner the outrage it should have, and Zach wondered if she indeed even had a clue as to what he inferred.

She squared those small shoulders once again and drew a long breath. "My lord, you named the amount your father pledged to me as a monthly allowance. I truly have no care to be supported by you but would ask that I be given two months of that bequest. That would allow me to lease rooms for Bethany and me for many, many months. I ask no more than that as I can work to support us. I—I assume it is not within your power to refuse me the coin that is, essentially, mine."

A muscle in his jaw began to twitch. No, he hadn't any power to refuse her the monies. Hell, he hadn't any *intention* of doing so. He just didn't want her gone from here, whatever Bethany's parentage might be. But he ignored her request for now.

"Explain to me, if you will, how it can be that Bethany is not your child. She bears the look of you—hair color aside—and those eyes are rather unmistakable."

A draining sigh preceded her answer. "My parents died when I was very small. My sister, who was seven years older than me, and I maintained a room at the King's Arms. Gretchen worked for the both of us while I was too young." She paused a moment then shrugged as she explained, "Gretchen had many admirers. She died bringing Bethany into this world. I—I couldn't very well place my sister's baby in one of those horrid orphanages. And the Smythes were wonderfully supportive."

"And my father?"

"Your father first came to the inn during a bad rain—his carriage was stuck up the road. I happened to be working the tap-room, as Alice was held back by the rains. Your father was nice. He was protective, actually, even before I knew him well. There was a brawl that night and I was caught in the middle of it. My finger was broken, and your father was kind enough to send for his own doctor. He returned a week later to check on me. He was smitten with Bethany. That is how it began."

"And?" There had to be more. A man didn't include a girl in his estate leavings unless there was more.

She shrugged again. "And... what? He visited us regularly after that. He took us to market in Lambeth. He showed us his new Landau. He bought Bethany a doll. He tried to persuade me to leave the inn."

Zachary added what most he needed verified. "And you had a relationship with him."

"Well, yes." She admitted, as if this needn't have been asked. "I loved Michael. He wasn't anything like the usual nabobs; he wasn't stuffy and full of himself. He might have been the kindest man I'd ever known."

Feeling something roil within at her confirmation, Zach knew not what else to say. Having this fact indeed established did not ease his mind at all, and it certainly did not make it easier to deal with this raging desire for her. He still wanted to taste her again. He still wanted to explore more. But he would not.

He could not.

He determined then that her *intent* had never been to swindle his father out of a living; in all probability, she had no idea the extent a man might reach just to care for her. One look at those haunting blue eyes and a man was likely to give up much to have her gaze rest happily upon him.

His decision was quick to come then. "I will assist you in the purchase of a house—you needn't live in common rooms." He held up his hand to forestall her coming objections. "That part is not debatable. But I insist that you remain at Benedict House until a proper and suitable residence can be found."

"Then I insist upon working for my keep."

My God! But she was stubborn. He almost smiled now, wondering if his own father had felt at wit's end over her endless obstinacy. "You have enough to do to take care of Bethany," he pointed out. When it was apparent that she would have argued further, Zachary decided to try a different approach. Brusquely, he announced, "I cannot have *my* staff caring for *your* child when they've their own work to do. No, I will not allow it. And as your stay here might only amount to a few weeks, at most, I cannot have you thrown into the household mix, only to be yanked out so quickly—that would disrupt too much."

Ah, so guilt was the weapon to use to best effect, he realized then, as Emma bit her cheek, but did accept this, as she was not eager to upset the household.

Zachary nearly laughed out loud at how easy that had been, determining that it was obvious his father had never used the guilt tactic to achieve his own desires for Emma Ainsley. Well, certainly not all of them. His mood soured once again—the thought of this girl having been his father's mistress a damnable thing—Zach told her then that he would have Mrs. Conklin fetch Bethany and that they should make ready to retire for the evening.

He noticed that she stood up often to him, at times not cowed by him, but when she knew she was beaten, as was the case presently, she became a rather meek thing. He frowned over this, deliberating if this were to his liking or not. Perhaps having lived her life always as part of the serving class, it was not easy to put forward a brave mien at all times.

Emma once again sat across from the Earl of Lindsey in his carriage, this one with an open top as the day was fine, the last vestiges of a cool and rainy spring seemingly evaporated altogether. As usual, she stole glances at him, still enamored of his handsomeness, if not his charm. Since his edict of three nights ago that she remain at Benedict House until a dwelling might be found for her, he had proven to be a foreboding presence. He'd insisted she dine with him, had been incensed when she politely refused, and then had proven a disagreeable host throughout the meal when she did appear in the Paneled Room, after he'd storm her apartments and angrily demanded her presence.

He'd presented her—via Mrs. Conklin, who was proud to effuse over 'his lordship's bounty'—with several more gowns and garments and slippers and cloaks, and so much more for Bethany. Again, she'd tried to resist, but to no avail. So she sat now across from him, dressed gaily in a white cotton empirewaist gown, with the most adorable shoes, adorned with pink ribbons; and she sported a thoroughly clever bonnet, such as she had never seen, trimmed with ribbons and pearls and protecting her not quite fair skin from the bright sun. She only wished she felt as merry as she was sure she looked.

They were on their way to a small property and house he'd found, thinking it a possibility for her new home. Emma was not excited. This would be their third venture out, visiting cottages for sale. Thus far, the earl had proven to be a very discriminating buyer, finding fault with everything from the size of the rooms ("too small"), to the state of the yard ("those tracks had looked like mole tunnels"), to the ineptness of the caretaker ("he was a drunkard, I tell you").

Presently, they sought out the Daisies Cottage, located on the edge of Hertfordshire, the closest village being Perry Green. The carriage ambled carefully down a leafy lane to the secluded property, both Zach and Emma turning their heads to view the house as it came into view. The stone and ivied house was nestled into a valley and Emma could see that coming out the front door, painted a merry shade of bright blue, would lead a person directly upon meandering lanes and within sight of breathtaking views of the valley and the farmland. On the north side, there was an apple and pear orchard and there sat within this, two wicker chairs and a small table.

She thought the place charming upon first sight, and possibly the perfect size for her plans, but dared not let her hopes rise as the earl was likely to find it unacceptable.

When the carriage stopped, the earl disembarked and offered his hand. Emma placed her gloved hand in his, attempting to pay no heed to the spark of heat that raced through her with every small touch of his. For three days, she'd steadfastly refused to recall his kiss, though had been successful in this endeavor only rarely, but determined that there be no repeat of that embrace; her body and mind had thrilled at his touch then, and this was apt to cause her nothing but heartache.

Mentally shaking herself, she stepped from the carriage and happily onto solid ground. The ride had not been overlong, but Emma found herself a bit stiff from holding such an immobile posture in his close company.

"This is lovely indeed," she said, waiting for the inevitable fault-finding mission to begin.

"So far, yes," he surprised her by agreeing.

A man appeared then from around the side of the cottage, moving slowly upon legs that seemed to present him knee-first. "You'd be the earl," he guessed. "This here is our Daisy cottage, though I ain't seen daisies here in thirty years."

He spoke as slowly as he walked and had perhaps seen years numbering more than seventy, Emma guessed. She watched him shift upon his bent legs, and tuck one hand into his rope belt while the other pushed the thin and longish hair off his forehead. "Oh," he said then, with a slap at his forehead. "I'd be Henry, the caretaker. Suppose you'd be wanting to see the inside." And without awaiting a reply, he sauntered leisurely toward the front door.

Emma passed an appreciative glance over the flower boxes that graced the two windows which flanked the front door. She frowned and looked to the earl to see if he'd noticed the prolific abundance of daisies within these boxes. He had, apparently, for he offered her a small yet disarming grin at their presence of the pretty blooms, certainly after Henry had specifically mentioned the lack thereof.

They followed Henry into the cottage and Emma was immediately delighted with the open floor plan. The foyer was set with well-kept flagstone and the walls were papered charmingly in a dainty floral print. Directly across from the door, a wooden staircase with engraved trim, uncarpeted, reached the second floor. To the left was a parlor with knotted beams upon the high ceiling, the room filled with pretty furniture. To the right was a small study, the walls lined with shelves and shelves of books, the room bright despite its heavy woodwork.

Henry said not a word but walked by these rooms, leading them down a wide hallway next to the staircase, to the rear of the house, where sat the kitchen. This room was small, but again the high ceiling afforded it a larger appearance and Emma saw that there was, aside from the usual kitchen fixtures, a pump within a tall and wide sink basin. They followed Henry, who continued on through a wide pantry and into the back hall. There, he painstakingly mounted a narrow spiral staircase and walked down the well-lit corridor upon the second floor. The earl pushed open each of the three doors to reveal three bed-chambers, all bright and pretty and well-furnished. A fourth door, open to reveal large windows presently letting in ample sunshine, showed a modest sitting room, which connected to one of the bed chambers.

Henry pointed slowly to another door, further down the hall. "Stairs to servants chambers, four of 'em, and maybe some storage or what have you."

At the end of the hallway, Henry turned a small corner and began to descend the stairs, which brought them back to the main foyer. "Well, there ye be," he said, and seemed to wait for an instant decision. Emma cast questioning eyes toward the earl. "Oh," Henry said then, "and the small dining room is through the parlor there." He pointed in the general direction with his thumb. "Meets the kitchen, too, after the pantry."

Emma nodded, thinking this was by far her favorite of the houses they had toured, but inwardly thought it silly to get her hopes up for surely this lease would be beyond her means, whatever they may be. And then she nearly collapsed when the earl looked at her and asked if she liked it. Had she not been so surprised by this solicitation, she might have better considered his motive here—he hadn't asked her opinion at the previous three cottages they'd seen. But she did like this place, very much so. "I do. It's very bright and the yard is lovely. It's not too far from Perry Green, within walking distance I imagine, on a fine day." She watched the earl nod at her. To Henry, she dared to ask, "How much to let the house month to month?" She watched Henry look to the earl and had a feeling he wasn't accustomed to discussing business with a female.

"Emma—" the earl began.

"For sale, milord, not to lease," Henry said at the same time, looking at the earl.

Emma's heart sank. She didn't know much about the cost of things, but she knew for sure an outright purchase was out of the question. "Oh," was all she said. Dejected, Emma felt her shoulders slump, supposing this perfectly charming place no longer an option. She lifted a re-animated gaze, however, when she heard the earl say, "We'll take it, then."

Emma turned sharply. "My lord?"

But he paid her no mind, other than to place his hand at the back of her arm when she neared him, telling Henry that he should inform his employer—Lord Darby, the current owner—that his solicitors would be 'round to make the deal. With that, Henry tipped his head politely at the earl and then again to Emma and the earl steered her out of the cottage.

"My Lord," Emma protested, "for Bethany's sake, I am not against accepting your father's bequest, but I don't think—"

"Good, then don't start," the earl clipped, causing Emma to frown yet more. "Trust me, there is plenty. And you've still quite enough left to see to your daily needs."

She had no idea what she'd done to incur this present ill-humor of his—he'd asked if she liked it; she answered yes, that was all. So why was he angry now? she wondered. She allowed him to hand her into the phaeton once more and they made the twenty-minute drive to Benedict House in complete silence, but she was ever aware of the ticking vein at his temple, as he allowed her to view only his profile.

Chapter Seven

Once returned to Benedict House, Emma clambered out of the phaeton before the earl might have been of assistance. She would be thrilled to be well gone from him. True, he'd done her a kindness to purchase so costly a house for her, but that benevolence, offered so abrasively, seemed then not a kindness at all. And she was reminded that it wasn't *his* kindness at all, but his father's. Emma began to believe that he was as anxious as she to have her gone from his home. She bothered not to hide her distress and made no excuse but ran directly up the stairs without even the politeness of a by-your-leave.

The man was insufferable, she decided, and found it then impossible not to compare his dastardly nature with that of his charming father, once again finding the present earl much lacking. And oh, how she missed Michael!

Emma reached her rooms just as Mrs. Conklin was exiting the nursery next door. The plump housekeeper put her index finger to her lips. "She's just gone down for her nap, Miss. She was an angel, to be sure."

"Thank you, Mrs. Conklin," Emma replied. "It was nice of you to look after her."

"'Tis no trouble, Miss, though truly I don't know how you'll manage when you leave."

Leave, she couldn't do soon enough, Emma thought irritably but showed this not to the kindly housekeeper. "We'll manage just fine, Mrs. Conklin. Truthfully, I'm not much used to having so much free time. We'll settle back into our old ways, just Bethany and me," she offered, though other ideas had recently come to her. She turned then, *feeling* him near. As Mrs. Conklin moved away from Emma and down the corridor, Emma saw that the earl had reached the second-floor landing. His face was set into the same scowl it had shown most of these last few days, yet his eyes seemed to devour her, and this severe stare sent Emma scurrying into her room.

Emma spent the remainder of the day by herself, and then with Bethany when the child awoke. She'd already decided that she would absolutely not join the earl for dinner and would bar the door if need be, but she needn't have bothered with these ponderings, for she was informed by Thurman later in the day that the earl had sent his apologies—he would be dining with friends this evening. Emma might have squealed her joy at this lucky turn, but instead enjoyed a more relaxed evening, having not to fear the earl's changeable moods and dark, brooding stare.

When Bethany had been sleeping for nearly an hour, Emma lifted her from her own bed and pushed open the door to the nursery, gently laying the babe into the tall crib. She left the door ajar, and then left her own room intent on finding Bethany's doll, which must have been abandoned or forgotten somewhere downstairs.

Tying the sash of her dressing gown more securely about her, she searched the darkened parlor and then the sitting room, but to no avail. The house was quiet at this hour, and honestly, she felt a little like a thief sneaking around, trying so hard since she'd come to this overwhelming house to go unnoticed. This was not a simple thing to do, Bethany making herself known even as Emma would rather not.

Actually, she hadn't been able to recall when last she'd seen the doll, and began to wonder if some tidy servant had only removed it from the floor of some room. She peeked into yet another room on the first floor, surprised to find what must be the earl's study. The room was large and gorgeous, with dark paneling and an entire wall of long windows, allowing moonlight to show her that indeed Bethany's doll was atop the desk at the far side of the room. She snuck in, not quite sure why she bothered to tip-toe and even less sure how the doll might have found its way here. She breathed a startled gasp as she saw that behind the desk on the wall of gleaming paneling hung a beautiful portrait of Michael.

"Oh," she moaned, and tears formed instantly. She covered her mouth with one hand just as the other grabbed hold of the doll from the desk. Oh, but wasn't he so handsome, and stately, and fine? The painting must have been done years before, as his hair showed not the liberal gray that he'd gained by the time she had known him; his eyes were as wonderfully kind as she remembered; he was depicted from the thighs up, dressed in a clever high-collared waistcoat and tailcoat and a finely tied cravat of sumptuous creamy silk. Emma smiled at the almost Byronian hairstyle, his darker locks swept forward and to the right across his forehead. "Oh, how I miss you." Her shoulders slumped. Aside from memories, too few at that, this was all she might ever have of him. She determined that she would bring Bethany here tomorrow, she would insist the child not forget this dear man.

She almost turned away, her sorrow heavy just now, but then decided to sit and visit with him for a while. With a pleased smile, thinking he might enjoy her company, she scooted behind the desk and turned the heavy side-armed chair all the way around until it faced the portrait. She sat in the chair, pulled her knees up to her chest, her feet just at the edge of the seat, and hugged the doll he'd bought for Bethany, being now within only feet of the painting.

"I wish you were here right now, my friend."

The portrait was perfect, in that it showed the hint of a smile that seemed always to hover about his lips. His eyes nearly danced, so that Emma imagined whoever had put his image to canvas must have known him fairly well. Emma smiled back at him.

Zachary Benedict stood frozen at the opposite side of the room, having risen from the very desk chair in which she now sat, simply to refill his brandy snifter. The door opening had lifted his gaze, and Miss Ainsley's creeping had kept him still, though a frown had come. Suspicion had faded as soon as she'd reached for the doll, which he had noticed upon his desk earlier.

Tucked in the shadows of the far corner, she had yet to notice his presence, and Zach hadn't moved a muscle to alert her that she was not alone in the room. Her gasp, when she'd spied his father's portrait had nearly startled him. And then she'd done the most remarkable thing, pivoting the chair and sitting down, staring at his father, seeming only to want to spend time with him.

Whispers of her soft words reached him. Honestly, he was a bit surprised at her referring to him as her friend. He might have supposed, as she thought herself alone with him, she might have been unguarded enough to perhaps refer to him as *my love* or some such nonsense. *My friend* gave him pause. And then all the words that followed, as she talked quietly to his father, laid out so many truths to him, most that he'd refused to see or believe until now.

"I'm going to bring Bethany here tomorrow," she was saying, "I don't want her to forget you." Zach thought she might be crying, her voice cracked as she continued, "I wish I had known the last time I saw you was going to be...the last time I saw you. I would have used the time to tell you how wonderful you were. I would have told you I cherished every minute we'd spent together. I'm sorry I was often so resistant to all the help you tried to give to me. Honestly, I didn't understand it. Maybe it frightened me a little—people are so rarely kind for no other reason than to be kind. But you were. So ridiculously kind."

Still immobile near the small liquor cabinet, the fine crystal glass held at waist height in one hand, the brandy decanter in the other, Zach waited, afforded only a view of the top of her head over the back of the chair. She was quiet for a long time, her head tilted against the leather of that chair, glancing upward. "I remember the first night you came to the inn, when my finger was broken. You were so natural, so gentle with Bethany. She'd known Mr. Smythe all her little life and had never taken to him as she had to you. Just like that. It was so remarkable to see. We don't need to talk again about the spoiling—you know well my thoughts on this, as I do yours." Zach thought he detected a hint of a smile in her voice.

Another long pause, and her tone changed, was less soft. "Your son, Michael—we should talk about your son. Honest to God, Michael," she was saying, "you did no favors to me by your descriptions of him. All that fatherly pride prepared me not at all for exactly...how different from you he is. He's so...angry, it seems. Or just obstinate, I don't rightly know. Were you like that at his age, and just mellowed throughout the years? I cannot imagine that your beloved Barbara instilled such hardness in him. Oh my God, Michael! Did you spoil him as well? Is that why he's so adamant about everything being done his way? Always being right? Looking down his nose at a person..."

Zach's eyes widened. So much revealed just here, so many opinions then to put to those sparse and wary looks she so often gave him.

She carried on, "It's not your fault though. He's a grown man, all his decisions—to be mean or not to be—are his own. But I tell you now, Michael, if I find out you somehow inferred, or outright said to your son that Bethany is your daughter, I promise you, we are going to have words when next we meet. I cannot, for the life of me, imagine where he came upon that notion—so, apologies to you, my friend, I'm blaming you until I hear or know otherwise. Yes, I've told him the truth. He doesn't believe me. I can see it in his eyes. Oh, and the best part, which I'm sure you are already aware of: he doesn't mind looking down his nose at me—a taproom jade, he thinks—but what does he do at first opportunity? He kisses me. Did you see that?" She harrumphed then, and God help him, Zach almost burst out laughing.

"You probably did. It may have appeared for a moment that I enjoyed his kiss, but Michael, I assure you I did not. Well, honestly, I—no! No. I did not enjoy it one bit. Dear Lord, he frightens the bejesus out of me. You told me he was intelligent beyond imagining, and that his honor was strung about him as armor, and something about...oh, what was it? Oh, yes, you said he 'was impressed neither by appearance nor rumors, but rather by the knowledge and character of a person, and if they had a humble heart'. I have to tell you, Michael, your son wouldn't know a humble heart if it thumped him upside the head. He's too busy being bossy and intractable, and making people feel awkward in his presence. Again, not your fault."

Intractable? Zach wondered. Was he? He didn't know, but damn if he weren't learning so very much right now. It was as good as being inside her head, he thought. But he chewed the inside of his cheek, believing it damnably unfortunate that she held such a low opinion of him.

He heard her yawn then, a vocal and lengthy yawn, and she was quiet for several more seconds until she said, a haunting melancholy tinting her words, "I hope you've been reunited with your Barbara. And maybe you've met Gretchen and have told her how adorable her daughter is. You always said I was a perfect mother to her," she said, and tears must have come for her voice broke once more, "but does Gretchen think so? Will you tell her I'm trying my best?" Long pause now while she sobbed into her hands. "I don't know what I'm doing," he thought she said, but could not be sure, muffled and cracked as the words were now.

Jesus, but it was enough to break his heart, even as he was quite sure she thought he hadn't one.

"I miss you," she whispered one more time and then was quiet and unmoving for so long, Zach was sure she must have fallen asleep in the chair.

He shifted his weight from one leg to another, so afraid to move if she were indeed still awake. But when another fifteen minutes or so had passed and she made no movement and uttered no more words, he gingerly and with excruciating slowness set the decanter and snifter onto the top of the cabinet. Only the smallest of noises accompanied this, but in this very still room, it might have been heard, if she were awake.

She was still yet.

Zach walked silently to where she sat. Just as he came around the side of the chair, he saw that her elbow was on one bent knee, her small hand fisted and holding up her chin while she slumbered. Her other arm was wrapped around the doll, clutched tightly to her. The moonlight, which had not reached the corner in which he'd hidden, offered just enough illumination that he could distinguish the trail of tears down her cheeks and the small furrow in her brow.

What am I going to do with you?

He moved all the way around the chair, so that he faced her. He leaned his back against the wall, just near the frame of the portrait, and watched her sleep.

Possibly, she wasn't real. She couldn't be. They weren't made like this, so very exquisite, and with that beautiful heart of hers, that missed his father, and her sister, and worried that she might be failing as the child's mother. And talked to portraits in the night. Glancing sideways, he looked at the picture of his father, who at this very moment, from this angle, looked as if he were smiling upon her, as if only satisfied to be watching her sleep.

Ah, but she was stubborn, even while calling *him* intractable. But she'd given the why of this: she was afraid. Frightened by kindness?

It was late. He was weary. And he considered that he had much to contemplate about everything she'd revealed to him, by way of her conversation with his sire.

Loath as he was to disturb her, he knew it needed to be done. As gently as possible, he shimmied his hands under her legs and around her back and lifted her into his arms. The doll settled perfectly against her chest, and he strode from his study and through the dark hall to the wide staircase. He knew when she roused and realized her circumstance by the stiffening of her form in his arms. He climbed the stairs, and murmured, "Shh." Though she said nothing, she remained fairly rigid in his grasp now.

Zach debated if any words from him now might put her at ease, decided it was unlikely and so extended none. He reached the top of the stairs and turned right to find her rooms. The door was ajar, allowing him to give a nudge with his foot to push it fully open. He set her on to the bed, and spared her only a glance and a murmured, "Good night," lest she think him only some mute monster, an intractable one perhaps. He supposed he was glad for the total darkness of her borrowed chamber, that he might not see what expression might have accompanied her severe posture in his arms.

He pulled the door closed as he left, closing his eyes for the space of a moment, trying to imagine what, if anything, he hoped might come of their very brief but icy relationship. Would he simply deposit her at the Daisies Cottage and be done with her? His immediate internal response to this was, it seemed most prudent. But why? Why was it prudent not to know her?

Therein, he supposed, was the real answer, that he didn't want to *not* know her.

Maybe that was all he needed to understand right now.

The last thing Emma wanted to do was accept charity from the Earl of Lindsey, even if it were originally conceived by that greater man, Michael Benedict. But fact was fact, and she hadn't a home, or an income, or a family, and so then had no choice but to accept that he had indeed purchased the Daisies Cottage for her and Bethany.

This morning, she was plagued by that decidedly uncomfortable remembrance of last night, when she'd woken to find herself in the earl's arms. God's wounds, but how could she have allowed for something so unbearably tortuous to have occurred? Never mind that his embrace, for all its utilitarian purpose, had been perceived as warm and safe and...not wholly unpleasant. *Ugh*.

She could not take up residence at the Daisies Cottage soon enough.

But she had a few things to take care of first. She approached Thurman bright and early one morning, holding Bethany's hand as the babe walked in yet another pair of new shoes, courtesy of the Earl. Emma had stopped refusing, had stopped insisting, and had stopped complaining about any purchases for Bethany. There simply was no point.

The butler waited expectantly.

"I wonder if I might have use of a buggy to take into town," she inquired of the aged man. She didn't tell him which town, so didn't therefore consider that she lied to the man.

"You can, perhaps, write down any items you were in need of, Miss," he answered quite solicitously, his bushy gray brows raising a bit at this offering. "Mrs. Conklin regularly sends a footman or such to town for shopping—fresh goods, and wardrobe items, and other sundries...."

"This is to be more of a visiting nature, making calls," she told him, while Bethany now uncurled her little fingers from Emma's hand, plopping down on her bottom on the immaculate tile floor to look at her new shoes again.

"I see," intoned Thurman, raising and lowering his head in a manner which Emma imagined only butlers managed to employ. "Peter would be available to drive you to your appointments, Miss."

"Oh, I shouldn't want to put someone out, Mr. Thurman. I'm certainly capable of handling a small buggy, pulled by any agreeable nag," she countered with a sweet smile.

"Be that as it may, Miss, Peter will take you in to town."

Emma considered arguing further, but judged the argument was perhaps more likely to succeed with a goat, rather than the almost formidable Mr. Thurman. "Thank you, sir." She scooped up Bethany. "We will ready ourselves and return momentarily."

Within the hour, Emma sat beside Peter, a man only slightly older than herself, with a pleasing personality. She held Bethany in her lap, not of a mind to further disturb the Earl's household by once again asking Mrs. Conklin to watch after the child. She had directed Peter to the King's Arms Inn—rather assertively, she'd thought—and if he was surprised by her destination, he gave no indication. She didn't know what she expected to find of her old home and workplace, but she needed to see the Smythe's and make sure they were well. Peter was indeed pleasant but not much for small talk, so Emma occupied herself with Bethany, as the trip took almost an hour. When they'd crested the last hill that would show the inn to them, Emma found herself holding her breath. But it was as she had feared, the inn was indeed still gone, only the burnt-out shell still remained; obviously no rebuilding had begun, or perhaps wasn't intended. But how would she find the Smythes?

"Miss," Peter said, when they'd stopped still a distance from the ruins, "did ye know this was gone?"

"I did," she answered, almost forlornly. "But I don't know how to find my friends—my family, really—and thought I should at least start here."

"Little Hadham would be the closest town," Peter said after a moment. "Might they have moved there?"

Emma shrugged sadly. "I just don't know." She took her eyes from the King's Arms Inn and looked at the young footman. "Would you mind driving there?"

Peter had snapped the reins over the lone horse in answer, and the gig moved again, now away from the inn. "We'll find 'em, miss. Never you fear."

Little Hadham boasted not much more than a lone mercantile, a few pubs, and only one inn, all lying in the village just south of Hadham Hall, ancient seat of the Capells, and the Earl of Essex. Emma suggested they begin their search at the inn. But only a moment after making this suggestion, while Peter maneuvered the gig through the narrow road and sparse traffic, Emma spied the young stable hand, Langdon, walking down the road, heading to the pier down at the River Ash.

Excitedly, she raised herself on the seat and called happily, "Langdon!"

The young man looked left and right upon hearing his name but saw no one familiar and so continued walking. "Langdon!" she called out again. This time, he turned, and finally saw Emma—her arm flailing wildly in the air—and company bearing down on him. He squinted but quickly recognized her. She'd not much recalled that he ever smiled, but he did now.

Langdon approached the gig just as Peter pulled up at the side of the road.

"Miss Emma! What are ye about? Are you coming back with us?" He wanted to know, his eyes hopeful.

His question enlivened Emma. "Are you all still together? Are you with the Smythes? And Alice, too?" She hoped it were true. She was encouraged by Langdon's excitement over seeing her.

"Sure, Miss—was cheaper to share one room than have to find one yerself," he told her. "We did stay at the stables those first few days, but it were rough. Alice never stopped crying. But Mr. Smythe and me, we came into town here to see what could be had. We all pooled our money—well those who had any—and well, at least got a real roof now. But we may have to go to another town, maybe a bigger one, to find some work... for any one of us. There's nothing here." And then he smiled and nodded at the three of them in the gig, having delivered all his news.

Emma was amazed, staring rather dumbstruck for a moment. Firstly, Langdon had never strung so many words together in her presence, or to anyone, as far as she knew. Next, she was surprised, though pleasantly so, that the four of them had stayed together. They really were a little family. Her eyes welled. "Where are they?"

Within minutes, Emma was following a still chatty Langdon into a cottage at the edge of the small town, having asked Peter to remain with the gig. It had a rough and ramshackle exterior, and even before entering there was an odor about the air that was decidedly unpleasant. Inside, Emma hugged Bethany tighter, her eyes adjusting to the dimness of the interior. She heard, before she saw Mrs. Smythe. The old woman let out a howl of glee upon spying Emma and the child, coming straight at her from what Emma imagined must be the kitchen, when her eyes finally settled.

"Oh, my dear," Mrs. Smythe cried, "never have I been happier to see a soul! So worried about ye, we've been." She stole Bethany abruptly but cheerfully out of Emma's arms, crying and fussing over the little girl. "And look at ye, dressed in your finery—the both of ye!—oh, I pray he's been good to ye. Seems as much, I daresay."

Emma glanced around the house, wondering at their arrangement here, as it appeared only a single dwelling, and one of improbable character.

"What have you—?" She began but was interrupted by the appearance of the innkeeper himself, Mr. Smythe. She smiled expectantly at him as he entered the front room. He'd never been a warm and fuzzy person, but Emma did decide that he looked rather pleased to see her. "Good afternoon, sir," she said.

"Emma, girl," he acknowledged. "You're well, then?"

"Oh, yes, sir!" She was quick to assure him. "I'm so very pleased to find you all. I've worried so!"

"Won't have an inn no more," Mr. Smythe said, with a bit of a shrug to his shoulders, and a pursing of his lips. "But we've a roof for now—until Mrs. Coombs returns from London next month and again takes up her residence here. So we've time still to figure out where best to land." And he nodded. He looked to Langdon, who nodded along with his boss—former boss, now housemate.

"But that's why I'm so happy to find you!" Emma said. She touched Mrs. Smythe's arm next to her. "What are your plans?

Will you rebuild? Will you find another inn to buy? Have you other property or...even monies to see you through?"

Mrs. Smythe lowered her eyes, offering only a weak smile. Mr. Smythe shuffled his feet a bit.

"Never did 'ave much for savings. And what we did was burned up in there," he said roughly, tossing his head in the general direction of the King's Arms Inn. "But I've a mind to head south, more toward London. We're thinking there might be a need of a good and experienced manager—if you will—for all those fancier public houses down there. Maybe have need of a cook and stablehand," he finished, but it was quite apparent from his lackluster tone that he hadn't really any hope of this. "Maybe another barmaid," he added when the light from one of the doorways was briefly blocked.

Emma turned to find Alice staring at her. The young woman did not look entirely happy to see Emma, but her moods were ever mercurial, and her face—when not serving in the taproom, hoping for coin—was often hard. She was different somehow, though, Emma realized instantly, her shoulders wilted, her eyes rather lifeless. She wore a gown of somber brown—dreary was more apt—with threads that looked to have seen better days, and Emma knew this to be a huge embarrassment to the girl; ever did she love her vivid colors and loud combinations.

"Hullo, Alice," she offered hesitantly, never quite sure of her reception.

Alice only nodded, her gaze raking over Emma's finery. If she did try to smile, it appeared only as a grimace. Awkwardly, she shoved her hands into the flap pockets of her borrowed, pilfered, or scrounged-for dress.

Emma turned back to the Smythes. She looked from one to the other. She guessed they'd aged about twenty years since the fire had taken everything they had in the world. Perhaps she'd never thought so much about their specific ages but guessed Smythe, with his balding, craggy head and long face, having once been tall and thick-chested though those days were long behind him now, to have seen about 60 years by now. And his wife, that dear Mrs. Smythe, with her short and stout form, and her wiry hair and kind eyes, might have seen just a few less than that.

She approached Mr. Smythe, putting her hand on the rough fabric of his sleeve. Momentarily, she wondered if she had ever touched him at all before. She'd known him almost a decade, had worked side by side with him, knew he truly did care for her, but this felt new.

"Come with me," she said shortly. "The old earl—Michael—truly did make provisions for me. Well, likely for Bethany really." She turned to look at Mrs. Smythe, who seemed to be waiting, interested, but not yet willing to be hopeful, it seemed. "His lordship—the new earl, that is—has purchased a house for us." Emma watched as Mrs. Smythe slapped a hand over her mouth, her eyes crinkling with her upset. "No, Mistress, not like that at all, I promise. The house is for Bethany and me. Just us. I truly didn't want his money, or his help. But...but I've Bethany to think of. And Michael, well, he wanted this for us." Emma turned, and looked at an expressionless Alice, and Langdon who was nodding again, apparently in agreement, and then to Mr. Smythe, who was frowning, seemingly not in annoyance but with consideration. She continued, talking quickly to convince them, to assure them, it could work, "The house is big enough. It's close to Perry Green—likely we can find work there, though I think Mr. and Mistress, you wouldn't need to work if you'd not mind helping to take care of the house," she said, hopefully. To Langdon, "There's space for you, too. An entire floor of bedrooms I'd not know what to do with. And there's a small barn, a stable, maybe we can find a horse and gig eventually." She turned to Alice, "Perry Green has a handful of pubs—there's even a modiste, and a milliner. We can find work, I'm sure." No one said a word. Emma turned to Mrs. Smythe, "Perhaps you wouldn't mind looking after Bethany if I'm to find a job."

When they remained silent, Emma spun around to Mr. Smythe again. "Our own house again," she imagined.

His eyes lifted over her to settle on his wife. After a moment of worrying the inside of his cheek, he asked, "What say ye, missus?"

When Emma turned back again, she found Mrs. Smythe crying into a squirming Bethany, who'd thus far had been intent enough on the people and the atmosphere of this room to have been quiet, but now was reaching for Emma with a whine.

"Shh," Emma cooed, and stroked her daughter's hair but did not take her. Emma kept her eyes on Mrs. Smythe. "Won't you come with me?"

Mrs. Smythe began to nod her head against a warm but still fussing Bethany. Emma let out a happy cry. Eventually Mrs. Smythe raised her wet and red eyes to Emma. "Oh, but ye always were the sweetest thing, Emma," she said through tears. "And here ye are, still thinking of everyone but yerself. Oh, but we thank ye!" And she leaned forward, kissing Emma's cheek, and Emma squeezed her tightly in a happy embrace. "We needn't fret no more, husband," she said to Mr. Smythe.

Emma looked at Mr. Smythe. He nodded at his wife's words, and surprised Emma by gently touching her arm, a gesture of appreciation.

A quick rapping sound brought all eyes to the door, where Peter stood, wringing his hat in his hand. He looked apologetic, but said, "Miss, I hate to hurry ye, but I'm needing to get back to Benedict House—ye as well, I imagine."

"Oh, yes, Peter," Emma answered hurriedly, "I'll be along shortly—very quickly," she amended, when he appeared unsure. Emma looked at Langdon and Alice, smiling hopefully. "You'll come, too, right?"

"Of course they will!" Mrs. Smythe insisted, her tone motherly.

Langdon shuffled his feet just for a moment, his face reddening with this attention, as all eyes rested on him. "Aw, miss, I ain't nowhere else to go. Yer all I have, I guess. I can be helpful."

Impulsively, Emma hugged him, so happy to have these people back in her life. "I know you can, Langdon. You're going to love the house!" She turned to Alice. "You will love the Daisies Cottage, it's just perfect—"

"I appreciate the offer, I truly do, Emma," Alice interrupted her. "But I will be all right here."

Emma thought she looked sincere. They had never been close, but they had shared so much over all these years passed. "Alice, you must," she said softly.

Mr. Smythe spoke up. "Alice, girl, there just isn't much opportunity here, we're finding out."

Alice raised her shoulders. "There could be. I'll be all right."

"Alice," Mrs. Smythe cried, "ye must come with us."

"You have always been fair to me, the both of you," Alice said, looking suddenly, uncharacteristically sheepish, "but I think it's time I moved on. I want—need—something other than a cottage in the dead of the country." With what appeared to be a false bravado, she added, "I've been thinking for some time now to be heading to London anyhow. What family I do have, they're all there."

Emma saw that Mrs. Smythe's bottom lip hung open. Mr. Smythe only nodded, saying nothing. Langdon was still staring at Emma.

Emma tried to think of something else to say to Alice to change her mind. But Mrs. Smythe spoke first.

"If yer sure, dear...?"

Alice nodded, trying to smile to back up her words. But to Emma, she only looked guarded and somehow peeved.

"Miss," Peter prompted again from the doorway. He seemed unperturbed, perhaps only uninterested in the scene he'd witnessed, but eager to be on his way.

Emma nodded, and retrieved Bethany from Mrs. Smythe. "I must go. I'll return, or send word, once we're settled at the house. Hopefully, it will be soon." She quickly kissed Mrs. Smythe and called goodbye to all. She stopped once more in front of Alice. "Be safe, Alice. Come back if you need to."

Alice nodded again. "Goodbye."

Chapter Eight

Some part of her—the part that wasn't hounded by so much intrigue over the earl—was happy to be informed that he was gone to London for the day, and would she mind taking her supper in her rooms. This suited Emma perfectly, as she had yet to find ease with the sometimes practice of handing the child off to a servant while she'd partaken of meals with the earl in the dining room.

Later that night, she tucked Bethany into her crib just as a wild summer storm began to kick up. Fortunately, Bethany had fallen asleep before the thunder began to sound in earnest. Emma stayed inside the nursery for quite a while, making sure she wasn't wakened and frightened by the storm. When the rains seemed to be moving away, and the thunder and lightning began to fade, Emma finally sought her own bed. She had no difficulty falling asleep herself, as she found herself of late to be rather emotionally exhausted by day's end.

She woke to the sound of a huge crack of thunder pealing across the night sky. She leapt from the bed, imagining that if this round of thunder and lightning had woken her, it might frighten Bethany as well. But she heard no crying as she quietly walked through the connecting door to the nursery, which she always left open. Stepping within the room, she stopped suddenly upon finding the earl already there.

Her heart beat faster at just the sight of him. Dressed only in his black trousers, he must have heard Bethany wake whilst in the midst of preparing for bed. His back was to Emma, and Bethany's sleepy head was just visible over the top of his shoulder.

He was soothing Bethany with a soft hum and a slight, fluid rocking motion.

Emma could only stare, half aghast at this picture—at the very fact that he seemed so tenderhearted as to be found rocking a frightened child to sleep—and half breathless as she hungrily absorbed the sight of his naked back and arms. The Earl of Lindsey boasted a magnificent figure; in the dim light, afforded by the open door to the connecting room she'd not yet dared to explore, he was a bronzed god of sinewy muscle; shadows danced merrily over this contour and that hollow of his skin; the very size and chiseled purpose of his arms alone brought her hand to her chest, as if that might still the rising rate of her heart. True it was that Emma had labored many years at an inn, but she had never seen a nearly naked man before, and still, somehow, she was quite sure that none could rival the form of this man.

Lightning streaked just as he moved to lay a sleeping Bethany down, and the noise paused him for a moment. He waited until he was certain she remained asleep and then did stretch his magnificent form over the edge of the baby's crib. Skin and muscle moved in conjunction with his reach, shapes appeared and disappeared, arms flexed and tightened.

Emma sighed just as he righted himself again, which did not go unnoticed; he turned rather sharply, affording her a fine view of his bare chest and lean abdomen. A sparse matting of hair was centered directly below his jaw, beginning at his chest and thinning to one straight line which stretched low and dipped beneath his trousers. His nipples, bare as a newborn come into the world, were dark and small, but peaked enticingly. The very shape of his chest was foreign to her, being that his was squarish while hers was round, his being firm while hers was soft.

She knew he watched her gawking at him but could not seem to move her eyes away from his person, being as entranced as she was. Only when he strode to her, Emma vaguely noticing the long and lean bare feet upon the carpet, did she finally look into his eyes. He kept coming though, seething, it appeared, breathing heavily through his nose. Without stopping, he grabbed her arm in a near-bruising grip, turned her around, and dragged her back into her own chambers. Dark eyes on her, he closed the door to the nursery almost completely with one hand, still holding her with the other.

Neither had yet to say a word, Emma having been rendered speechless while under the profound influence of his glorious form. When she spun around, and they faced each other so closely, she still could neither manage words nor take her eyes from his chest. A rare boldness, called forth by the intoxicating sight of him raised her free hand and set it on his chest. Slender fingers grazed the short, wiry hair of his chest, short tapered nails found the heated skin there. He drew a deep breath at her tentative foray. This drew her eyes to his, reading him, trying to interpret that feral gleam.

And then reality, and embarrassment, flooded her. Yanking her hand away, she curled her fingers into her palm just as he said, "Don't stop."

Emma shook her head, mortified, even more so as she was quite sure she discerned a lazy smile in his tone.

A taproom jade, indeed! She'd just unknowingly vindicated him of any outrage she might have felt or sustained from the kiss he'd taken from her only days ago. Closing her eyes against a shame that, while powerful, was unlikely to aid her in undoing the last few moments and her unseemly behavior.

She pulled at the hand he still held and pivoted. But he would not allow her to turn away from him.

She couldn't—wouldn't—look at him now. She heard his heavy breathing, felt the stiffness come to him with her actions. And reactions. She swallowed hard, and shook her head again, lest he think to pursue this madness further.

"I don't know why I—" Staring at the huge and rumpled bed, she was only peripherally aware of his nod, controlled, silent. He glared at her a moment more. He wanted to say something, she knew, but he did not. Finally, he released her hand, turned on his heel and left her room, slipping through the nursery door the way he had come.

The next morning, Emma approached the earl in the breakfast room, her cheeks unpleasantly flushed, her lips dry with distaste, and her stomach filled with dread. She'd mumbled through some atrocious apology, excuses such as "I haven't a notion what I was thinking...I was imbued with sleep yet," and, "You so caught me by surprise...having no shirt..." coming not so pluckily as she'd have liked them to. He'd lifted his head from his morning paper, considering her with a mute starkness about him that frightened her yet more. When he'd made no immediate response, even as his gaze had seemed to soften, Emma had flown from the room, nearly in tears, heedless of his eventual call for her to return.

She had avoided him for the next several days, quite sure that mortification alone might send her to an early grave. Never in her life had she behaved so wantonly as she had that eve with him. To her own self, she admitted that never before had she reason to be so tempted into shamelessness. She constantly chided herself, since then, that his figure alone should not have sent her into such depravity, and that his supreme gentleness and regard for Bethany was his *only* saving grace. Considering the man as a whole, Emma determined that he'd been rude and oppressive and autocratic since the very moment they had met. She wasn't so naïve as to not understand what he thought of her. And now her own actions supported his belief!

Three days after what Emma now privately referred to as *Her Inglorious and Reckless Blunder*, the earl came upon her and Bethany taking a stroll, off the terrace and around the well-manicured grounds of Benedict House.

As his stride was quite purposeful across the trim and tidy lawns, Emma was immediately sent into a dither, gathering Bethany into her arms, turning slightly so that the wind stopped blowing the frill of her pretty bonnet into her face.

He stopped, several feet away from them, bending one knee while he kept weight on the other, his fine tall hat in his hand, tapped against his thigh. He was dressed formally and must have then, she presumed, just returned from London, as he so often favored fawn breeches and muslin shirts when here in the country.

When he seemed content only to stare at her, she lifted a brow to him, imagining—hoping—that his arrival was occasioned by some intent other than raking her rather severely with his inscrutable gaze.

He cleared his throat.

"I thought to take Bethany riding with me today," he said.

Emma did not know what to make of what sounded like uncertainty in his voice. She wondered if any living soul could claim to have ever heard such hesitancy from this man.

And then he said, "Mayhap you would like to accompany me as well. Riding, that is," which served only to confound Emma yet more. She was acutely aware that she knew nothing about anything, but didn't this just sound so fantastically like a polite invitation?

An invitation. From the earl. To spend time with him.

She felt that wicked wind send the skirts of her fine cotton gown firmly against her thighs. It whipped the fabric into a caress, pushing the skirts out and away from her, surely highlighting every curve and line of her legs. His gaze dipped there and then retreated as the wind faded, finding her eyes again as he awaited a reply.

Mulishness was the only motivation she could conceive to refuse him. But she thought he should know, "Of course I don't ride, my lord." She couldn't imagine why he might think that she could. "But I'm sure Bethany would enjoy the occasion." Truly, there was no reason to deny the child any experience merely to save herself from awkward situations, which seemed to consist of any time spent in the earl's presence.

She wouldn't have said he appeared, then, particularly disappointed as he strode toward her and lifted his hands to Bethany, who happily removed her arms from around Emma's neck and reached for him.

"Would you care to learn to ride?" He surprised Emma by asking then.

As she imagined she might never own her own horse, and while the idea took flight that she could never hope to have control over such a large beast, she shook her head. "I think not." As he stood there, just watching her once more, she wondered if he only awaited more words from her, that she thought to add, "But I thank you for the offer." His expression did not change. And he did not move, not even to bear himself and Bethany to the stables to find a mount. Awkwardly, Emma gave a brief smile and lifted her skirts. "I'll await Bethany's return at the house then." And she walked away—which seemed a perfectly acceptable thing to do, given that he'd said so little, and had just stated that he aimed to ride just now. Without turning back to see, she knew that he hadn't moved yet, and had the unnerving and cheek-pinkening notion that he still stared at her, that it took so much more effort to walk straight and with seeming calmness. Meanwhile, the wind continued to bedevil her, at one point lifting her skirts nearly to her knees.

Once returned to the house, and without a chore to attend, she wondered to Mrs. Conklin if she might only wander around the house, curious about the stately home but unwilling to trespass if it might be frowned upon.

Mrs. Conklin only shrugged. "It is only the earl and yourself in residence, miss. Aside from his personal chambers, if a door should be unlocked, feel free to explore. Of course, the ground floor is all servants' quarters but the first and second and third stories will show you some very pretty rooms, even if they rarely see any visitors these days."

"Does the earl not ever entertain?" Emma asked.

"The earl finds all his entertainments in the city, miss. Haven't hosted an event here since the countess lived, and that's more than a decade ago."

Emma guessed she might have only assumed that people of wealth and consequence regularly held dinner parties and soirees, or similar frivolities. She thanked the housekeeper and found her own chambers, where she discarded her bonnet and jacket and then returned to the hall. With her hands on her hips, she glanced up and down the corridor, choosing where to start. Surely, this floor was mostly or only bedchambers, the Lindsey family apartments. She walked to the end of the hall and ascended a narrow flight of stairs to the third floor, peeking inside the first door she came upon. A disappointing beginning, as this room might well have at one time been a small but pretty bedroom but seemed now to have been relegated to that of a catchall. Boxes and crates and furniture crammed every inch of floor space, appearing as if each new addition was only set just inside the door and pushed forward into an ever-growing mountain of discarded things.

Hoping to find something of greater interest, Emma proceeded to the next door. And then the next and the next, each of which showed only many bedchambers, grander than any servants' accommodations but not as stately as the second floor apartments. She had never seen so many chambers all under one roof. To some degree, almost every chamber had, over the years, been inhabited or suffused with odd furniture and more items of storage, that not one of them held particular appeal to Emma. Save for the third-to-the-last door she might have peeked inside. She paused just inside this room, taken aback by how much finer and frillier this room was than any other, made especially appealing as it had escaped the notice or intent of persons looking to stash no longer needed household elements.

She stepped fully inside, taking in the overall pink tone, still dominant despite the advent of dusty linens covering so much of the furniture and even the bed. The walls and carpets and window treatments all bore some design of pink, striped curtains and chintz floral wallpaper and a thick Aubusson carpet which once might well have been as bright as magenta.

Emma lifted the edges of one piece of linen, showing the subtly glossed wood of an armoire. Another lifted linen showed a pretty carved wood writing desk. Absently, Emma flipped the linen completely out of the way and opened the desk drawer. Or tried to. The drawer stuck but she had the impression that it only did so because too many papers were trapped inside, a hint of these seen from the barely open drawer. Facing the desk squarely, she gave another good tug, and then slipped her fingers within until she moved enough of the impediment away that it finally pulled open. It was indeed crammed with papers, flat and folded letters in a bold, hard-pressed script.

Emma withdrew the topmost letter, turning over the heavy paper to reveal it had been signed and sent by a George Fiske. A quick glance at the others indicated the lettering was all the same, the messages having come from the same person.

A scrawled phrase, *until we meet again*, caught Emma's eye. The date at the top of the letter read January, 1774. Curious, yet considering the aged letters fair game as she could likely injure no living person with her snooping, Emma read the entire letter, finding that whoever George Fiske was, he suffered quite a distant passion for "My darling Caralyn", who was, the envelopes said, a Caralyn Withers.

My love has made me selfish. Were that your hand were fast in mine.

Thus intrigued, Emma scooped up the entire contents of the drawer, all the letters, and found a pretty pink ribbon strewn and crinkled within the stack. At one time, these love notes had been tied neatly together. Emma considered that she'd found the drawer untidy, and immovable because of the messy business within. Had someone, at some time, come looking for a particular missive? Had they been frantic, ripping away the ribbon, and leaving the chaos behind?

Turning, Emma walked across the room and sat on the floor just at the edge of the once bright rug and beneath the set of double windows which afforded plenty of sunshine for reading. Thinking George and Caralyn's story would reveal itself more efficiently if the letters were put in order by the date of their writing, she took the time to do this, trying to keep any remaining envelopes still connected to its rightful contents. When she'd organized them, she counted twenty-eight letters. Leaning her back against the side of the linen shrouded bed, Emma began to read George Fiske's words.

Zach returned to the house almost an hour after stealing Bethany from Emma. Truly, he delighted in the child. She was easy to please, had taken to the riding as well as he'd expected, and hadn't fussed at all when he'd told her they were done for the day.

"We had ourselves a bit of fun, didn't we?" He asked her, as they swept through different rooms upon the ground floor, but found Miss Ainsley nowhere.

Bethany didn't answer and Zach was thinking she was tired. He marched up the stairs and knocked upon Emma's door but heard no call for entrance. A quick peek inside showed him only an empty chamber. Returning to the first floor, he finally saw another person, his housekeeper, stepping out of the dining room, a notepad and pencil in hand.

"Ah, Mrs. Conklin," he called to her. "Have you any idea where Miss Ainsley might be?

When Mrs. Conklin had informed him that Miss Ainsley had asked to tour the entire house, he'd wondered idly what might be done with the child now.

His housekeeper laughed at this, and Zach himself grinned, as he supposed it did rather sound as if he'd only questioned, *Now what do I do with her?*

"She will be ready for her afternoon nap, I daresay," suggested Mrs. Conklin, about to reach for the child.

"What does that involve?" Zach inquired, which had his housekeeper dropping her arms again.

A bit taken aback by his query and his interest, Mrs. Conklin had lifted a brow and told him, "Miss Ainsley likes to read to her in the nursery, while rocking. The sweet thing rarely resists—truly, she has the most wonderful temperament. And then she's put to bed and usually sleeps for more than an hour."

"Doesn't sound very difficult," Zach surmised. And he left the housekeeper, with a sleepy Bethany in his arms still, calling over his shoulder, "Look lively, Mrs. Conklin. I may return for assistance. But if you don't see me in the next half hour, you may assume I've successfully managed to put a toddler in for a nap."

He did just that.

Inside the nursery, on a small table beside the rocker sat a neat stack of books. Zach picked up the first one and settled into the chair. *Tommy Thumb's Pretty Song Book,* according to the frontispiece of the apparently well-loved and well-used tome, is what he employed to lull Bethany to sleep. Her little blonde finger pointed to the pen and ink drawings on the pages while Zach read different rhymes to her, some of which he'd not ever heard before, or recalled. Soon, her hand was still upon the open book in his lap, and Zach rocked a few more minutes to be sure she slept before depositing her into the short bed. He straightened and stared down at her, thinking that she was very dear to him already, and then feeling quite accomplished for the feat he'd just managed.

Of course, it could be argued that their vigorous outing and the excitement of their pursuit had just as much a hand in getting Bethany to sleep, but Zach was willing to share in the glory of the job well done. He set the book down and wondered still where Miss Ainsley had gotten to. He'd been disappointed that she'd had no interest in horseback riding with him, and apparently no interest in learning either. But she'd denied him her company politely, and seemingly without an agenda, that he could find no reason to be sore about it.

Touring the house, was she? Of course, it was possible that she remembered little of her own family's home, or maybe it had always been the inn, that Benedict House must appear a palace to her with it's endless passageways and corridors, and more rooms than a household of one hundred could properly utilize.

Poking his head into the library, drawing room, billiards room, and several others offered no sighting of Miss Ainsley. He had no specific reason to seek her out, but that he'd been plagued of late with the memory of the sensation of her fingers on his chest. He'd allowed her space for several days, her mumbled apology the morning after having been, he'd been convinced, akin to swallowing sand. Truth be told, it was in her best interests for him to have avoided her as well. He'd relived the moment so many times, had played out so many different endings in his head—none of which saw him actually leaving her that night—that he was certain being in her company before he'd managed to dispel the idea that he was a fool for not having swept her up in his arms and kissed her senseless would have seen him doing just that.

Now was safe. Daylight. Fully Clothed.

She would be safe from his desire, he was sure.

He wouldn't have guessed that the third floor would have called her attention, being that it housed only rarely used smaller chambers. Zach himself hadn't ventured upstairs since he was in short pants, but as he'd not found her upon the second floor, he was soon glancing inside different rooms on the top floor.

He almost missed her, even as he'd come upon the slightly ajar door and assumed she must be within, he immediately saw no sign of her and was already turning his shoulders away when he spotted the top of her head. Just the crown of her head, the contrast of her shiny mahogany locks against the linen covering the bed caught his notice. She was sitting on the floor on the far side of the bed, he mused.

Curiously, Zach strode around the bed, his footsteps muffled upon the faded rug.

Emma sat with her legs tucked neatly beneath her, scores of papers floating all around her, her head bent as she perused the paper she held. In her right hand, holding one side of the paper, she held also a length of pink ribbon.

His tall Hessians were surely the first thing she saw as he came around the bed, alerting her to his presence. She gasped and lifted her eyes. Having discerned she was surrounded and engrossed in dozens of letters, he was about to tease her that she seemed to have accumulated an astonishing amount of mail in the short time she'd been here.

But the face she turned up to him—shimmering eyes shuttered by spiky wet lashes, red-stained nose, and sad little turn of her lips—brought a frown instead of a grin. Zach stepped fully in front of her, her gaze following him.

"Miss Ainsley? Dear God, what has happened? Have these letters delivered bad news?"

She nodded, and dropped her chin to her chest, holding out one hand to indicate the mass of correspondence. "Oh, it's just awful," she said and wept.

Zach went down onto his haunches, but she did not raise her tear-stained face to him. He thought the letters must be from a man, the script he briefly noticed being neither delicate nor pretty. His lip curled, presuming some undeserving blighter had just broken her heart.

"Now, now, Miss Ainsley," he soothed awkwardly. "No man is worth this painful weeping —and certainly not one who doesn't realize how rare a prize—"

Her expression changed, in the midst of his cajoling words, going rather blank so that he stopped speaking. Perhaps, in her mind, some chap *was* worth these tears.

But no. An uneasy giggle came next. And then the giggle evolved into a cheery if nervous laugh. She covered her mouth and her laughter with one hand, waving the other which still held a letter, flapping the paper rather jerkily. Above the hand covering her mouth, her watery blue eyes danced with merriment.

Finally, she apprised him, "These aren't mine." While Zach returned her gaze blankly, it was another few seconds before she settled her laughter and explained, "I was snooping and came across these old letters in the writing desk." She pulled the hand away from her face and indicated the small piece of furniture in his periphery.

He blew out a relieved burst of laughter and sat on the floor, beneath the window, putting his back against the wall. She was beautiful when she cried. Honestly, the redness seemed only to highlight the perfect blue of her eyes, making them brighter, more intense, so very animated. And that smile—surely she might ask for stars from the sky or water from a desert, and there would likely be many a man eager to delight her with at least an effort, if this smile be the reward.

"But then why do you cry?" He wondered, even as he was now so entranced by that gorgeous smile.

Her shoulders slumped. She lowered her head again, taking in all the letters covering her skirt and the carpet and the floor. "This man, George Fiske, is writing these notes to a woman named Caralyn—" the blue eyes found his again. "Do you know a Caralyn Withers? Is she of the Lindsey family? A relative? A servant? She must have stayed here or lived here. But something awful must have happened, for she does not give George the love he craves—though he seems to believe she wants to—and then these letters were just left here, scattered. I cannot believe she would have willingly abandoned all this love."

"Hmm," Zach said, giving it some thought, still more mesmerized by the shimmering blue of her eyes. "There is no Caralyn in our family, not that I'm aware. And Withers is unfamiliar to me, as well."

"These were written in 1774."

"I see," he said, though it helped to define this Caralyn not at all. "That would make it even more difficult to identify this person. I don't even think any of the staff here now would have been here then."

"More than forty years ago," she said. "But listen to this." She moved her hands over the papers on the floor, sifting through the letters until she found what she was looking for and read to him. "*I saw you last eve at Winthrops' less than fascinating dinner. You knew I watched you. My darling, you couldn't not have known. Surely your neck tingled with awareness. Surely your breath caught with wonder. Our hearts speak, even when we do not. But why, oh why, do you persist and resist? You said it yourself: the heart wants what the heart wants. Yet, you allow yourself not the chance to explore this. And still, your kiss lingers in my memory and, indeed, my own broken heart.*"

Zach thought it sounded like a lot of drivel, and immediately thought he understood the entire circumstance: a lady allowed herself to be kissed by besotted man, then regretted the decision, and could not rid herself of the man's attention. How very... tedious. Save for the fascination instilled within Miss Ainsley at such heartfelt nonsense. He chose not to rain on her charming, lovesick parade and refrained from offering his own opinion on the matter.

She plucked another letter from the haphazard pile, and read, "*'Tis mercy, 'tis shame, 'tis joy and unbearable grief, to have* that moment—'twas only a moment I now see—to share love, and give love, and be loved. And then you were gone." She looked up at Zach again, heaved a breathy and tortured sigh. "Oh, poor Mr. Fiske. And this part—" she consulted the paper again. "I had a dream and it was you." Her hand fluttered over her heart.

Zach grinned, convinced more than not of the swain's unrequited love, wondering indeed if the uncompromising Miss Caralyn only thought the correspondence tiresome and overdone.

On the other hand, he considered Miss Ainsley's very keen reaction, and alleged with a lazy grin and no small amount of amused charity, "You are a romantic, Miss Ainsley." It was so unnatural to him. Women of his acquaintance wasted precious little time on such fancy. Love was only a lucky by-product of a solid union, not at all the sole reason for being. He couldn't say he was aware of or acquainted with any couple who was truly in love. Several friends might have initially lusted after their arranged wives, some might have genuine affection even, but no man, and rarely a woman in today's day and age squandered their dreams on so nebulous a notion. Certainly not with such tortuous ardor as the glib Mr. Fiske.

Miss Ainsley did not take exception to his accusation, only grinned and admitted, "I daresay you'd be hard-pressed to find a woman who might read these words, and not wish them to have been penned by her own object of affection." Her tone hinted at practicality, as if she only stated fact, and was not imbued what any sense of drama and gave no hint if this be her wish as well. She added, with a shrug of her slim shoulders, "Whether or not she might admit to this would be an entirely different matter altogether."

"You have a very tender heart, Miss Ainsley." *Despite your constant stubbornness in regard to all things having to do with me.* He was filled with a sudden desire to know so much about her. He recognized the wonder of this, as he could not ever recall another person in whose presence he had been, which had found him craving...more. More knowledge, more time, more of her.

He shook himself, chastising himself internally. Good Lord, but ol' Mr. Fiske's covetous words must have left an impression indeed. Yet, he found himself asking of her, "Have you dreams of receiving words such as these from your beloved, Miss Ainsley?"

He'd employed a cautious tone, to give no indication of his own thoughts, but felt some censure had crept in there anyway, as evidenced by her evasive reply of, "Dreams are not for everyone."

Her entire manner changed then. With a suddenly tightened jaw, she began to gather up the many letters, putting them in some sort of order, as she did not simply collect them haphazardly, but consulted each paper and inserted it into the stack in her hands with some care, and at different places. "I am sorry for having snooped, for having made a mess."

Zach felt like a heel. "Miss Ainsley."

"And how shameful of me, to not have even inquired of your ride or—"

"Miss Ainsley."

"Or, my heavens, where is Bethany? How silly and irresponsible of me, to have forgotten—oh, but is she with Mrs. Conklin?"

Firmly now, "Miss Ainsley." And he reached forward and stilled her fretful hands with the touch of his own. "Bethany is napping."

She looked up and nodded, her cheeks now a becoming shade of pink. She moved not at all now so that Zach retrieved the last few letters near his own legs and neatened them before handing them to her.

"Thank you."

"Have you no dreams, Miss Ainsley?" The want of this answer seemed to override everything else, including her sudden embarrassment, and his desire to kick himself for having caused it. At her blank stare, he clarified, "When you were a child, surely you must have dreamed of...something?"

"I didn't have any dreams," she supposed in a small voice. "Dreams of what?"

"Dreams of what you hoped your life to be."

A small grin, one without humor, curved her beautiful lips. "Perhaps you are not aware, my lord, that people from the lower classes don't really have accessible dreams. I had no dreams, my lord. I just imagined I'd get taller and older and hoped the Smythes lived forever so that I might always have the roof and the work."

"That reeks of a lack of imagination," he said, a frown hovering, "of which I'm somehow convinced you are not wanting."

She only shrugged, her lips rolled inward, as if to prevent herself from speaking.

Zach chewed on this, determining that she surely must be omitting something. No young girl, possessing the heart she obviously did, spent all her youth on such practical matters, giving no quarter to more personal desires.

When he only stared at her, seeking truth in the depths of her blue eyes, she allowed her own brows to crunch as she asked,

"What did you dream of as a child? Did you dream to become a member of parliament?

"No, I thought for sure I was going to be a beekeeper when I grew up."

"A beekeeper?" She laughed, despite herself. "Like bumble-bees?"

He shook his head. "Like honey bees." He offered a disarming grin. "When I was very young, my tutor, Mr. Fellows, had an ardent interest in beekeeping, and was allowed to do so right here, at Benedict House. We bred and cared for our own bees, made our own honey, it was all very exciting and...worthy, it seemed." He tapped his hand against his thigh, pursed his lips with some fond remembrance, and said, "My parents were indulgent, and truthfully, I cannot recall that they ever tried to dissuade me."

"So...what happened to the dream?"

"Life, I suppose. I went off to Eton and Cambridge, and Mr. Fellows moved onto to another lucky young man, who perhaps now laments that he wears a wig and listens all day to political blowhards hurling polite ridicule at each other while so few agendas are truly ever met, rather than ducking under the bee-keeper's helmet and stepping into the beautiful buzz of thousands of honey bees."

"But why don't you have—keep? Is that the word—bees now? You've the means, and—oh, does it take up so very much time? You are gone often and regularly." But even this, she waved off, "But you've servants that you might train to help."

"I've thought about it. Seems to lose some of its allure, if I'm only to be paying a person to do the job—and that would be all it was to them, a chore, labor."

"You're a fairly clever man," she said, "so I must admit to some surprise that you wrestle with this. My lord, parliament is not in session all year round. So find the perfect person, perhaps among the staff, who shares the passion. And when you're available, you enjoy all the benefits that come with doing something that you love, and when you are otherwise engaged, you have faith that whomever you've entrusted with the chore will give it the same passion as you."

"Having no dreams, what might you know of *all the benefits that come with doing something that you love*?" He wondered, not at all immune to the charm of Emma Ainsley, who declared she hadn't her own dreams but now smartly demanded he make his come true.

"I have Bethany, so everyday I have something I love."

He allowed this to be her response, even as they both knew it was unrelated, and mused, "But now your circumstance has changed. You will ever have a roof over your head and needn't worry about any occupation—despite your claims to the contrary—so have you the luxury now of dreams?"

Mildly, with a ponderous tone, she said to him, "I shall have to give some thought to that and return an answer to you at another time."

Zach raised a brow to this and was sorry that she stood now and returned the tidy pack of letters to the drawer. He sensed about her some inner debate, to leave or to stay, to speak or to not, and he reluctantly aided this, by offering her escape, "I will see you at dinner this evening."

It appeared she released her breath at these words. Without looking at him again, she bobbed a hasty curtsy and with a bare, "Good day," exited the room.

Zach lifted a knee and draped his arm over it, considering Emma Ainsley just now, rather than the substance of the time they'd just shared. It wasn't easy to separate the woman from her beauty, but then he decided that even as she appeared to have no idea of the spell she cast, her physical loveliness was as much a part of her as was that tender heart, as was her innate sense of responsibility, as was her belief that she was so undeserving of dreams.

He sighed, not without some frustration. He couldn't deny he was attracted to her, couldn't deny he wouldn't mind exploring the fascination. But the allure had been born when he believed her so much less innocent than he now knew her to be. And his present desires merited no more time in his head, as they were now judged inappropriate, and ultimately would prove ruinous to Emma, if acted upon. When he'd kissed her previously, he questioned why he should feel poorly about it. And even as he knew the answer now—that he had no business dallying with so unsophisticated a creature, that the attraction would fade as had so many others before—he was teeming still with a desire to know more and show her more.

Ah, but that would be a dangerous thing.

She would leave soon, take that cottage as her own, be away from him. He wondered how a little nobody like Emma Ainsley would get on in the not quite sleepy town of Perry Green. It did not sit well with him, her living by herself. He thought it imprudent and dangerous, thought her too naïve and too soft. But he hadn't cause to gainsay her, or his father's will. She couldn't stay on at Benedict House, not without causing ruin to herself as an unattached young woman. This short-term arrangement was acceptable, but if extended, it would only bring her trouble.

If she'd been reared within the city limits, if she had even a scrap of the stained and spoiled mentality of any person, nobility or otherwise, so necessary to escape life uninjured, he'd feel less uneasy with her being on her own. He should take her to London, give her a good dose of what people were really like, surprised she wasn't more jaded, having grown up in a traveler's inn. Credit to her mother and her sister, and even the Smythes then, for having recognized the pureness of her heart that she had been kept sheltered.

Take her to London?

Jesus, but it was perfect.

He could conceivably kill the proverbial two birds with one stone. He could introduce her to a larger population, one not always kind—but only briefly, as he'd not be happy to see her lose her untainted perception of people and things—and give her just enough of a taste of the true character of so much of the public. She would then be perhaps better equipped to live life on her own, and he would feel as if he'd had some part in preparing her better for the role.

In addition, the other bird in need of killing might be tackled, if he could convince Miss Ainsley to help him out with a rather frustrating issue he'd been dealing with of late.

Chapter Nine

"I wanted to ask a favor of you," the earl said to Emma, across the length of the dining table that evening.

"Me?" Her surprise, determined so easily from both her tone and her arched brows, did nothing to diminish how absolutely entrancing she appeared tonight. This, then, must be the best of the lot, from the gowns Mrs. Conklin had acquired, under his instruction and from the dressmaker in Perry Green. While simple, as necessitated by their country setting, the pale blue of the gown was a perfect backdrop to the creaminess of her skin, and the luster of her dark hair.

Zach grinned. "Yes. You."

"I cannot think of anything you might need from me." This, with tremendous wariness.

Ah, if only she knew. Zach consulted his plate, pretending a great interest in the lamb cutlets. "I have a dinner party to attend in London. I would like you to accompany me." He speared a piece of lamb onto his fork and raised his gaze to her.

She stared blankly at him. Almost comically void of any expression, save for her gaping jaw. He had decided to be candid with her when issuing the invitation. Candid, as it were, about one of his goals. "The dinner is at the home of a senior member of parliament, whose support is vital to a bill coming up for a vote in the very near future. A bill I have sponsored."

She closed her mouth and swallowed. "But why would I attend? I know nothing about bills put before parliament or dining in fine company. I haven't the wardrobe to do justice to such an occasion, despite how generous you've been thus far." She be-

117

gan shaking her head. "I would only embarrass you. I know nothing of mingling in...those kinds of circles."

Sorry as he was for her near distressed state, he persisted, "Miss Ainsley, you do yourself an injustice. I assure you, you can more than hold your own." Meeting her gaze steadily, he admitted, "I asked it as a favor, as the invitation has an objective. May I explain further?" This had been planned as well, having expected her refusal. He'd learned a few things about Miss Ainsley, one of which was that she could not resist giving aid to a person in need. He would exploit that now, and without shame.

She nodded, a small frown coming for his asking permission, he was sure.

"The host and parliamentarian, Lord Kingsley, has a daughter." Her frown deepened, her mind surely whirring at the speed of light, he believed. "The daughter is—I can think of no kind words, sadly—a hindrance to my goal of speaking to the man in a setting and in a mood that might find him more agreeable to the policy I hope to explain more persuasively."

"A hindrance?" Now her lovely arched brows rose, high into her forehead.

"She has developed a *tendre* for me," he informed her in a level tone. A *tendre* was putting it mildly. The insufferable lady gave new meaning to the word tenacious, had caused Zach several instances where he'd wished that he could somehow escape any disastrous consequence if he but begged her to close her mouth for five blessed minutes. "Her father has insinuated that he might well find his way to lending his favor to my bill if I could manage to return the...affection—presumably by way of a betrothal. Of course, I have no intention of selling myself to gain votes inside the walls, so I thought—" He stopped as her darling lips began to curve in a mischievous smile.

"You want to bring me along, so the man thinks you have already formed an...attachment elsewhere," she guessed. Correctly.

He imagined his returned grin might have appeared sheepish just then. Aiming for a more formal, foreboding mien, he straightened and rested his wrists on the edge of the table, reining in the grin. "You have the right of it, Miss Ainsley." He hoped her seeming merriment over his predicament boded well for whatever her response might be. "I thought if I arrived with someone who seemed to have captured my...affection, it would remove that obstacle from gaining his support."

She continued to grin, the blue of her eyes brightening as the smile widened. Then she bit her lips, attempting to contain her mirth just as Zach decided she might actually be laughing at him.

"Poor Lord Lindsey, the object of an unrequited affection," she teased. "How very...pedestrian."

He rolled his eyes at his, but without rancor, and allowed her to have her fun.

"Honestly, my lord, the idea of so formal a gathering, where I will no doubt stand out like a sore thumb, scares me half to death. Likely I will regret this, but I must say yes, simply because my very inquisitive nature demands that I meet this woman who has so befuddled your political aspirations with her untimely and lamentable fascination with you."

Aside from the very obvious fact that she was finding great amusement in his predicament, Zach was realizing fantastic pleasure in her just now. He liked that she dropped the mien of suspicion and uneasiness usually worn in his presence, had teased him and smiled so spontaneously in front of him. With him. He liked how her eyes brightened so amazingly with her smile. He liked tremendously her spirit, that this girl who so feared that she would be a fish out of water amongst the *ton* was willing to accommodate him, because she thought it might prove entertaining and because, he knew, she wanted very much to be useful and necessary.

His gaze settled on her lips, still smiling so prettily, so damn temptingly.

He liked so many things about her.

They departed the very next day for London, Emma seated across from the earl in his fine carriage once again. She fidgeted nervously, plucking at invisible specks from her skirt, aligning the sleeves of her jacket so that they were the exact distance from her wrists, moving her bonnet so that the fringe visible across her forehead was equidistant from left to right.

Oh, but she had not thought this through. She'd agreed under some spell, intrigued by the earl's near bashful attitude last evening at dinner, as if he'd never in his life asked a favor of another person. Charmed as well by the very idea that she might be of some assistance to him. However, this part was of a more dubious nature, as she couldn't imagine how anyone might think the magnificent Earl of Lindsey might somehow have formed an attachment to a nobody such as herself.

And then, as if she'd not been nervous enough, as if she'd not already been considering she'd certainly bitten off more than she could ever chew, he'd let it be known today that Bethany would not be able to travel with them, as his townhome hadn't anyone to look after her while they were out and about. He'd said that his housekeeper there was not the 'warm and fuzzy type'.

"Calm yourself, Miss Ainsley," he said now.

Emma raised her gaze from the curled fists in her lap to his eyes, finding the gray to be softer today, the usual intensity lessened. Taking a deep breath, she smiled at him, or tried to. She had said she would help him, and so she would.

He looked incredibly handsome, or more so, in his brocade waistcoat and breeches of buckskin, covered with a claw hammer coat and finished with his usual Hessians. Next to him, and despite her fashionable gown and spencer which she thought unbearably lovely, Emma felt quite gauche, or at least, fraudulent.

"We might contrive to agree upon some back story," he suggested, "as people may have questions, how we met, how long has it been going on, things of that nature."

"A fake narrative to give credibility to our fake...attachment?"

He acknowledged her apt sarcasm with a tip of his head. "As it is, the simpler the tale, the easier it is to recall, and to pose as truth. Do not embellish—the less said the better. Let us just agree that we are cousins, of a sort, on my mother's side. The Morrissey family is much less known than the Benedicts," he explained. "And you've kept to the family home in Hertfordshire until just this year, caring for your ailing mother, which will explain why no one in London is familiar with you."

"Do I use my own name?" Dear Lord, it sounded dangerously convoluted already.

He frowned. "Of course."

Emma nodded. *Cousins. Morrissey. Hertfordshire. Ailing mother.* "All right." It was here and now that she considered that this scheme seemed suddenly less like fun and more like true deception, and something woeful twisted in her belly.

Her anxiety was quelled somewhat as they neared and then entered the city, and Emma found she could not take it all in, the size and the scope and the height of London. She glanced out the left window and then the right, her gaze filled with wonder. Having never been to London, she truly hadn't any idea what to expect, but reality gave no legitimacy to any of her previous imaginings. It was loud and big and bustling, as the carriage meandered down city streets, and drivers and pedestrians squawked and chattered, and the roads and sidewalks teemed with people, and the buildings were close and tall and so overwhelming. But she smiled as she soaked it all in. It was all just so fascinating.

As the carriage slowed, to accommodate for the crush of traffic, Emma's gaze was captured by a couple outside walking upon the sidewalk. The gentleman sported a bright orange tailcoat and a hat longer than his head, while pushing forth a stick of shiny wood with each of his steps. The woman wore the most sumptuous long coat, held together with frog closures and being the exact shade of fresh spring grass. Atop her head sat the most amazing hat Emma had ever seen, being closed about her face with hard scalloped sides, and sporting what seemed like an entire garden at her brow and crown. Their walk was perfectly in tune, even as their garish color choices were not, his left leg and the stick moving at the same time as the woman's right leg, their stride similar that it appeared almost rehearsed.

Emma pulled her eyes from the stunning couple and met the earl's gaze, wondering if he'd witnessed so spectacular a sight, but he was not looking out the window as she had been. He was watching her. And the storminess had returned to his gaze, as he watched her so intently.

"What is it?" She asked, believing surely something must have happened since their last words had been exchanged to have wrought such a severe change in him. Gone the affability, gone the near pleasantness, replaced by what she deemed a brooding and quite unnerving glare.

"What is what?" And just like that, his expression was shuttered. The darkness left his gaze, he unclenched his jaw, and he lifted a brow at her with his countering query.

Emma shook herself, loosened her own frown, and turned again to look out the window. She sat primly now, intent on being less the country girl come to town, presuming it was her animated fascination with all the sights and sounds that had instigated his sour countenance of a moment ago.

She nearly startled, only seconds later, when he rapped his walking stick upon the roof of the carriage. But this was only a notice to the driver to stop, and Emma leaned once more toward the window to see what their destination might be.

The earl sprung from the carriage nearly before it had stopped, and well before the driver might have come to open the door. He supposed it would not have been in good form to accost his artless houseguest, and counterfeit sweetheart, within the confines of the carriage and before she'd actually enjoyed even one small part of the city. But damn if his little country miss was not the most amazingly alluring creature, and then even more so when her face lit with such enthusiasm at things to which he'd not give a second notice, including one garish carroty coat and a hat which might draw the attention of as many birds as it did people.

He hadn't meant to be brusque, or appear surly, but she'd caught him unawares, and in the middle of raking her quite mindfully with his hungry eyes. She'd turned to him, her animated smile a thing to behold, her expressive gaze so damnably appealing. He did not care at all to have been caught gawking at her, as it were. He liked even less that he had, in the first place, been reduced to those simmering and ravenous long looks at her, all the while wondering how he might seduce her and make her his, even as he knew he would—could—promise her nothing.

Ah, if only he were a rogue with less of a conscience.

She hadn't asked why they had stopped, or where they might be going, only put her hand into his as he helped her alight and continued to swivel her head about, taking in every detail of the dirty, pretentious city.

He guided her into the closest storefront, whose shingle pronounced it as Mrs. Shabner's modiste. A bell tinkled above the door as he pushed it open and steered Miss Ainsley within. Zach did not visit modiste's often enough to say that the shop was busy or not, but the front room showed several ladies and one portly and unamused gentleman idling around tables with ready made wares, scarves and gloves and a table of fabric swatches.

Understanding where they were and what they were about, Emma turned and showed another nervous gaze to him. He immediately put her at ease, "It is all very necessary to the ruse, Miss Ainsley." He held her hand still, because it would show the modiste—who had just come from a back room and noted the arrival of a *person of importance* and pasted on her prettiest smile—that Miss Ainsley was favored, and thus her treatment would be polite, nearly fawning. He held her hand yet, as well, because he liked the feel of it in his, like the way their hands fit, and how soft her skin was.

But he did release her hand, after it had been noticed by the shop owner, who ignored the other people browsing to shimmy her way around tables and persons to stand before the earl. Modiste's had a particular talent, a gift he might have said, for discerning who was monied, and who would be spending.

"My lord," she greeted him, her painted lips spread wide in her face.

"Mrs. Shabner, I bring you Miss Ainsley," Zach said. The woman's gaze raked Emma with enormous judgment from head to toe. "She will need to be outfitted for three days in London."

He was quite sure he could see her doing math in her head. Her smile grew. "Of course, my lord. Any particular events?"

"One dinner party and one ball. Several daytime—"

"A ball?" Emma turned her face up to him. "Truly?" Her excitement was so palpable, so contagious, he could not help but smile, even as he knew the total cost for this undertaking just went up, as Mrs. Shabner's gaze was keen as she considered his indulgence.

"Shoes? Hats? Gloves? Undergarments?" Clarified the modiste, with a lift of her brow.

Zach waved the gloves in his hands with some ennui, as was expected of him. "A complete outfitting, if you please. Dinner gown by tomorrow night, and ball gown for Saturday."

And now the modiste showed a hint of alarm, at which Zach raised a challenging brow. Her gaze narrowed and her smile was tight, knowing he would exit her shop if she could not accommodate him. He could find several who would in a very close proximity.

"As you wish, my lord. Come, my dear." She led Emma away from Zach, calling over her shoulder as she stopped with Emma near the table of fabrics, "Have you a preference to color?"

"Blues," he said, decisively.

"Bold?" Wondered the modiste.

Zach leveled her with a decisive frown. "Pastels," he clarified, answering her unasked question of Emma's role in his life, paramour or beloved. Supposed beloved, he amended.

"Cut?" The modiste persisted.

"Tasteful."

"Style?" Mrs. Shabner lifted a hand to indicate the attention-grabbing hat atop a mannequin.

"Elegant," he corrected. "She needs no decoration, as you can plainly see."

"Mm," agreed the modiste, considering Emma's fair and perfect skin. She reached out and touched a lock of Emma's hair, escaped from her hat. And then to Zach, "Very well. I'll need her for an hour at least."

He nodded. To Emma, he said, "I shall take up some business nearby and return for you."

"Oh...all right. Thank you, my lord." Of course, her eyes said that it was not all right, that she would rather he stayed with her. But she needed to learn how to go about on her own.

With a curt nod, he pivoted and walked to the door, hearing the modiste say to Emma, in a tone that was not quite a whisper, "You've got him sewn up quite nicely, Miss Ainsley."

To which Emma replied, clearly having no inkling of the woman's inference, "We're cousins. Of a sort."

"I'll bet you are," the modiste tittered just as Zach closed the door behind him.

Emma was happy that evening to remain within the earl's Mayfair townhome, not quite sure she was ready to face the masses, so to speak, at a public outing. She was immediately enamored of the residence though it bore little resemblance to Benedict House, with its stark and cool feel. The floors were tiled, the doors were painted black, and there was not a stitch of wallpaper in the entire home. She'd been shown to a neat but plain room of blue, which was still prettier than her apartments in the King's Arms Inn.

The earl had not been far off the mark when he'd mentioned that his city housekeeper, Mrs. Downing, was certainly not warm and fuzzy. The woman was tall and lanky, her face long, her mouth drawn down at the corners, not even lifting at Emma's pretty greeting. Emma was glad then that she'd not brought along Bethany, as she couldn't imagine being at ease leaving her daughter in this woman's care.

"Dinner is prompt, at seven o'clock," the woman said, or rather called over her shoulder as she led Emma up the stairs while the earl remained in the foyer, looking immediately at messages and letters that had piled up since last he visited. Upon the second floor, still walking stiffly ahead of Emma, the woman asked, "Where is your maid, Miss Ainsley?"

"I haven't one."

This, now, turned the starched woman around, so suddenly that Emma nearly crashed into her.

"No ladies maid?" All of the abhorrence of a hundred faces seemed crammed into only this woman's.

Emma's initial thought was to reply that she'd never had her own maid, that in fact she was a maid. But recalling what they were about here in the city, and her role, she shrugged as casually as she supposed the woman's frigid glare would tolerate and brushed it off. "By necessity, the poor dear was forced to remain...at home," was all she could think to say.

She was rewarded for her lie with a harrumph which suggested she was not believed at all, or that if she was believed, she was thought a ninny. Emma wondered if she would know, by the woman's expression—so far she'd been witnessed to only two, her frown and her heavier frown—what she thought of the earl's houseguest. Deciding she didn't care, she thanked her for showing her to her room and received only a curt reminder of the dinner time. Emma closed the door after the woman and made a face, which properly revealed her own opinion of so cold a fish.

It was just past four now, so she imagined she might have a lie-down before supper and so removed her shoes and jacket.

She imagined a footman might deliver her small, borrowed valise with her pitiful few belongings that she might hang the only gown likely to pass muster with Mrs. Downing's critical eye for dinner.

When Emma had stepped from the carriage in front of the townhome, she'd thought to gather the valise then, but had recalled from the hundreds of carriages that had stopped at the King's Arms Inn that a lady never carried her own luggage. Emma was sure that however she might get through the next few days in the city, she would rely heavily upon what she had witnessed of the upper class that had graced the rooms of the inn over the years. The ladies held their chins high and behaved with an air about them that all their needs should be met before they had been voiced. Mostly, Emma and all the employees of the inn were invisible to the nobles, man or woman. This had suited Emma perfectly and it was usually a sad day when she was not unseen, as this had indicated that the person had homed in on her as their own personal fetcher and getter, as she and Gretchen used to say. People were rarely outright nasty, but they never let it be forgotten on which side of the coin she was on.

As it was, Emma would make good use of her many years in service to the inn, as she was fairly certain she might be able to successfully emulate a fine lady. Or at least a poor cousin of a fine lady.

A rap at the door bade her call for entry, expecting a footman. She was surprised when the earl pushed open the door. He was followed by a footman, however, who quietly bobbed his head at Emma and set her lone valise onto the bed.

"My lord," she said to the earl, without a hint of cleverness.

He frowned. He was always frowning. She hadn't any idea what this moment's cause might be. Ignoring him, she opened her valise and began to withdraw her few possessions.

"I was going to take you for a ride through the park," he said, his gaze passing over the bed where lay her jacket and then the floor where sat her slippers.

"Oh, well, I hadn't known—but you still can," she amended quickly when the brow did not unfurrow. Having no inkling then that she was making a grievous misstep, she sat on the little stool which later would be used to climb into the bed and put her small heeled slippers back on. She swept the skirts of her gown out of the way, up to her knee, and tied the ribbons tightly as the shoes were, truthfully, one size too large. Placing her hands on her knees, she pushed herself to her feet and caught sight of the earl's expression. Still glowering.

Thumping her hands onto her hips, and with no small amount of impatience, she wondered, "What now? Why are you frowning?"

He opened his mouth twice, but no words came forth. On the third try, he managed in a tight voice, "Miss Ainsley, do not ever dress yourself—any part of yourself—in front of a gentleman. In front of *any* man!"

She rolled her eyes and reached for her pretty long-sleeved spencer of blue cotton.

"I wouldn't have done so in front of *any* gentleman," she defended, donning the jacket, and closing the three buttons at her chest.

"Am I not any gentleman?" he wondered, less affronted than still annoyed with her lack of decorum, she decided.

"You are different," she said vaguely and faced him again. "You've seen me in my shift, And on several occasions, my lord. I'm sure the sight of my stocking-ed shins needn't send you into a dither."

His expression changed. First his mouth lost its scowl and soon enough the darkness left his gaze, and his brows relaxed. She liked him so much better when he wore almost anything but that scowl of his.

"You'll need a hat or bonnet...or something," he suggested.

"Must I?"

"Absolutely. It would be akin to appearing at dinner without a dress to go driving in the park without a hat."

"Oh, bother." She grabbed up the closest one, atop the pile of clothes she'd unpacked, and quickly plopped in upon her head and tied the strings beneath her chin. Seemingly satisfied, the earl offered his arm, through which Emma threaded her hand.

They left her chambers and Emma wondered, "My lord, is it appropriate for you to be inside my bedchamber?" And before he might have answered, she went on, "Seems a larger crime than me baring my ankles to you."

"Touché, Miss Ainsley."

The earl's fancy carriage stood at the ready just off the curb from his front door. A different coachman, this one aged and portly, sat patiently atop the driver's seat. Emma allowed the earl to hand her up into the barouche, whose hood remained lowered, and took note of the high-quality horse team attached to the rig.

The earl sat next to her and they were off.

"Why did we not simply use the carriage and horses we arrived in less than half an hour ago?" Emma wondered.

"The point of driving is Hyde Park is to be seen, and be seen well," the earl enlightened her.

Ah. "Hence the fancy vehicle and expensive horses?"

"Precisely."

"Do you visit Hyde Park often? Like this?"

"Not at all," he admitted, glancing sideways at her. "I thought you might enjoy all the pandering and posing of the *beau monde* during the fashionable hour."

Emma was struck immediately with two thoughts about this. First, it was very kind of him—which was not specifically in keeping with what she believed of him—to consider that she might enjoy this outing. And then, as hinted by his rather sardonic tone and word choice, she imagined he thought it all very silly, which made her even more grateful that he'd indulged her so.

She was not prepared however, for exactly what he'd meant by *pandering and posing*, and then neither was she prepared for the number of people doing just that. As they entered a queue of carriages crawling along one road just inside the park, Emma was again made aware of her own gaucheness, feeling terribly underdressed for this occasion.

A greater number of carriages than she had ever seen assembled all at once, were gathered just here, inside the park: two-wheeled and four-wheeled vehicles; led by a pair or a foursome; some with drivers, some without; and a few sporting the family crests identifying the riders. And within these fine carriages, a dazzling display of color and fabric and design were shown to the best advantage by persons who sat regally, their noses tilted skyward, their marked condescension clearly in contrast to their very attendance.

Additionally, people crowded and ambled along the sidewalks, and single mounted riders easily maneuvered in between and around the wheeled conveyances to reach different people.

"Posing, indeed," Emma muttered, watching one young woman rapping her closed parasol against the side of her own carriage. A man, riding close and gripping the door of her open carriage, yanked his hand away as if he'd actually been wounded, and the young lady erupted into a stomach-turning fit of giggling.

The earl laughed and pointed across Emma, to bring her gaze to a woman walking a dog that stood as tall as her hip. Both lady and pet wore matching spencers of pink plaid.

"Oh, my," Emma gasped.

"Lindsey!" Came a call from their left, which turned both Emma's and Zach's gaze in that direction. "Do my eyes deceive me?"

"Lady Marston," said the earl, amiably to an older woman, riding solo inside an ancient carriage that moved in the opposite direction, but stopped just now beside them.

"Never thought I'd see the day the much-admired Earl of Lindsey toured the park with the rest of us commoners."

"Pity the man who believes there is anything common about you, Lady Marston," returned the earl.

Emma considered his tone quite favorable, understanding that he must admire or enjoy the Lady Marston very much, as she sensed in his voice a genuine affection.

"Allow me to introduce Miss Ainsley," the earl said. "She has graciously consented to spend a few days in London with me."

Emma smiled at the matron and offered a, "How do you do?"

The woman, dressed severely in dark gray, and in many layers it appeared, that surely underneath she must be wilted in the fine June sun, passed a critical green-eyed glance over Emma. For her part, Emma had the immediate impression that the woman only appeared malevolent, narrowing her eyes, and pursing her lips as she took her sweet time forming opinions of the earl's present company. However, when her perusal persisted, becoming almost rude, Emma dared to lift a brow at the woman.

And only then did her lips loosen and crease in a smile. "I do very well, my girl. The question is, how did you do it? Get *this* man into *this* park at *this* time of day?"

Emma shrugged. "He invited me."

"Oh, did he now?" Asked the woman with a lifted brow aimed at the earl. She held a cane in both hands, just in front of her knees. She thumped this into the floor of her carriage, and her smile grew. "I suppose that does well to answer any other questions I might have had."

Unperturbed by the lady's presumptions, the earl informed her, "My cousin had just come up from Hertfordshire and, as she's never been to London, I thought it a fine way to introduce her to the pageantry of our city."

"Pageantry? You mean vile spectacle," harrumphed Lady Marston.

"Oh, but I think it's splendid," Emma joined. "I don't know any of the persons here today but find myself enamored of their...zeal for so simple an occasion as riding in a park."

The lady's lips blew out a bemused snort. "Ah, a diplomat. You're to be commended, Lindsey. Only you could manage to attract so similar a character that her words sound so pretty until you assess all of them to know the slander tangled within. Well done. Now off with you! I dislike those carriages who park too long, making useless small talk when no one listens to what we say anyway." She spanked the cane onto the back of her driver's seat and off they went, the woman not even calling out a respectable farewell.

They moved on, the carriage crawling forward. The earl tipped his tall hat to several persons, both men and women. Emma caught the interest of more than one pretty young lady steadied breathlessly upon his person. Of course, this came as no surprise to her. Zachary Benedict was an enormously handsome man, clearly meriting second glances. And third, it seemed. Emma rolled her lips inward, preventing a knowing grin, while she wondered what some of these fawning ladies might have thought or done if they had come upon Zachary Benedict, shirtless and god-like, as she so marvelously had. Marvelous, it had been until it had become *Her Inglorious and Reckless Blunder,* that is. Invariably, the besotted gazes left the earl and fixed on Emma, their brows immediately dropping, leaving no doubt that they considered Emma's person unworthy of the company she kept.

Emma shook herself. She needed to stop fretting about her own inadequacies. It was unlikely she would ever again have an opportunity or the need to visit London. She wanted to enjoy every aspect of the experience, and not have it ruined by her childish and dour insecurities.

They passed over a small bridge which spanned a narrow stretch of water. On either side of the road over the bridge, stood many artists, painters with their easels and canvases set just so, facing the water. Their deft hands twirled and dotted and swiped paint-filled brushes across their works-in-progress. Several ladies posed along the bridge, their parasols open, their gazes tipped toward an artist while he rendered their image into the foreground of his picture. The carriages slowed with the congested traffic. Emma shifted toward her right, leaning her arms upon the side of the vehicle to better view each painting as they crawled past.

One artist, mixing paints upon his palette, caught sight of her as the carriage ambled by. Emma smiled at him. The man in the beige linen smock let his jaw gape while his brush jammed carelessly into his cerulean blue. He pursed his lips into a kiss, which he sent along to Emma followed by an oily but roguish grin.

Emma laughed at this and waved to him as the carriage moved slowly away from the bridge. When the painter had turned back to his subject, Emma pivoted and found the earl watching her, surprising her with a generous grin.

They took almost a full turn around the park, exiting after the earl consulted his time piece and announced today's session would start within the hour and they should call it a day.

Emma spent the evening alone, missing Bethany already, and loathe to occupy her time with snooping around this house for fear of running up against the formidable Mrs. Downing. With little else to do after taking dinner in her room, she dressed for bed and retired early, though wrestled for some time with anxieties and unease. And thoughts of Zachary Benedict, the source of most of her disquiet.

Chapter Ten

Glancing around the sumptuous private parlor of Lady Marston's immense city home, Zach ignored the tea waiting for him upon a near table and waited his godmother's inimitable presence. Aside from happening upon her in Hyde Park yesterday, he hadn't seen her since his father's funeral.

Leticia Durham, nee Brent, and his own mother had been bosom confidantes since before they were married. Leticia was as hard and cynical as Barbara Benedict had been soft and comely, was icy compared to Barbara's warmth, but they had been inseparable. Zach recalled that his father had never much use for Lady Marston, not while his wife lived, though well he tolerated her friend to keep peace. Ironically, his mother's passing had seen a shift in the relationship of his father and his godmother. They'd become their own sort of bosom pals, finding each other often at events, and Lady Marston, a widow for many years, sometimes serving as hostess for his father at Benedict House and here in the city. He'd not ever thought there was anything to their relationship other than their need to hold on to each other as a means of hanging on to the memory of his mother.

"He was the best of men," Lady Marston had shocked him, having uttered these words to him at the grave of his father.

Lady Marston just now stepped into the well-appointed room, reserved strictly for family and close confidantes, her daughters-in-law excluded, Zach recalled with some hint of absurdity.

He stood, just as Lady Marston barked, "It's a damn good thing you didn't make me have to hunt you down inside this city, boy."

His lips quirked. Her private person was so much more amusing than her still hard public persona, though remained more bark than bite, he knew.

"I imagined you would have questions," he acknowledged, taking her hand, leading her to the blue damask wing chair. "Alas, I need your help as well."

She barked out a laugh. "I'm not sure you do, boy. I don't know that I've ever been witness to a pair going so far out of their way to make unseen eyes at each other."

Zach laughed and sat in the matching chair across a small table from her. He admitted, "I'm not entirely sure I care to know exactly what that might mean, ma'am."

She sighed and gave him a look riddled with exasperation. "I'll leave off commenting on that bit of nonsense and allow you to tell me where you came upon so dangerously pitiable an ingénue."

Zach cocked a brow. "Pitiable? Emma?"

"I don't care how remarkable you think she is, that girl is no match for you," barked the dowager, finally taking a moment to fix her tea, the set having sat untouched between them until now.

He debated this, considering the context of the lady's statement against what he knew of Emma Ainsley's stubbornness.

"My father left her a pretty sum in his will."

This raised the mighty woman's brow, until it lowered and her lips parted. "Pray do not tell me she is the imp from some inn down near Hertfordshire."

"He told you about her?" Zach was aghast.

But Lady Marston quickly shook her head. "I'd taken him to task for having defaulted on a dinner party I'd had. Said he'd been waylaid down there—but wait, he specifically said by a *charming and dimpled blonde*. Those were his words. Oh, I gave him hell, told him he was too old for things of that nature. But your Miss Ainsley, while admittedly alluring, is neither blonde nor dimpled." Her eyes skinnied with shrewdness.

Zach was rather pleased to be able to baffle his godmother with the news, "Ah, but her daughter is."

Lady Marston sat back in her overstuffed chair, while so many manifestations of emotions crossed her face: jaw gaping with disbelief; eyes narrowing with calculation; nose wrinkling with displeasure.

"Bloody Hades, what did he do?"

To save her further erroneous assumptions, Zach laid out the truth of Emma's tale, and his father's connection to her, or at least the truth as he understood it. His father had happened upon her while his carriage was stuck. He'd been perhaps initially taken with Emma's decency, and then more so by darling Bethany, that he'd visited often, regularly, and had benevolently thought to increase her circumstance by way of his final bequest.

Lady Marston rolled both her eyes and her head when the telling was done.

Another sigh preceded her assessment, "He was a fool. I say that with love, you know that. God's wounds, he was softhearted. But there is good news, in that the child is not his. Are we sure about this?"

Zach shrugged. "Relatively."

The blue eyes rolled again. She considered Zach for a long moment, giving him a good glare while she assessed the situation and her thoughts on it. Finally, she said, "So where are we now? You're aloof and brooding, boy, but you've not quite managed to hide your simmering—dare I say, longing?—glances at the poor thing." She sounded particularly displeased about this part. "Why bring her to London? Why not leave her tucked away down there in that cottage? You can't marry her. And I know you'd not stoop so low as to despoil that sweet thing. So what, then?"

"My intention was twofold," he said, and added sheepishly, "but only part of it was not entirely selfish."

"Not surprising."

Zach briefly sketched his purpose in bringing Emma to London. He focused more on the assistance her very presence might give to his hopes of avoiding the hindrance of Lady Prudence Kingsley while still garnering her father's support. Stubbornly, he put less emphasis on his plan to briefly expose Emma to the *beau monde*, that she might not so much forfeit any part of herself but rather gain a bit of an understanding about people outside her own little sphere of life.

"So you've said all that and I'm telling you right now that's the grandest load of twaddle I've ever heard. I'm supposed to believe your stated altruistic intent, when I personally witnessed how you absolutely chewed her up with your eyes. Don't you dare insult me, Zachary Benedict. You've brought her here for my approval. You want me to somehow change the laws of polite society, or give you leave to ignore them, so that you can...what? Marry her?" She scoffed. "You are the Earl of Lindsey. You may not marry a commoner. A country cousin, maybe, and even that I would advise against. But a chambermaid? You've a fine future in politics, boy, that shouldn't be driven off by some trifle, who are—let's be honest—ten a penny."

"Are they, though? Ten a penny?"

Lady Marston gasped. "Dear Lord, you're in love with her."

Zach said nothing. His jaw tightened. Something inside would not allow him to refute her supposition, even as that precise idea had never so much as entered the periphery of his mind.

He could literally see his godmother composing herself, forcing slow breaths, straightening her shoulders. Levelly, she pronounced, "No, they are not, I suppose, not ten a penny. They are rare, and wasn't I and your parents lucky enough to know it? But Zachary, dear, this is different. She is worthy only in your eyes. They'll eat her up. She would never rise above it—they wouldn't allow it. Is that what you want to do to her? It wouldn't end well."

He sat silent, frustrated.

"I know it's not what you wanted to hear. But you are to be a great statesman. You need a partner of strength and wiliness, someone willing to play the game at your side. She's not it. It would wipe out everything you love about her now."

Zachary gave in to his own thoughtful perusal of his godmother, chewing the inside of his cheek as he did. "All that, gathered in so short a meeting? Quite remarkable, even for you, my lady."

When the dowager only smacked him with a withering glare, he waved a negligent hand. "Be that as it may, I need an invitation for her for Kingsley's dinner this evening," he said. His godmother was no great fan of Lady Kingsley, but she was a society matron few would dare to refuse. "Additionally, I need you to sponsor her tomorrow night at Clarendon's ball."

A slow, calming blink of her eyes preceded her nod. "Very well. I will collect her at eight. And *you* will not arrive until nine. At least give some show of insouciance." As an afterthought, her forefinger raised swiftly from her cane, she added, "And you may dance only once with her! In that regard, I will not be budged."

Zach grinned at his godmother. "Honestly, my lady, I haven't any idea if she even knows how to dance."

Thin, arched brows rose nearly into her hairline. "You are going to be the death of me, boy," was issued in a slow and seething tone.

Zach left shortly thereafter, having amused himself greatly at the woman's expense. But once seated inside his carriage and driving away, his grin faded.

In love with Emma Ainsley?

She tried very hard not to let the earl see exactly how nervous she was, how close to begging him to release her from her promise to help him.

As ever, he seemed to read her so well, though she'd not said a word within the confines of the carriage as of yet.

"Miss Ainsley, please do not trouble yourself," he said into the darkness. "It is simply a dinner. Perhaps only twenty people or so."

Emma attempted a smile and was glad for the shadows and the probability that he actually could not see what she was sure emerged as a pained grimace.

He added, a bit consolingly, "Think of it as similar to being in the midst of the crowded dining room or taproom at the King's Arms Inn. Filled to the brim with persons infused with an appreciation for their own importance, who will want to talk about themselves, who will no doubt not give any regard to any answers you might make to the indifferent questions they may or may not put forth. You should expect to be bored to tears for all the talk of politics, and I apologize in advance for that."

Only a few minutes later, they stood just inside the terraced house of Lord and Lady Kingsley. The foyer was a study of classic English design; black and white tiled floor, pilasters of rich marble, and wall coverings of muted gold silk.

The earl assisted her in the removal of her cape, which had arrived today with the gown she now wore. When her shoulders were freed of the luxurious sky blue cape of soft and light velvet, Emma turned to the earl but gave her gown a swift perusal, brushing away what she thought might be wrinkles in a certain spot in the skirt. Never in her life had she owned or worn silk, and here she was surrounded by it tonight. The sweet silk of the dress was of a summer blue, the skirt and bodice generously adorned with embroidered *fleur de lis,* fashioned with shiny gold threads. The peasant bodice was trimmed with a gold cord and the hem of the skirts, touching just at her ankle, showed a single layer of gold *fleur de lis* lace. Beneath her gown, her legs were caressed by sumptuous silk hose and her feet were tucked into low-heeled slippers of gold satin.

She felt like a princess and had delighted at the earl's initial response when she'd joined him in the foyer of his Mayfair home earlier. His gaze had raked her with fascination, the smile that had lifted his gorgeous lips had come slowly and had thrilled her so much more than it should have.

He offered her the crook of his arm now, tucking his other hand over the fingers she placed on his sleeve and they moved as one to be received by their hosts.

Emma almost forgot to be nervous then, as the earl ducked his head and whispered at her ear, his breath teasing the curls there, "You are ravishing, Miss Ainsley," which Emma personally thought entirely more exhilarating than his earlier generic, albeit appreciative statement of, "Well done, Miss Ainsley."

"Lindsey," said their host, a portly man not much taller than Emma herself. Lord Kingsley was easily twice the age of the earl, with thinning hair and a face that seemed to be folding in around its features, compressing his eyes and lips inside his puffy skin.

"Lord Kingsley, may I present Miss Emma Ainsley," said the earl.

The elderly man arched a thick and untamed brow, throwing the earl a look of quickly tamped down displeasure before he flashed a thin smile to Emma. Taking his slowly proffered hand, she sank into a respectable curtsy.

Next to her squat husband, Lady Kingsley appeared quite long, though was stuffed so harshly into her silk gown of tangerine, Emma feared any sharp exhale might send buttons or flounces or trim scattering away from the ensemble. Likely, the gown had fit the lady perfectly a decade ago, but tonight it appeared its purpose was not so very different than that of the butcher's sausage casing. She looked about as pleased as her husband with Emma's introduction, casting a narrowed glance all over Emma's fine gown.

The lady recovered quickly, however, and accepted Emma's greeting and curtsy with a pinched and painted-lip smile. Inclining her head, she said to the earl, "I was pleased to be able to accommodate Lady Marston's request for the addition of one guest to my table." Her next words, and the lofty tone in which they were delivered, shriveled Emma's excitement fairly quickly. "Even as it befuddled my numbers, as it would have any hostess with such short notice." She tittered then, as if that additional sound would have eased the severity of her statement.

The earl responded smoothly, "Lady Marston did not misspeak about you, Lady Kingsley, having assured me of your generous charm and hospitable spirit."

Emma glanced sharply up at the earl, never having heard such a pretentious and servile voice from him. However, this seemed to effectively mollify the woman, if only for the time being. Emma began to imagine that Lord Kingsley and his daughter, the Hindrance, were not the only ones eager to entice the earl into their family.

They were directed to the upstairs drawing room, where other guests gathered and milled about, awaiting dinner. This room had not the tall ceilings or classic design of the immense foyer but was charming, nonetheless, with its pretty Queen Anne furniture and soft hues of blue and ivory.

Emma thought she detected a slight and brief hush to the room as the earl, with his hand at the small of her back, guided her within. There were perhaps a dozen people already assembled. Several heads turned their way, several gazes abandoned the newly arrived couple when Emma moved her eyes over these persons.

A lively, nervous laugh reached her, and a young woman stepped before her.

"You look as if you were made—or dressed—specifically for this room," said the young lady. She indicated Emma's blue and gold dress and then the room in general, showing similar shades, before pointing specifically to a settee of a gold striped pattern, enlivened with soft blue *fleur de lis*.

Emma laughed at this happenstance, meeting the pretty green eyes of the young woman.

"I am Lady Margaret," said the girl, her smile seeming both genuine and friendly.

"Emma Ainsley," she introduced herself, as a young man had pounced upon the earl and had his ear to her right.

"And that's Lindsey?" Asked Lady Margaret, whom Emma decided might be several years younger than herself.

Emma lowered her voice as Lady Margaret had, ducking toward her a bit. "It is."

"My sister will be happy for his coming," she said. "Good heavens, but that's all she's talked about today. Oh my, and apologies to you, but she will not appreciate the challenge you represent."

"Challenge?" Emma wondered.

Lady Margaret took Emma's hand and pulled her away from the earl, still engaged by the other man. "Challenge for the earl's affections. Are you in love with him as well?"

Startled, and slightly unprepared for having to respond to questions about her relationship with the earl so soon into the evening, Emma gulped and said, "Well, he and I are—"

Lady Margaret giggled and interrupted. "Oh, it will be so much fun to see Prudence thwarted. Ever has she talked as if he loved her already when anyone with even half a brain inside their head might tell you that he has yet to notice her existence."

"I'm sure that the earl—"

"Prudence makes excuses for all the opportunities he has had to call upon her, or make a date with her, failing to embrace the truth that he is not interested." Lady Margaret snickered again. "Tonight is going to be very entertaining after all!" Still holding Emma's hand, she pulled her along, moving further into the room. "Come, I'll introduce you to the people who matter."

As she was led away, Emma threw a glance back at the earl, not quite sure if she wanted to be separated from him so soon. Now surrounded by two gentlemen, he watched her yet, inclining his head just enough to let Emma know he would offer no objection to her being so hastily whisked away and paraded around by the Lady Margaret.

Lady Margaret proved to be her own little whirlwind, interrupting her introduction of Emma to a statuesque woman named Lady Stanhope with the query, "Is it your own maid who so cleverly arranged your hair, Miss Ainsley?" And when Emma was presented to an oily middle-aged man titled Lord Shirley, Lady Margaret followed the introduction with, "You should limit your conversation to only the hello, my lord, as she has come on the arm of Lindsey."

Emma was sure she had never met anyone quite like Lady Margaret. And when ten minutes had passed, and Emma had thankfully been saved from having to answer any questions about herself, or her arrival with the earl—Margaret having answered many queries herself—she stood in front of *the Hindrance*, Lady Prudence, Margaret's older sister, and the reason Emma had been brought to London.

Lady Prudence was taller than Emma, with shiny blonde hair and a rosebud mouth. Emma's initial impression was, *very handsome even as she wished she were beautiful; deliberate; outwardly confident.*

And then she opened her mouth.

In a tone laced with reprimand, she first chastised her sister to kindly use her polite indoor voice, and then turned an inhospitable smirk onto Emma when her sister introduced her.

"Was it your aim, then, Miss Ainsley, to upstage your hostess with your choice of dress, or was it your intent to remain unnoticed?"

Emma recalculated. *Angry, insecure, and similar to Alice, in the sense that she'd likely put a person down if she thought it would increase her own significance.* But Emma had dealt with enough of her type over the years at the inn, Alice included, that she needed only a moment to collect herself and reply with, "I do rather blend in, do I not?" And then, pointedly, "I shall take Lindsey to task for the frightful fact that I might well be mistaken as only the draperies."

Lady Margaret giggled uproariously at this quip.

Lady Prudence minced no words. "And what, pray tell, is your relationship with Zachary?"

Emma smiled at the lady's very transparent attempt to presume a more intimate relationship with the earl than was real.

"The earl and I are cousins—"

"Barely, I would imagine," the imperious woman charged in, "as the Benedicts are quite a small—"

"On his mother's side," Emma finished evenly and then lifted a polite and curious brow to Lady Prudence. "Are you acquainted with any of the Morrissey relations? Oh, but you must be, as we are such a prolific family." And she laughed, as charmingly and as innocently as Lady Margaret had. This only saved her further verbal condemnation, but not so much from the lady's scornful scowl.

Lady Kingsley, having joined her guests in the drawing room with her husband, strode with some purpose toward her daughters and Emma just as a low gong of a bell was sounded. Two footmen pushed open the double doors, insinuating that the party would now be going down to dinner.

"Oh, Mr. Pickering," called Lady Kingsley, her eyes on Emma even as she said to the man who strode toward her, "Won't you be so kind as to see Miss Ainsley down to dinner?"

Emma's gaze was suspended upon the straining bodice of Lady Kingsley, wondering if the seams might survive the meal. When Mr. Pickering stood before her with a pleased smile and proffered arm, Emma met his warm gaze and gave him a gracious smile.

"Thank you, sir." She set her hand atop his and not through his elbow, as she'd noticed Lady Stanhope had done in front of her, and they followed the other pairs out of the drawing room.

"You will suffer my company at dinner, Miss Ainsley?" Mr. Pickering inquired.

"I shall not suffer, but enjoy it very much," She answered, entirely aware that Lady Kingsley, or Prudence herself, had arranged for the earl to lead the Hindrance into dinner. "Are you, sir, a member of parliament?"

"I proudly represent Ockendon in Commons, Miss Ainsley. But surely, you must believe that my appearance at Lady Kingsley's table is reliant more probably upon my clever wit and happy banter."

Emma liked him, and the merry glint in his eye. "Quite so, I should imagine. I expect to be satisfyingly entertained, sir, throughout the meal."

Inside the dining room, whose earlier closed doors had kept this room secreted from the guests as they'd arrived, Emma's eyes widened at the sight of the luxurious table and settings. Mr. Pickering led her around to the far side and held a chair for her near the middle of the table, taking a seat next to her.

She'd set enough tables at the inn to have a fair amount of knowledge about the service set before her, but fair at best. With a growing sense of dread, she counted eleven pieces of cutlery, seven items of gold-rimmed china, and three different crystal glasses. Her eye found the earl's, as he set Prudence in one spot and then—purposefully, Emma thought—made several remarks to another man, moving away from the Hindrance, and then almost absently taking a chair several seats down from the woman, directly across from Emma. Perhaps Emma's expression gave away her concern in regard to the lavish settings, that he said in a low voice, across the width of the table, "It will be fine," which seemed to go unheard by any other, as people settled into their seats.

"I say, Miss Ainsley," said Mr. Pickering at her side, "I have daughters about your age who, all three, were headed out this evening to some public ball. I ask you, my dear, is it truly necessary that the dressing of three women should involve fourteen different persons in my household and more than seven hours of time?"

"Oh, dear," said Emma with a sympathetic smile toward the possibly harried man.

"You seem put together rather remarkably," he noted, politely keeping his eyes on hers. "I have a feeling you required no such nonsense as all that."

"Every girl dreams to be the princess at the ball, I dare say," she reasoned.

"Would that any one of them had been born with their mother's looks, rather than my own." He gave her a long-suffering sigh, and then advised her to try the stuffed sole when a footman stood between them with that platter.

Thus charmed, Emma was happily engaged by Mr. Pickering as each course, seven in all, were brought to the table, now crowded with twenty-four persons, Emma counted. She watched either the earl or Mr. Pickering and copied whatever action they made, choosing her utensil appropriately, she was sure, all evening.

Damn, but he hadn't thought this through at all. Firstly, he'd been led to believe the dinner guests would be members of parliament and their spouses or partners. Lord Kingsley had pulled him aside just last week outside chambers, had insisted he must attend the dinner, had specifically said, "there'll be much discussion about that bill of yours, Lindsey." As it was, this formal gathering was more a husband hunting expedition, likely arranged by Kingsley's wife, as there were—aside from the clinging and disenchanting oldest daughter, Prudence—two more daughters, equally in need of husbands and about as likely to land one as their older sister. Kingsley and his wife likely imagined they might as well throw all three into the mix, hope at least one beckoned some interest. Zachary peered across the table at the middle daughter, he couldn't remember her name, who was making eyes at Simon Fenton beside her. Fenton, for his part, appeared about as interested as any other man present, giving his white soup a zealous amount of attention in an effort to remain oblivious.

The other part, which he absolutely should have expected but had failed to take into consideration, was the amount of attention Emma was drawing. Of a certain, he was not surprised, and honest to God, he knew a sense of pride that she was so well received, making him the envy of many a man here tonight. And just as he'd entertained this self-satisfied thought, Simon Fenton raised his face from the soup finally. He gave no heed to the Kingsley girl, but let his wistful gaze fall onto Emma, which in turn curled Zach's lip. Neither unhappily nor by accident, Zach allowed the young man to notice his reaction when that man's covetous eyes left Emma momentarily to land on Zach. Not surprisingly, the soup suddenly engaged Fenton's regard once more.

Zach was convinced of the true agenda of this gathering when dinner had finished, and Lady Kingsley did not insist the ladies take themselves off to the drawing room that the men might enjoy their cigars and brandy and weightier discussions. Instead, their hostess pronounced with a cackle that much resembled a nervous hen, "You gentlemen get on with your smoke and your drink. We ladies won't mind, the party being so small that it seems pointless to break it in two."

A lazier, more obvious excuse, Zach was sure he had never heard. With a sigh, imagining he might as well shelve his plans for a private chat with Lord Kingsley, Zach rose from the table and thought to join two acquaintances in the corner of the room, where they were already availing themselves to the butler's tray of half-filled snifters of what he was sure was a very fine brandy.

Emma was still in deep conversation with the gentleman, Mr. Sydney Pickering, next to her. He might at some point educate her on the proper form of showing equal attention to the persons on either side of you during dinner. But as he'd noted Lord Middleham's absorption with the widow Stanhope and her cleverly displayed charms to his left, it seemed a worthless matter currently.

He joined Lords Wharton and Ryley around the brandy, waving off a footman's offer of a tray of superb cigars and cheroots.

"I say, Lindsey," said Ryley, a young viscount who always seemed to Zach to be on the verge of laughter, even while in chambers, "did you bring along the charming Miss Ainsley only to negate the schemes of Lady Kingsley?"

"Quite the impediment to the hopes of three certain ladies and their well-intentioned mama," added Wharton. He held his head high and tilted to the right, a curious affectation that flaunted an air of haughtiness, though he was usually a congenial sort.

Zach sipped his brandy, his gaze following that of these two men, settling upon Emma once more. While she still sat and faced Pickering, Lord Shirley now stood behind and between the pair, bent attentively to her speech. Zach's nostrils flared as he watched Shirley's gaze dip to the provocative arrangement of Emma's bosom in the pretty pale blue gown. Of course he wouldn't comment, wouldn't discuss Miss Ainsley with persons not worthy of the conversation.

He felt a growl of displeasure grow within him as Prudence Kingsley walked in his direction, being not so subtle as to leave any doubt of her intention, but rather bent upon the purpose of gaining his side and his attention. As it was unavoidable, he only pivoted to receive her company that he might have a clear view of Emma, just as the brash young woman stopped before him.

"Lord Lindsey," she said, "father tells me you've taken a certain interest in the Irish Roman Catholic bill."

Inwardly, Zach rolled his eyes. He had no intention of squandering his speech on the bill in which he'd invested so much time and energy on this gushing woman.

She went on, "He declares that the loyalty those people had manifested throughout the war should avail them to any and all benefit to them. Do you, my lord, feel as if they have been deprived too long of essential constitutional privileges?"

This was her gambit, one she'd used previously and with about as much effect. She pretended an interest in politics, thought herself clever and well-versed, and hoped to convey as much. The truth was, however, that she was capable only of parroting her father, hadn't a sincere fascination in what she spoke, but only hoped to garner attention for what she projected as her keen mind.

His gaze stretched just beyond the top of her head, fixed on Emma still. That bounder Shirley yet danced attendance, smiling benevolently at Emma as if it were he who graced her with his notice. Emma was smiling, all but ignoring Shirley—good for her—speaking earnestly to Pickering, with whom Zach could find no fault. The fact that he was more than twice Zach's age aided in his charitable assessment.

He lifted a brow at Emma, delighted by the widening of her smile when her eye met his, even as he replied to Lady Prudence with a deliberately astute, "Miss Kingsley, pray do not trouble your gentle mind with political affairs, certainly not when your dear mama has other, more pressing ambitions for this evening."

Ryley choked back a bark of laughter.

Wharton had just taken a drag of his cigar and coughed and sputtered on the interrupted exhale.

And then Zach read Emma's lips, from the span of the twenty or so feet that separated them as she began to rise and said to the gentlemen in her company, "Excuse me, sirs," all the while keeping eye contact with Zach. He found it exhilarating, watching her stand and detach herself from those men and walk around the table and toward him, her gaze never leaving him.

"I say," Wharton murmured, facing the same direction as Zach, possibly having observed exactly what Zach did, what caught his breath.

She reached his side, at which Zach stepped left to allow her space between himself and the sulking and thwarted Prudence Kingsley. Excepting the fact that he nearly failed to remember that Emma merely played a role, and at his invitation, Zach was otherwise captivated beyond measure when she slid her hand into the crook of his elbow and smiled up at him as if he hung the moon.

"I feel I've monopolized poor Mr. Pickering's time longer than I should," she said, her fabulous blue eyes still holding Zach's very appreciative gaze, "so I've come to collect some of yours, my lord. Lady Kingsley had suggested Mr. Pickering take me strolling through the gardens just outside those doors—"

Zach just bet she had, the cunning old goat!

"—but poor Mr. Pickering deferred, with some complaint of allergies, that I thought to beg a tour of you."

God's blood, but weren't these words, uttered so charmingly from this woman, just about the most bedeviling thing he'd ever heard?

Save that it was all a ruse, he knew, and of his own making.

With a quick glance and tip of his head to those around him—which showed both Ryley and Wharton beset by some exposed sense of envy, while the unfortunate Lady Prudence, as of yet unrecovered from Zach's most recent indifference, revealed skinny eyes and a pinched mouth—Zach pulled Emma away from the group and toward the French doors to the terrace.

She pulled her fingers from his arm as he opened the door and steered her through with his hand lightly upon the small of her back. Leaving the doors ajar, Zach directed her to the far side of the terrace, where the Kingsley gardens might best be viewed.

But Emma gave no heed to the abundance of colorful blooms vying for attention within the undeniably vast and excellent garden but turned on Zach, her eyes shining.

And the smile—the one that bedeviled and teased him into a dastardly hunger only moments ago—disappeared, replaced by a conspirator's grin.

"Did I manage that successfully, do you think? Truth be told, I was enjoying tremendously Mr. Pickering's company—he is an avid outdoorsman and tells the most remarkably entertaining tales—but thankfully recalled my purpose and came to your rescue." And then she teased, "You're welcome."

Jesus, but he wanted to kiss her right now. Kiss her thoroughly, have that be the reason behind so delighted a face and smile.

Instead, he said, "You're very good at this. Surprisingly good."

"I begin to believe I fretted needlessly. Everyone is so very kind and so long as I listen attentively and comment appropriately, this is all very...agreeable. And it's no inconvenience to attend and remark to Mr. Pickering; surely he was quite a charmer in his prime."

Everyone was so kind because she was a fresh-faced beauty whose smile might bring men to their knees. She imagined she played a role, but Zach was quite sure she was just being herself, being considerate and engaging and so very disarming.

"And Lord Shirley?" He wondered if her good opinion extended to that man as well.

She shrugged and acknowledged, "That one requires a bit more playacting, if you will. But I think I pulled it off."

"I'm certain you did."

Her smile faded. "But you have not talked privately with Lord Kingsley," she lamented. "Rather defeats the whole purpose."

He considered her fallen expression, that his goal was not yet met.

"Generally frustrated by Lady Kingsley's attempts to find husbands for her daughters."

"The youngest, Lady Margaret, is very sweet," she allowed. "Seems to get rather lost in the shuffle of two older sisters and an overbearing mother. Mayhap you should be speaking to Lady Kingsley about your bill. I daresay she wears pants under her gown. Lady Prudence as well."

Zach stared at her. Christ, but she might have the right of it. A slow grin evolved, while ideas formed in his head. He'd gone so far out of his way to avoid Prudence Kingsley, he hadn't considered that she might actually be useful.

Emma's eyes sparkled. "Oh, but your mind is whirring. Are we changing tactics then?"

He nodded, and thus enlivened, he pounced on her, kissing her firmly, his hands on either side of her face. He stopped, pulled his mouth away, and was completely still while only inches separated their lips. He hadn't meant to do that, was only so thankful for her reasoning it through better than he had.

Bloody hell. Lady Marston's word screamed inside his head. *Dear Lord, you're in love with her.*

They remained motionless, his fingers still threaded over her ears, into her hair. She'd gasped at his kiss, stared now only at his chin, even as her own hand lifted and covered one of his. Her fingers sat not softly, but rather dug into the skin of his hand.

Zach breathed heavily, and then released her with excruciating slowness. His hands slid away from her while her fingernails lifted from the back of his hand and she dropped her arms.

"I am...sorry," he murmured. She swallowed. He saw the very hard and strained motion of it travel from her jaw and down her slim neck.

She lifted her eyes, gave him a weak smile, and shook her head, in some attempt to relieve him of his guilt. Sadly, guilt was not at all the dominant emotion right now. Need. Want. Hunger. All of these raged through him.

Voices came to them, dispelling the breathless moment, pushing them further away. The young Lady Margaret stood just inside the open doors with a clearly displeased Lord Shirley, suggesting Lady Kingsley was hard at work even now.

Straightening, gnashing his teeth, Zach touched his hand to Emma's elbow and led her back inside.

They spent the next few hours in dedicated discussion with first, Lady Prudence and then Lady Kingsley. Emma was aware that initially, her presence was noted with something akin to disdain, and thus disregarded. The ladies themselves did not include her in conversation. She only participated when one of the gentlemen, sometimes the earl, invited her opinion. She was happy to remain on the sidelines initially, intent on learning about the earl's bill before she opened her mouth on the subject. For his part, he laid out a persuasive case, she thought, though found herself more engaged by his demeanor, yet not any less so his argument; he was charming and practical, garnering support for the truth and the facts, only sparingly using emotion.

This Earl Lindsey, the one seeking backing for something he was clearly passionate about, presented the first occasion when she felt, *he is very much like his father.* And then she thought it odd, that she felt particularly proud of him, and to be with him, however tenuously.

And at the end of the evening, when they'd returned to the earl's townhouse, and he had solicitously relieved her of the pretty velvet cape, he showed some annoyance again, one to which she'd been a witness previously. His brow crunched over his dark eyes, his cheeks twitching in such a way as to suggest clenched teeth while he only stared at her. His butler, who now held both their cloaks slung over his arm, stood at attention, keeping his eyes away from the pair, while Emma questioned once more what she might have done to have wrought such displeasure from him. Or, had something untoward happened or been said to have taken away that fierce but mesmerizing look he'd bestowed upon her when he'd kissed her? The same look she'd caught upon him several times throughout the remainder of the evening, the one that indeed made her want to be in his arms. Or, had she misread what she'd perceived to be desire? She had only the earl's countenance by which to judge.

Emma found herself presently wondering if he were once again thinking about their kiss, which all but begged the question, was he angry at himself for having kissed her, or upset that he'd not pursued it more thoroughly?

She knew her own answer to this quandary, but dared not speak it, even inside her own mind.

Chapter Eleven

Emma dashed down the stairs, her feet light in her luxurious silk slippers. Her smile was bright while her hand held out the skirt of her gown to better display it to dramatic effect. While last night she'd found humor when Mr. Pickering had lamented how long and arduous his own daughter's preparations for a ball had been, Emma herself had just spent three hours being readied. Secretly, she'd found it exhausting and overdone, but would never have said that to the earl, as he'd made arrangements that her ensemble for this evening had been delivered with two maids to dress her, and her hair. Having withstood their ministrations for the past three hours—to beauteous effect, she was happy to admit—and knowing she would likely never again be dressed so fine, Emma stubbornly planned to milk every ounce of fun and frivolity out of this circumstance. And she hadn't any intention of allowing the earl's sometimes mercurial moods to rain on her proverbial parade.

The earl waited at the bottom of the stairs, resplendent in his all-black formal wear. His gaze warmed—indeed, thrilled—Emma even more so than her own finery did. Yet the sheer splendor of the gown enlivened her, and she danced around the earl when she reached the first floor.

"Isn't it lovely? I've never worn a gown so beautiful."

She was very pleased with the fabrics she and Mrs. Shabner had chosen, and as lovely as she had thought her gown to yesterday's dinner, she imagined this one more fairy-tale like, with its round Circassian robe of pale blue crepe over a white satin slip, fringed full at the feet with blue satin tassels. A peasant's bodice of blue silk, laced in the front with silver gave way to capped, Spanish slash sleeves, embellished with white crepe foldings, and finished at its edges with bands of silver. It was ridiculously gorgeous, and Emma had been happy to have her hair arranged to do it justice, and the spare ringlets left outside the bundled chignon, bounced near her cheeks and forehead as she danced around the earl.

He did not turn as she glided around him, but she caught his grin as she twice twirled around his front.

"Very lovely, indeed," he said.

"I have also never had another person attend my hair," she said, her smile infectious. "It's terribly boring, just sitting there, but look at the darling curls they managed." She stopped in front of him, and gave her head a little shake, making the curls move still.

The earl was kind enough to smile indulgently at her devotedness to her entire costume, but then he ruined everything with his next words.

"While this prancing is indeed graceful, Miss Ainsley, I fear I must ask, are you acquainted with the dances likely to be employed at tonight's gala?"

Emma went completely still and stared at him. "Oh bother." Aside from being silly with Gretchen, and that had been years ago, Emma had never truly danced. "Perhaps we should have spent more time in preparation for this ruse we've brought to London." Her shoulders dropped, the smile left her face. "I'm so sorry. You should have chosen someone who knew better how to go about in society. You should have—"

"I wanted you."

Emma's breath stopped coming right then.

The earl cleared his throat. "I wanted you to see London, and you were conveniently at hand," he clarified to great effect.

"Yes, of course."

"Too late to worry about dancing—"

"But it's a *ball*."

He allowed only a slight and momentary frustration to cross his features. "Lady Marston will give us an assist, I'm sure."

"Lady Marston?"

"Yes." He glanced at the tall clock near the pillars of the staircase. "She will arrive at any minute. She will escort you, as it would be unseemly for me to do so." At Emma's blank look, he explained, "Essentially, you need a sponsor. You may not simply crash into the *ton* with neither an invite nor a supporter."

"Oh."

"The dowager countess's carriage has just pulled up, my lord," said the butler, near the door. He grabbed the handle but did not pull it open immediately.

The earl stepped around Emma and received her cloak for the evening, which the butler had been holding.

Emma stared rather blindly at the stairs she'd cavorted down only moments before. How could she not have considered that she didn't know the first thing about dancing?

The earl, laying her cloak about her shoulders just as the aged butler pulled open the door, caused Emma to startle. He turned her around to face him and left his hands on her arms, over the soft velvet of the cloak. "I am not concerned, and you shouldn't be either. We'll figure it out."

Emma was sure her expression conveyed adequately her disbelief in this, but as she supposed it was too late to bow out, she smiled grimly at the earl and allowed him to lead her outside and to the matron's shiny black carriage.

"There she is," said Lady Marston, from within the vehicle as the door was opened, "the extraordinary chit who dragged the jaundiced Lindsey into the park only two days ago."

"Be kind, my lady," the earl chided with a grin as he passed Emma into the carriage.

"You can count on it," said the lady in such a way that Emma thought she should not count on this at all.

"I'll see you within the hour," he promised to Emma, and closed the door.

Emma faced the dowager countess and gave her a nervous smile, before she thought to thank her for her sponsorship.

Lady Marston spoke up as the carriage rolled away from the earl's home. "Jaundiced, as in cynical, my dear," the lady explained.

"I gathered," Emma announced, though wouldn't exactly have said the earl was cynical. Not all the time. "My lady, while I thank you for your support for me this evening, I fear I must reveal to you what I've only now shared with the earl, that I haven't any experience or knowledge of dancing."

Lady Marston, cane in hand and wearing a matronly gown of royal blue, made a noise that seemed to have no purpose, or rather none that Emma might interpret.

"This comes as no surprise, Miss Ainsley. At least less so to me than to your very benevolent earl." Her shoulders lifted and fell.

Emma liked her somehow, despite the tinge of sarcasm that seemed to never be far away and now surrounded the word *benevolent*. She smiled prettily at the matron, even as she lifted a brow at the woman's words. She knew her not at all, but suspected Lady Marston did not fret about many things in her life.

"My godson tells me you were acquainted with his father," she said.

As Emma had to assume, by virtue of her personality, that this was not a woman you lied to, she imagined the earl had laid out the entire truth. "I was. He was a wonderful man."

"Yes, he was. And I've been told that you have a child, as well."

Ah, so it was to be an inquisition. Having just learned that the earl was her godson might explain this present line of questioning. Emma would not presume outwardly to know where it was going, but privately thought she had a pretty good idea. Indeed, the suspicious and knowing tone, which Lady Marston bothered not to hide, said nearly as much as the words themselves.

"I do. Her name is Bethany."

"Charming," was replied in such a way that Emma was convinced that the lady did not actually think so. "And what is it you hope to gain, if you should find your efforts to keep the very sharp and unpleasant claws of Lady Prudence out of Lindsey's person are actually or somehow successful?"

"Gain? I haven't anything to gain, but that I've helped the earl, as he—by way of his father—has helped me."

"And now you've made your presence known—driving in the park, dinner with the Kingsleys, and tonight the Clarendon ball. Made your presence known amazingly. The drive through Hyde Park alone has the tongues wagging. Tonight ought to send them into a lather."

Emma bit her lip, unsure what the good lady expected as a reply.

"Do I misspeak, Miss Ainsley?" Lady Marston queried, pressing her hands upon the top of her cane, which she employed more as an affectation, Emma was sure. "Perhaps you are unused to being the subject of so many rumors, but then your unprecedented descent into the park rather contradicts that, does it not?"

Emma demurred, her smile intact, "You do not misspeak, Lady Marston. The truth never upsets me. But rumors... how is that even possible?" She tilted her head, not daring so much as to point out to Lady Marston that she was the only person they'd spoken to inside the park.

A sly grin twisted the old woman's mouth. "You were seen, and by hundreds. Or rather, Lindsey was seen, and your presence was noted. Rumors abound." She leaned forward, her eyes begging Emma to do the same, which she did. "And it is more than probable that I was not the only one who made note of how his gaze all but devoured you. A dog salivating after his bone."

Emma sat straight, removing her eyes from the woman, with a great lack of appreciation for the correlation. When she faced the woman again, she realized some bit of her apprehension about the woman had slipped, as had some of her respect. "What is it you would like to say to me, my lady, that has you beating around the bush so poorly and with such crass comparisons?"

Lady Marston arched a thin brow.

"He is toying with you, nothing more. He won't marry you. He cannot marry *you*." She let that settle before adding, "It's just the way it is, girl. I tell you that not to upset your dreams, but to bring reality to the fore. He just cannot. He and I have already discussed it, and he knows his career is too promising, too important, to trifle with, and certainly not for something so fleeting as lust. And with that said, I think the following less necessary, but I'll drive the point home regardless—he won't marry you, so do not allow him any opportunity to make you promises he won't keep. He'll say he will, or would, wed with you, of course; that's part of the game. Do you understand me? Yes, I can see that you do. That's a pretty flush, Miss Ainsley. It comes with innocence and naivete and hope, all dangerous things to possess in a city teeming with dissolutes and bounders."

"'Tis a good thing then, that after tomorrow I shall likely never see it again, this city." Fairly seething now, for the woman's obvious judgments and false assumptions, Emma informed her, "As I'd said to the earl only a few days ago, my lady, people like me aren't afforded the privilege of dreams. Your godson is safe from any manipulations by me."

The carriage slowed then and lined up in the queue at the grand house of Lord and Lady Clarendon.

"See that it remains so," Lady Marston said after a long silence, and only seconds before the door to the vehicle was pulled open.

Emma, then, was prepared not to enjoy herself at all, Lady Marston having stripped her of all giddy anticipation for the evening. And yet, once they stepped inside the home of the Duke of Clarendon, Lady Marston's demeanor toward Emma changed. Perhaps having said her peace, having gotten that out of the way, the matron did what the earl obviously had asked of her: introduced Emma prettily, as if she were someone of no small consequence; smiled at her at times as if she'd known her forever and actually enjoyed her company; and once, even commented that, "If not for the fact that you depart London tomorrow, I'd put odds on you becoming the taste of the season. But damn that Lindsey, I'll not know a moment's peace tonight."

Having followed Lady Marston through the foyer and around the first floor, they had eventually found their way up to the second-floor ballroom. Emma gasped and twirled around, taking in the splendor of the room. The ceilings were so high, the room so large, she thought the entire structure of the King's Arms Inn might have stood inside it. Curious paper lanterns were strung all about, many potted greens and fresh flowers were grouped all around the room, and Emma's jaw dropped when she realized the floor had been painted with a chalk picture. The room was crowded already, leaving Emma only to guess what the entire sketch might have been, but she saw clearly several spots that showed trees and a setting sun and a mounted horse, and the figure of a man gallantly depicted in an English military uniform.

She frowned, though. As lovely as the chalk art was, she watched several women with longer trains sweep across the floor, disturbing and blurring the scene with the hems of their gowns.

"Expensive, but wasteful," Lady Marston commented at her side, seeing where Emma's gaze had been. "Ah, here comes your new friend, Lady Prudence," she said then, lowering her voice. "She thinks I enjoy her, hopes to gain favor with Lindsey by way of my appreciation. Will never happen." And when the lady stood before them, garbed resplendently in a frothy pale-yellow confection, Lady Marston smiled widely and said, "You've met our sweet Miss Ainsley, I am to understand."

"I have," said Lady Prudence, literally looking down her nose at Emma, her gaze raking over Emma's gown as if she found it distasteful.

She might have said more, but a young man approached them, his gaze on Emma with a lavish amount of appreciation, his mouth opened to speak before Lady Marston said sharply to him, "Off with you, Yeardley. You can make your exceptional presence known to Miss Ainsley when she is available. Presently, she is occupied."

Thus thwarted, and gape-jawed still, the man sent one last glance to Emma, who offered him a sympathetic smile, before he pivoted and skittered away.

Lady Prudence said then to Lady Marston, "At some point, I should like to have discussion with you about—"

Another man stepped within their small circle, bowing politely to the matron, ignoring the Hindrance, and smiling eagerly at Emma.

"Hullo," said Emma, when he seemed intent only on staring at her, and not actually presenting words.

"God's wounds, Rutherford, say something to Miss Ainsley, lest she think you a bigger idiot than this lousy first impression," Lady Marston barked with no small amount of impatience.

The man, with beautiful, large blue eyes, stuttered, "I—that is...how do you do?"

Emma smiled at him and his face all but melted. "Very well, kind sir."

"He is the *Marquess* of Dorcester," snapped Lady Prudence, "hence, *my lord*."

"I will be whatever the fair Miss Ainsley wishes me to be," he said, having composed himself, and proving himself a fine gentleman for having staved off Emma's blushing embarrassment that had accompanied her regretful gaffe. "First, I am hoping to be a partner this evening for a dance." His eyes never left Emma's.

"Quite so," Lady Marston said smoothly, "but return later, Rutherford, for that honor. Miss Ainsley has many introductions to make first."

Lord Rutherford bowed, his eyes only for Emma still, and backed away.

"I won't have a moment's peace tonight, will I?" Asked Lady Marston, her smile indicating something akin to a motherly pride, even as it did not quite reach her eyes. All for show, Emma suspected.

Lady Prudence was not to be deterred. "As I was saying, I would like—"

Turning her wrinkled face to the Hindrance, Lady Marston lifted a hand from her cane and waved it dismissively. "It appears, my dear, that there will be no time this evening for any dialogue that is not directly related to the uproar caused by Miss Ainsley's debut." Even as she said this and noted the frown of disfavor upon Lady Prudence's pinched face, two more men strode with purpose toward the trio.

Lady Marston discouraged or outright denied any request for a dance with Emma in a similar, near discourteous fashion for the next half hour. Lady Marston did generously and favorably introduce her to ladies of consequence, having escaped the watchful eye and dour company of Lady Prudence. The ladies did not go out of their way to know or make conversation with Emma, but rather talked around and about her, as if she stood not so close to them. She smiled politely, the expression becom-

ing rather stiff after some time, until she spied finally the arrival
of the earl.

"And here is Lindsey now," said one of the women currently
gossiping with Lady Marston. "I see the rumors have not misspo-
ken. Like a bird of prey, the way his gaze found your Miss Ainsley
with such fantastic haste."

Emma straightened and cast her eyes toward the door. Yes,
there he was, in the company of two men, both of whom put
forth a practiced posture of boredom, while the earl's gaze was
indeed fixed upon Emma, though she could ascribe no emotion
to the slight frown that accompanied his regard. She gave him
a smile, tinted with some exasperation and a dramatic rolling of
her eye, to give her opinion of all the tedious chatter, tucked
as she was in the bosom of Lady Marston and her cronies. She
turned back to the women, but not before she caught sight of the
barely discernable loosening of his frown. Just briefly, the dark
eyes lightened, his lips twitched as if they might lift.

Emma grinned at the ladies around her, while several brows
were raised at her, though no questions attended these curious
looks. Not too many seconds later, several sets of eyes widened
and stared over Emma's shoulder. A prickle of awareness, a warm-
ing tingle caressing her neck, told her the earl was moving her
way. Squaring her shoulders, she rolled her lips inward, tamping
down the smile that wanted to come.

Emma did not turn, just stared ahead at Lady Walcott, an
immense woman both in height and girth, whom she would forever recall as the Gray Lady, her gown, her complexion, her hair
all a similar shade. The Gray Lady's eyes moved swiftly under
her lowered brows, back and forth from Emma to whom she assumed was the earl standing behind her now.

"Lady Marston, Lady Walcott, Lady Chester."

The earl indeed. His voice warmed her as she was sure no other person's ever would. Finally allowing the smile the come, she turned, finding him to be very close, that her hand brushed his while he held a fluted glass of some dark liquid.

"Miss Ainsley," he greeted, as if he had not tucked her into Lady Marston's carriage just over an hour ago.

"Lord Lindsey." She detected a hint of a smile within his gaze, which struck her as unlikely, as if ever she'd read something hidden deep in his gaze, it was more often than not anger or one of a host of likewise dark emotions.

Later, she would blame his decadent and good-natured gaze for putting her in the position of having to dance at this crush of a ball, in the arms of the man she was very afraid was stealing her heart, and without a hint of knowledge about the steps of any dance, least of all a waltz.

As it was, he said simply, holding her gaze, "You will dance with me, Miss Ainsley." Not an invitation, not with any hopeful expectancy, but delivered as a statement, as if only inevitable, which had Emma swallowing and nodding against the onslaught of so masterful and confident the persona of Zachary Benedict, Earl of Lindsey.

And then her hand was in his and he turned her toward the dance floor, where only small colorful patches, hazy and lightened, remained of the pricey chalk painting.

Walking away from the not-quite-pleasant matrons brought about a sense of calm that was immediately disrupted by her recollection that she still did not know how to dance. She brought this to the earl's attention. "I hope you are not under the erroneous assumption, that between the time I stepped into your godmother's carriage until this moment now, I had somehow managed to acquire any skill that might be useful upon the dance floor."

The earl set his emptied glass upon the tray of a passing servant and faced Emma as the musicians began to play. He stepped backward, onto the perimeter of the dance floor, pulling Emma along with him.

"I have some suspicion that I might be able to steer you properly through a respectable waltz." He lifted his hand to the height of his shoulder, his palm open.

"I haven't any idea why I might trust that you are correct," said Emma. She considered his strong hand, waiting for hers. Slowly, and with a deep and brave breath, she put her hand into his. "But I do."

Zach's lips curved. She thought he might have been proud of her boldness.

"Put your other hand on the top of my arm," he said, and when she complied, he pulled her incrementally closer and placed his free hand under her arm and around her back.

Emma lifted her eyes to his, while lamenting the loss of her even breathing and bravery.

"I will guide you. Don't think about steps or where you should be going. Hear the music and feel my movements, under your hands and at your back. It's a very simple step-slide-step motion, beginning with your right foot stepping back."

Emma nodded. She closed her eyes, concentrating on the feel of him, a dangerous proposition to begin with, only marginally less so because of the task he'd set her. She sank her fingers into the firm hardness of his upper arm. When he began to move, she kept her eyes closed.

And stepped back just as he moved forward. Her touch did perceive his intent, that she knew by the subtle shifting of his left hand that she needed to move toward her left. And then the hand at the right side of her back squeezed slightly and sent her in that direction. She hadn't opened her eyes yet, letting the earls' movements instruct her own. Admittedly, it took several turns until she mastered the slide-step but felt a certain confidence in this fairly quickly.

Finally, Emma opened her eyes and found his smoldering gaze upon her, lit with some inscrutable light.

"That's a very brave thing you did there, rather throwing caution to the wind," he said, still twirling her around with such ease it seemed almost second nature to him.

Emma shrugged, more so inwardly than outwardly. "I haven't anything to lose, save from bringing embarrassment onto you. I will leave London tomorrow, and if you're not worried about being associated with some girl whose name will likely be forgotten before I'm even returned to Hertfordshire, then I will not be either."

"You could stay a few more days."

Here, she did falter. But his hold was steady, and their timing quickly recovered.

"Step, slide, step," he reminded her. "I think you are enjoying yourself and London."

Not *I like having you here*. Not *please stay with me*. How silly she was to just now understand that these were the words she craved!

She could only hope she was successful in hiding the sorrow from her smile. "I would be lying if I said I was not relishing this visit to London. But I miss Bethany, as I'm sure you can imagine.

More than anything, I am looking forward to seeing her tomorrow."

"Ah, I somehow expected that might be your response," he said lightly.

"Do you think we've accomplished our mission? In regard to the Hindrance?"

Zach let out a short chuckle.

Emma defended with a grin, "You hadn't given me her name when first we discussed this plot, that she was only—your words—a hindrance. Truth be told, even after I met her, she was still *The Hindrance* inside my head."

"She is at that," Zach agreed. "Yet, I dare say, we've made a point. Waltzing abets our cause, as it will have been noted that neither you nor I had or will dance with any other tonight."

"That sounds rather presumptuous, my lord," Emma returned with another grin. "I think I've gotten the hang of this dancing. I might try out these newly acquired skills on some poor—"

"Don't do that," he said, all good humor departed.

Emma clamped her lips. No. He wasn't allowed to do that. She would not permit him to dampen this evening with his constant and bewildering desire to control her. "Lord Lindsey, I—"

The music ended. Abruptly, Emma thought, though she really hadn't heard the notes in several minutes. The earl stopped moving but did not release her, in fact squeezed his fingers around her hand.

"It won't come as easily, as perfectly, with anyone other than me," he said. "Dancing, that is."

Aiming for a lightness she certainly did not feel, she teased, "You are many things, my lord—overbearing, stubborn, dictatorial, to name a few. I will add arrogant to the list."

He grinned and there was something knowing, defiant in his gaze. "Have I any good qualities? In your eyes?"

Emma tugged at her hand, and he allowed it to slip away. The floor had cleared of all but a few couples. Good qualities? Painfully handsome. Undeniably appealing. Sometimes very kind. Maybe what she'd dreamed of when she was a child, before she knew that noblemen did not fall in love with chambermaids.

"You are a very fine dancer." She gave him one last sad smile and left him standing on the now nearly invisible chalked horse's head on the dance floor.

Chapter Twelve

An hour later, bored and somewhat disillusioned, as Lady Marston would barely permit her to speak to any persons and had threatened and taunted and embarrassed several swains away when they'd dared to approach, Emma wished the evening might end. The sooner she was back at the earl's townhome, the sooner she might sleep, and then the sooner the morning would come, and she could be away. She might have liked to dance again, but feared the earl might be correct, that she would fail miserably unless in his arms. She'd watched with some delight several of the reels and cotillions but did not feel that she was prepared to put herself upon the floor with only an unsupported hope that she could properly perform any of the steps.

She glanced at the very ornate clock above the arched entryway. The lateness partially explained her fatigue; she was normally abed by now, as she was typically up with the sun. Dear Lord, but she would be tired tomorrow.

"We shall head downstairs for supper now," said Lady Marston then. "I dislike standing in line like some beggar come to the soup kitchen. If we move now, we might find ourselves near to the front as it will not be served for a quarter hour, at least."

Emma demurred. "Honestly, I cannot imagine putting anything in my belly at this hour of night."

Lady Marston harrumphed. "That would explain your waif-like figure. Very well, stay here with Lady Walcott. Do not leave her side."

"Yes, my lady."

The old woman waddled away, using the cane more than she had for most of the night, causing Emma to wonder if she truly did have need of it. Feeling guilty that she'd left the lady to her own devices, Emma was just about the chase after her, offer her arm for added security when she saw that a man approached Lady Marston. They shared a laugh over something, and the gentleman extended his arm, which Lady Marston latched onto without hesitation.

The Gray Lady was deep in conversation with another matron, all but ignoring or forgetting Emma's presence that when a man approached and stood before Emma, she smiled automatically, welcoming the diversion. He was exceedingly handsome, almost too handsome, if such a thing were possible.

"I have made inquiries," the man said. "I couldn't *not* wonder who you might be, and how I might possibly be able to know you, Miss Ainsley."

"You have me at a disadvantage," she replied, facing him fully. He stood about the same height as the earl, with shoulders nearly as wide, and leveled a pair of vivid blue eyes upon her. The eyes, she noted, held evidence of frequent good humor, as told by the tiny, crinkled laugh lines in their corners.

"Tristan Noel, and please excuse my bluntness, but let us talk about you." He leaned forward and said in a quiet voice, "I fear the minutes available to me for this audience will be cut short once Lady M gets wind of it."

Emma bit her lip, smiling. "Have you been spying on me, sir? Or, is it *my lord*?"

"Call me *sir* or *mister* or the *right honorable*, or perhaps *my beloved*. Whatever pleases you."

"Very fanciful."

"I *have* been spying on you. But only most of the evening. Couldn't believe my good fortune when Lady M dared to leave you unattended, even as it is common knowledge that she never met a buffet she did not like. And Lindsey seems to have quit scowling at you from across the room, that I deemed it a fine time to make myself known."

"You are very observant, I should say, Sir Mr. Right Honorable Tristan Noel."

"You left off the *my beloved*." He winked at her. "Shall you dance with me?"

"I shall not."

He thumped his hand over his heart, as if mortally wounded.

"Lady M, as you say, would not take kindly to that," Emma explained. "But I might walk with you."

"That will do. For now. Even as I don't suppose you will allow me to direct you away from this crush, somewhere private."

"I would not."

They began walking, Emma hoping that the Gray Lady did not call out that she was to remain in her presence. They stayed to the perimeter of the room, the man's hand at her elbow when it was required that they move around other persons.

"Miss Ainsley must come complete with some wondrous name between those two very impersonal words."

"It does."

"And shall you tell me what that word might be?"

"That word would be my given name," she answered evasively, unable to keep the smile from her face. "I believe yours is Tristan. I have one as well. Everyone does, usually bestowed at birth."

"You are teasing me horrifically, Miss Ainsley."

"Actually, I am thinking what a clever man you are, to have made so simple a question resound with such whimsy."

"And yet this very clever man has yet to learn your name, indicating that my dreams will now be so damnably anonymous, with only a Miss Ainsley dancing through them. So now we are walking, but I beg that you not let us be waylaid by others, who may have also noted Lady M's absence and would be tempted to make use of this time."

"I shall not. Tell me, Sir Mr. Right Honorable Tristan Noel, is this how you find yourself in the company of many young women? Pouncing on them when no chaperone is near?"

"I should think, Miss Ainsley, that my methods might be applauded, for their creativity and for the vast amount of patience I have displayed."

"Poor Sir Mr. Right Honorable Tristan Noel —"

"Your beloved."

"—whose schemes are so vastly under-appreciated."

"Miss Ainsley of the secret given name, what brings you to London? And how long might the city be charmed by your presence?"

"I've come on a mission, actually."

"Of the mysterious sort?"

"Naturally. Is there any other kind worth the mention?"

"There is not."

Oh, but she liked Tristan Noel very much. What good company!

"And this would normally be the moment when you revealed your secret mission," he prompted.

"Sir Mr. Right Honorable Tristan Noel, it wouldn't be very secret if I bandied it about now, would it?"

"It would not. Unless, of course, you knew for sure that the ears into which you might speak it, would not, in turn, speak further of it."

"I know of no ears that can speak, Sir Mr. Right Honorable Tristan Noel."

"Oh, Miss Ainsley," he uttered, his grin at the moment devilishly handsome. "I am so glad you've come to London on a secret mission, but we are wasting time just now, and we must desist with this tomfoolery that I may—"

Emma clamped a hand over her mouth, stifling a burst of a giggle.

"What have I said?"

"Tomfoolery. What a fabulous word. I wish people used it more. Thank you for doing so, Sir Mr. Right Honorable Tristan Noel."

"Anything to please you, Miss Ainsley." He stopped walking and took her hand to hold her near. When next he spoke, and while Emma still smiled at him, he moved his gaze back and forth from her face to something over her shoulder. His own smile faded, his tone became serious, and his speech came quickly. "I fear our time is about to be abruptly and sorrowfully cut short. I will call on you on the morrow. Tell me where and say that you'll receive me."

"I will be gone on the morrow."

"You must not be."

"But I will."

"I will find you—"

"Beckwith."

Emma froze, the sound of the earl's voice behind her causing quite a panic, and no small amount of guilt.

She and Tristan Noel turned at the same time. He released her hand as they did. The earl stood there, glaring at them, having watched their hands separate. Well, more specifically, he glared at Sir Mr. Right Honorable Tristan Noel, who must actually be *my lord Beckwith*.

"Lindsey," Beckwith returned, employing the same frosty tone.

"Hello again, my lord," said Emma.

The earl spent a few more seconds leering with malevolence at Lord Beckwith before saying, "Come, Miss Ainsley, Lady Marston requests your presence." He lifted his hand.

Emma stared at his hand, actually debating refusing him. But no, she could not. She'd come to London to help him, not cause him...whatever it was that had hardened his expression and lit that fire in his eye.

Placing her hand in his, she turned to Lord Beckwith and smiled at him once more. "It has been a pleasure, my lord."

Beckwith's gaze held hers. He nodded but she could see that he wanted very much to say more. She made note of the pulsing cords in his neck, above his creamy silk cravat. With a fierce scowl that he bothered not to hide, he glanced again at the earl, and then bowed to Emma, his gaze softening.

"The pleasure was entirely mine, Miss Ainsley."

And then the earl pulled her away from the man, and the ballroom, leading her downstairs, where Emma assumed Lady M waited.

His hand upon her arm was firm—not painful, but rather noticeably weighty—as he steered her down the steps and then, surprisingly, into a darkened room upon the first floor, nowhere near the buffet and his godmother. Once inside the room, lighted only by the bare moonlight spilling in through a wall of windows, the earl closed the door and spun her around.

Through gritted teeth, he declared, "You may not—must not!—find yourself alone, and holding hands, and giggling for Christ's sake, with any man. And never—not ever!—with Beckwith. And you absolutely may not allow him or any other to avail himself so easily of your charms."

"I did not—"

"You did," he clipped. "You smiled at him, and goddammit, he ate it up, took it as the invitation it was meant to be."

Emma stared, aghast. And very angry. He was being unreasonably ridiculous. "You have accosted me and stolen me from the public room, and whisked me away into a darkened and vacant room, and have used this wretched tone with me, and now think to instruct *me* on what I may or may not do...because I smiled at a person?"

And here was that famous scowl again, the breathing through his nose, tick in his cheek, stormy-eyed look of which she been the recipient on too many occasions to count. My God, did he dislike her that much? As noted previously when he'd favored her with so many similar looks, his eyes moved from her angry gaze to her lips and back again.

And then his hand, still holding hers, yanked her toward him, and with such might that she all but crashed into his chest. Only her free hand, lifted and pressed between them, saved her from actually colliding with him. She opened her mouth to protest this savage treatment, but found her words swallowed by his kiss.

He crushed his mouth to hers, over hers, releasing her hand now to wrap her up in his arms, his hold strong, his kiss punishing. Emma whimpered under his lips, which instantly diminished the severity of his embrace, though he did not abandon the kiss. His hands splayed across her back, one reached up to the bare skin above the back of her gown, his fingers leaving prickling flames in their wake. His mouth glided over hers, his tongue was thrust between her lips. She moaned again, but not in fear. Her fingers clung to the thin lapels of his jacket, her face was lifted to him, her tongue met his and a heat began to build in the pit of her belly. Awkwardly, knowing only what his previous kiss had taught her, Emma pushed her hands up his jacket, over his broad shoulders, and into the hair at his nape. She slanted her head, giving him better access, returning his kiss with equal fervor, while pressing herself against the hard length of him. He kissed and licked and teased and savored, and she could do no more than follow his lead, happy to go wherever he might take her.

One of his hands left her back, slid around the front, between their bodies, and cupped the full weight of her breast at the exact moment that Emma was aware of his growing erection, pressing just below her belly.

Awareness gripped her. She lowered her hands and used all her wobbly strength to push him away. Gasping, she touched her fingers to her swollen lips and stared at him. He was breathing heavily, and that scowl was still in place, or was returned.

And finally, Emma thought she understood. The scowls and darkened looks were not particularly portraying anger at her. She had to truly consider that all those times she'd caught him staring so feverishly, so frighteningly at her, he was only besieged by this need. To kiss her. Were they not scowls at all, but only the earl fighting himself, trying not to kiss her? Dear Lord, that suggested so many occasions of an internal battle, waged with himself, to...not kiss her? Could this be true?

But why would he not want to kiss her? She knew her own practical and cautious reasons for hoping he did not kiss her, even as so many parts of her wished that he would. But what might his reasons be for not allowing himself to kiss her?

Her own response—dear God, his kisses were dangerous!—was another baffling thing altogether.

Lady M's earlier words, her warnings uttered inside her fine carriage trilled in Emma's mind just now. *He is toying with you, nothing more.*

She took out her frustration on him, the annoyance of not really knowing what was happening between them, the fear that Lady M had simply told the truth. In a ragged whisper, she insisted, "You need to make up your mind what it is you're doing with me, or what you think of me, or what....You cannot one day tell me I look ravishing and then kiss me. But manage to look as if you don't want to kiss me. And then act like nothing had happened. And then so wonderfully dance a waltz with me and now scold me for only speaking to a man and then...and then kiss me again even as you look as if you cannot stand the sight of me. I don't understand this behavior. Do you? Do you even understand what you're about? What motivates your kisses and your surliness and your sometimes very pleasant treatment of me?"

He stared at her hard. Finally, when she thought he might make some apology to her, he spoke, but his words only left her more befuddled.

"Are the kisses in any way related to the *sometimes very pleasant treatment*?"

It was perfect, actually, his flippant response. Perhaps she'd only just this evening, in the midst of that kiss and the immediate aftermath, convinced herself that he might have genuine and serious interest in her; maybe he, too, was plagued by thoughts of her, as she was so bloody often about him; maybe his wanting to kiss her was rooted in true affection; maybe this would not be her one and only visit to London, maybe she would be on his arm again.

Reality crashed, with his words, and just in time.

How ridiculous I am. I am falling in love with him, and I remain only a passing fancy to him, still the chambermaid from Hertfordshire that may or may not have been his father's mistress.

So the part of him that wrestled so often, trying not to kiss her—if she now understood everything accurately—was only whatever small amount of honor he did possess that would refuse him the opportunity to ruin her? Perhaps—and what did she know, really?—his baser self was attracted to the chambermaid, but his righteous self would not condone acting upon it, taking up with so low a creature.

It didn't matter. From the day she'd met him, they'd rather been at odds. It was wisest and safest that it remain that way.

"I will, for the remainder of the evening, comport myself with greater restraint," she told him, mentally shaking herself free of his hold, though he touched her not at all just now. Giving him what she truly hoped was a disdainful scowl, she turned on her heel and left him.

She did not seek out Lady M, but found a quiet place upstairs, a room removed from the ballroom. The music room, she surmised easily, as a grand piano sat in one corner of the red papered room, and close to that, sat a tall and golden harpsicord, whose strings she idly plucked as she passed.

"Ah, a melancholy note, if ever I heard one."

Emma jumped, yanking both her hands to her chest, and turned to find an elderly man sitting by himself upon an over-sized red striped settee.

"I'm so sorry," she stammered. "I didn't realize the room was occupied."

The man lifted tired green eyes to her, under thick brows that likely showed more hair than the top of his head, though above and around his ears, wiry gray hair was combed fashionably forward, toward his cheeks.

"Do not apologize, my dear," he said kindly.

"Are you all right, sir?" She wondered and stepped much closer, concerned as he seemed to be listing to the left.

At her voiced worry, he straightened himself. "Oh, I'm just fine. Biding time until we might go home." He put his arm upon the roll arm of the settee and propped his chin in his hand.

"May I?" Emma asked, and sat in the middle of the settee when he nodded and smiled at her. "Who might you be waiting for? Who is the other part of *we*?"

"My son," he said, his tone suggesting he'd been waiting for a while.

"Have you eaten? I can fetch you—"

He lifted a wrinkled hand and fluttered his fingers. "You are kindness itself, my dear, but I am not very hungry."

Emma thought to ask, "Do you mind the company, or shall I leave you alone?"

The man pulled his chin from the palm of his hand and turned sideways to really look at her. "You are a very sweet young lady. I wouldn't mind keeping company, but a nice girl like you probably wants to be dancing and watching some young fools fight over her."

Emma laughed at this. "This girl does not, sir. I am Emma Ainsley, and I am happy to keep you company. I think I've had enough of the fools, young and old, for the evening."

"Pardon me for truly being too weary to stand and make a respectable bow to you, Miss Ainsley." But he shifted slightly and offered his right hand. "Hadlee. Very nice to meet you."

Emma put her hand in his and he squeezed it politely.

"May I ask you something? It's a little embarrassing."

He straightened, seemed livelier, suddenly. One thick brow rose above widened eyes. "Sounds intriguing. Ask away."

"I am not...anybody, rather an imposter here, truth be told, though I've come with the sponsorship of Lady Marston," she was quick to clarify, as his brow had furrowed with her first words. "I don't want to shame myself or the good lady, but when you introduce yourself as simply Hadlee...what does that mean? Is that your title? Your surname? And how should I address you?" As he appeared non-plussed, she bit her lip and covered her face with her hands. "How humiliating," she murmured into her hands.

"Now, now, Miss Ainsley," the old man said, reaching over to pat her hands, pulling one away from her face. "You only surprised me, that is all. Do not fret. I gave you my title, Hadlee. When a person introduces themselves with only one name, you should assume a *my lord*. If I were not of the nobility, I would, I suppose, present myself with my given name and surname." He scrunched up his lips. "Maybe just the surname. I am not entirely sure. *Very pleased to meet you. I am Mr. Fiske.*" He seemed to consider this further. "I don't think anyone outside the peerage would say, *Hullo, I am George Fiske*."

Emma slapped her hand against her chest. "George Fiske?"

The man laughed, the sound ancient and craggy. "Haven't heard that in many years. I've been Hadlee for so long."

"But you are George Fiske?"

He nodded. "Yes, have been my whole life. But you cannot address me as such in front of other persons. They tend to get a little—"

Emma blurted out, "I found your letters. I have your letters to Caralyn Withers."

And now it was his turn to be astonished, to have his jaw fall open and stare at her as if she'd just announced she'd found the Holy Grail. But Emma nodded at him, her heart pounding with excitement.

"How do you know Caralyn—who *are* you?"

Shaking her head, Emma assured him, "I am nobody, I promise. But I'd been...staying with the Earl of Lindsey, at his house in Hertfordshire. I was...well, I was snooping one day, just looking around such a grand old house, and I found a stack of letters. I found the letters you wrote to Caralyn." She smiled at him, while his face had gone as white as the marble floor. "What happened? Is she your wife?" Her eyes widened. "Is she here?"

His entire thin body seemed to sink into the furniture, his shoulders slumped, his hands fell to his sides, his gaze dropped to his lap.

"My lord?" Caralyn Withers was not his wife, she surmised. Emma's heart and shoulders sank as well. "I'm sorry. How thoughtless of me. But I was so excited to know it was you—I didn't even think that maybe...." She stopped when he began to shake his head.

"Do not be sorry. I was only startled. I-I haven't heard that name in forty years."

Emma sat silently, allowing the old man to collect himself and his thoughts.

After many long minutes, his shiny gaze found hers. "Forty years."

Softly, Emma said, "I cried over those letters. They were so beautiful."

He gave a grimaced smile. "I was mad about her."

"I know. It's all written so plainly. What—may I ask what happened?"

His frail shoulders lifted in a shrug. "She didn't love me."

"That cannot be true," Emma insisted, though wasn't sure of this at all. But it mustn't be true. With a nervous laugh, she admitted, "I fell a little in love with the George Fiske who penned those gorgeous words."

He sat back, straightening himself, slid his hands up and down his thighs. "I loved her the very moment I first saw her. She had come to London with Lady Julianne Morrissey, as her companion. She wasn't of the nobility."

Emma did not interrupt but knew that name, Morrissey. It was, essentially, who she was pretending to be, a Morrissey relation.

George Fiske turned and favored Emma with a kindly smile. "Like you, she stood out. You couldn't not notice her. Of course, so many were turned off by her lack of good family, being only the poor relation. Ah, but she was remarkable, had the most amazing eyes, and her laugh was akin to angels singing, I swear to

God." He grinned again, at his own fancy, Emma was sure. "We met, we talked, we fell in love. Or so I thought. When the season was nearing an end, I begged her hand. She turned me down."

"But why?" Had been the burning question inside Emma for so long.

"She never said," he answered, his voice cracking. "All those letters and I had only one reply...asking me to stop." He stared straight ahead, seeing only the past perhaps. "God, but she was stubborn, was so sure I was not sincere, meant only a dalliance." With a smirk toward Emma, he admitted, "I was, truth be known, a bit of a rogue back then."

Emma smiled. George Fiske was very kind, perhaps mellowed with his advanced age. She tried to imagine what he might have been like, or looked like, in his youth.

"But where is she? I had a sense she left Benedict House rather in a hurry."

George Fiske sighed, a great sadness oozing out of him. "I visited that house, and Caralyn just before Christmas, 1774. Lady Morrissey was very ill. Caralyn could, or would, barely make time for me. When her lady died three days before Christmas, she just disappeared—no notice, no word of where she might be going. She just...up and left...me."

"Lord Hadlee, I am so very sorry."

"You needn't be. It was so very long ago."

"But you miss her still."

He made a face. "Only when I think of her." He turned to Emma then, shifted actually to face her. "But you said you currently have the sponsorship of Lady Marston? *She* knew Caralyn Withers. They were rather brought up together, along with Lind-

sey's mother, Barbara Morrissey. Lady Julianne was Barbara's
great aunt, if I recall correctly."

"Then Lady M might know what became of your Caralyn,"
Emma suggested with some hopefulness.

He shook his head. "I badgered her at the time. She hadn't
any more of a clue than I had. Curiously, Lady Marston—she was
simply Lady Leticia back then—and I were expected to marry at
one time. But I'd found Caralyn and she'd latched onto Marston,
that we'd both begged off. Families weren't too happy, but they
allowed it—the Marstons were a very wealthy family."

"But you have a son, so you must have married after all."

A slow and thoughtful nod preceded his response. "Amelia
Frere. Few years older than I. Seemed a safe choice, wouldn't try
to steal my heart from Caralyn, not that she could have. She
wasn't...awful. She just wasn't Caralyn. Been gone now a decade,
maybe more."

Emma chewed upon her lip as well as a thought. "Lord
Hadlee, would you like to have those letters returned to you?"

His face brightened, his brows lifted. "Do you think I
might?"

Emma laughed, "They are yours, my lord. Of course, you
should have them."

He inclined his head and rubbed his hands on his thighs
once again. "I would like that."

Emma passed the remainder of the night with George Fiske
in the music room, barely giving any thought to the earl or Lady
Marston, who may or may not be searching for her, or at least
wondering where she might be. People came and went from the
music room, others looking for quiet, away from the crush and
noise of the ball itself. More than once, a young couple burst into

the room, clearly hopeful of finding it empty, quickly departing when they realized it was not. After about a half hour, in which time Lord Hadlee and Emma traded more life tales and anecdotes of years gone by, a man stepped into the room, and did not leave upon spying the unlikely pair upon the settee but strode with purpose toward them.

"My son," Hadlee announced. As lively as he had been in the last half hour, his tone now soured. "Too much like his mother," he whispered to Emma, then increased the volume of his voice to say, "Ah, there you are, Peter."

The man, whom Emma decided was not at all a younger version of George Fiske, stood before the settee and ogled Emma with a practiced leer. It was quite discomfiting.

"Bloody Hades, Peter," Lord Hadlee groused, "leave off with...whatever that pitiable expression is meant to convey. I read only desperation and nonsense."

"But won't you introduce me, Father?"

Peter Fiske was short where his father was lanky, was round as his sire was thin, and possessed a complexion of some misfortune, being blotchy and pocked. But his eyes, Emma noted, repelled her the most; dark and wild, alternating nervously from narrowed to widened, he gawked at Emma as if she were naught but a delicacy upon the buffet, and he a starving man.

George Fiske stood from the seat. "I will not. She's untarnished yet, to know persons such as you." He extended his hand to Emma, bringing her to her feet as well. "I will see you returned safely to your Lord Lindsey."

"I can take her," offered Peter, while spittle followed this suggestion out of his mouth.

Both Lord Hadlee and Emma rather towered over Peter Fiske.

"She's not a pet, in need of a stroll," Lord Hadlee sniped at his son and pulled Emma away from him. "I swear to God, Miss Ainsley, I tried for years to like him. I just cannot."

Emma pursed her lips at this sad circumstance, though she had recognized relatively quickly how different were Lord Hadlee and his son.

They stepped out into the hall and actually ran into Lady Marston and the earl, who was settling the woman's cloak about her shoulders near the front door.

"There she is!" Lady M called out, sounding none too pleased. And then her breath noticeably caught as she saw who escorted Emma presently.

"I've been looking for you for twenty minutes," the earl said with some reprimand, seeming unconcerned that they had an audience.

Perhaps they did not. Emma ignored the earl and watched the silent exchange between Lady M and Lord Hadlee, hardly believing her eyes when she spied a flush creeping up the old woman's cheeks.

"Been a while, eh, Leticia?" Asked Lord Hadlee.

"It has, George."

Emma's head whipped around, looking at Lady M, trying to imagine from where this unknown person, of the quiet and lyrical voice and the blushing cheeks and soft eyes, had come. Emma covered her mouth with her hand, quieting her little snicker. Lady M was behaving like an overcome fifteen-year-old.

She's in love with him, Emma realized, her lip dropping open. *Oh, my.*

"We might be getting a little too old for this, Letty," said Lord Hadlee, his brow wiggling, his grin crooked.

"Speak for yourself, Georgie," Lady M returned, stomping her cane playfully. "This thing will see me through many more years. That, and two snifters of brandy daily."

Lord Hadlee chuckled. "Good to see you, Letty."

"You as well, old man."

Emma watched Lady M walk away, appearing straighter and taller than she thought she actually was. She glanced up at Lord Hadlee. He hadn't a clue, she realized, watching him put the woman out of his mind the minute she'd turned away. He faced Emma and asked, "Shall I really come down to your little cottage and collect my letters?"

Emma took his hands in hers and smiled up at the dear old man. "You absolutely must." She turned and found the earl, standing with Emma's cloak tossed over his arm, watching her exchange with Hadlee. "Might Lord Hadlee be welcomed at Benedict House?"

"Of course," allowed the earl, clearly befuddled, even as he was so politely agreeable.

Emma smiled at Lord Hadlee. "Send word to Benedict House of your plans. They will get any note to me." She reached up and kissed his weathered cheeks, left then right. Squeezing his hands, she nearly squealed, "I am so thrilled to have met you. I cannot wait for your visit."

"What's this? Benedict House?" Peter Fiske, having come into the foyer as well, wanted to know.

George Fiske ignored his son. "You have made my day—my year, I daresay," he said to Emma, tightening his cool fingers around hers. "I shall see you sometime in the next few weeks."

Emma allowed the earl to place her cloak over her shoulders. She further allowed his hands to settle there for a moment longer than they should have. She waved to Lord Hadlee and turned to leave with the earl, catching sight of Tristan Noel, idly lounging near a pillar by the stairs. He was grinning at her, and then dared to wink at her, even as she was sure the earl might have noticed this. And suddenly she didn't care. She smiled at Tristan Noel, and waved to him as well.

"Good night, Sir Mr. Right Honorable Tristan Noel," she called out as she took the earl's arm and stepped out of the grand house.

Of course, her brazenness did not go unchastised. Once inside the earl's black-as-night carriage, with only the lantern hanging and swaying within to give light, the earl announced, in a frosty tone, "Miss Ainsley, it would behoove you to recall whose sponsorship you bear. You should not have behaved so…familiarly with a man as esteemed as Lord Hadlee. And you certainly should not have been so careless with Beckwith. He is a libertine of the first water."

"Yes, my lord," she agreed readily, which seemed to both surprise him and mollify him. She didn't care for his—or Lady M's—attitudes for what they deemed proper behavior. Beckwith and Lord Hadlee had been the highlight of her evening. And while she was unaccustomed to the *beau monde's* mindset regarding public behavior—

"Just like that? No argument?" The earl interrupted her musing.

Emma let out a weary sigh. But gave him what he wanted. "Lady M spent the evening being progressively nastier to any person who attempted to speak with me, that it became rather embarrassing and bade me wish the floor might open up beneath me. You chased away a man with a feral scowl and only because he spoke with me—that man being so bold as to actually talk to me rather as if our minds and persons were of equal rank—the gall of him! And then, if I recall correctly, it was you who actually accosted me in a dark room, laying your hands and your lips upon my person in a most intimate and scandalous manner—which by the way, Lord Beckwith did not do. Please do go on, my lord, instructing *me* on genteel and acceptable conduct. I am all ears."

The entirety of the ride, after Emma's remarks, was made in complete silence.

Chapter Thirteen

Somehow, the next morning, Emma was not entirely shocked when Mrs. Downing coolly informed her that the earl had already left the house and that she would be travelling back to Benedict House by herself.

Praise the Lord! Had been her silent response to this news.

She wasted no time but advised the housekeeper that she could be ready within the hour. She bounded up the stairs immediately after breakfast and packed her own small bag.

Some despicable melancholy made her leave behind the fabulous blue ball gown, spread out on the bed, when she left. She gave one final caress to the tassels at its hem and grabbed up her bag and cloak and left the room.

Almost two hours later, she arrived at Benedict House. They must have seen the carriage sending up a cloud of dust upon the high road, that Mrs. Conklin and SueEllen and Thurman waited for her upon the front steps. Emma only had eyes for Bethany, held so sweetly in the housekeeper's arms. Although Emma was sure Mrs. Conklin must have told Bethany for whom they waited, her daughter's eyes did not light until Emma actually stepped from the carriage.

She ran straight to her, Mrs. Conklin coming forward, happy to assist in the reunion. Bethany wailed and giggled, and then squirmed when Emma squeezed her so tight.

"Did you enjoy London, Miss?" Mrs. Conklin wanted to know, hovering over the pair, brushing Emma's sagging hair out of her face, even as she still had her head buried in Bethany's little face.

Emma took a deep breath and lifted her gaze to Mrs. Conklin. "Honest to goodness, it was as wonderful as it was awful."

The housekeeper and the butler smirked at this.

"That's probably the general perception," Mrs. Conklin said.

One week after her return from London, in which time his seat in Parliament kept the earl often away from Benedict House, Emma was informed—via Thurman, as was usual these days—that the transaction was completed, and the house had been readied for her immediate occupancy. Emma took this to mean, *Leave, now.*

Having not a whit of belongings to pack aside from one borrowed valise for their newly purchased garments, Emma had hastily and happily replied to Thurman that she was ready now to depart. If the butler were surprised by this announcement, he gave no pause, but nodded affably and told her he'd have the carriage brought out front.

Hence, Emma and Bethany, having said their goodbyes to Mrs. Conklin and several of the maids, had climbed into the open carriage and had left Benedict House without a backward glance. Mrs. Conklin had fretted at their leaving, wondering that she shouldn't wait for his lordship to return from London. As Peter and the carriage waited, Emma had only pretended not to hear this and climbed inside, with Bethany wanting to do her own climbing and sit upon her own seat. And so she did, and Emma and Bethany waved merrily at those few staff members come to the yard to see them off.

Twenty minutes later, she stood inside her new home, still mystified by her good fortune, silently blessing Michael Benedict for the beautiful person that he was and praying—half-heartedly—that she might never see the present earl again. She thought she might have come upon Henry, the caretaker, but found the odd little man nowhere about.

Needing then to be busy, Emma carried Bethany up the stairs and made decisions about what rooms to take and searched for and found fresh linens for the beds. She thought it a good time for Bethany to graduate from the cradle to the child's bed in the front bedroom, and chose for herself the bedroom next to that, facing the east. She liked sunshine upon her first thing in the morning and had been fortunate to have had this arrangement at the King's Arms Inn formerly. As it had previously been her profession, it took Emma no time at all to make the beds, even while she kept one eye on a very curious Bethany, exploring her new surroundings. She worried for a moment about the effect of these recent upheavals upon so small a child, but considered Bethany's perpetually cheery mood, and was reminded again of dear Mrs. Smythe's idea, that a child took its cues from the adult and if she portrayed happiness and strength, so too would the child.

When this task was done, they explored the first floor more, Emma surprised to find that the larder and pantry had been stocked, and fresh vegetables and fruits sat in various bowls and baskets upon the cutting table in the middle of the kitchen. Picking up and squeezing briefly a tomato, testing its firmness, Emma turned then rather sharply at hearing the kitchen door open. She relaxed immediately upon finding Henry in the doorway, his knees bent in such a way as to suggest they were ready to sit, even if the whole of him were not.

"Good day to ye, Miss," he addressed her. He then spotted Bethany, trying to scamper upon a high-legged stool near the cutting table. "And a little miss, too."

"Hello, Henry," said Emma and introduced Bethany only by name. She was unfamiliar with this protocol; did she need to give Bethany's history to persons to whom it shouldn't matter?

"I thought mayhap tomorrow I'd take ye into the village, show ye where ye need to be to make yer purchases for this and that and whatnot," he offered.

Emma's brow crinkled. "Henry, do you not move on with the family who previously owned this cottage?" She feared what his answer might be because Emma certainly hadn't monies to pay for his time or work.

"It were arranged by yer earl that I stay with the Daisies, Miss, perhaps for just a few weeks to see ye settled." he answered.

This came as happy news to Emma, and she wondered at the earl's thoughtfulness in this regard. Seemed rather uncharacteristic of him. Quickly, she determined that was uncharitable of her and pushed those thoughts out of her head. "I'm happy to have you for whatever time, Henry, and hope not to be an inconvenience to you."

But Henry only waved her off, watching Bethany and her continued efforts to gain the seat of the stool. "Part of the deal, miss, whether yer trouble or not."

"Oh...well, that is good," Emma said, but then caught the old man's smirk and breathed a little easier. Briefly, she considered that she should ask the earl of the specific arrangement with Henry, to clarify.

And just as his name scurried through her mind, his image appeared before her, standing at the same doorway through which Henry had come.

"Aye, there ye be, milord," Henry said, by way of greeting. "I'll be off then, Miss. Until tomorrow."

"Thank you, Henry," she called as he left the cottage, nodding to Zachary Benedict as he moved by him. She wished Henry might have stayed—the look on the earl's face spoke clearly of his displeasure, though she could only guess at its cause.

He spoke immediately and brusquely. "I felt you had left London with some air of enmity between us. I didn't—I do not—care to have it remain."

And just when she thought she might latch onto that olive branch, he spoke again, giving her reason to assume he actually did enjoy the hostility.

"But then I'd ridden hard from London at the first break we had, and found you had left Benedict House, without so much as a by-your-leave."

Emma bristled, at both his tone and his words. Nearly through clenched teeth, she spoke before truly thinking better of it. "My lord, I was not aware that I owed you anything at all. I hadn't been informed that *your father's* bequest came with attached strings."

This only seemed to perturb him yet more. "Common courtesy alone might have insisted upon some thoughtfulness, perhaps at least waiting until I returned before you left."

"And you came here now to enlighten me in this regard?" Why—dear Lord, why!—did this man provoke her to this degree of hostility?

But this last bit of unkindness appeared to invoke no rebuke. For just the space of a moment, he appeared rather nonplussed. This, in turn, softened Emma's frigidity. Truly, she owed him not this animosity.

Emma drew in a deep breath and began anew. "I'm sorry, my lord. I certainly don't owe you such shrewishness. I do apologize. We seem ever to be at odds. Perhaps I only assumed I would for certain be seeing you again. My excitement that the cottage was ready for us overrode...my good sense."

By now, Bethany had successfully reached the prize of the stool top and sat herself at the cutting table, pounding the flat of her hands upon the wooden tabletop in her joy. Apparently, her pains to reach this height were so great that she hadn't even heard the earl and having been at the opposite side of the table, she had not seen him, and now her eyes lighted on him with glee. She lifted her chubby hands and clapped them together at the sight of the earl.

His scowl, so often present in the company of Emma, eased immediately upon seeing the child, and then yet more when he saw her enthusiasm at seeing him. "Hullo, moppet," he said and strode to her and lifted her up in his arms.

"Zach'ry! Zach'ry!" She chimed, and immediately set to destroying his neatly tied cravat.

Emma nearly blanched at Bethany's joy—however was she to take the man from her life when all else she'd known was gone as well? Watching the earl entertain Bethany now, Emma felt immediately that strange and uncomfortable feeling one gets when they realize they haven't any choice but to do something not to their liking, something they deem quite dangerous. Dread, she thought it might be.

With a sigh that she hoped went unnoticed, Emma asked, "Had you come only to reprimand me?"

This brought the earl's head up, his eyes, less stormy now, leveled on her. He nearly smiled. "I came as well to be sure you were settling in all right. To see if you had need of anything."

She had a need, that was for sure. She needed to not be so disturbed by the very presence of this man. She needed to think of him not at all when he wasn't near her. She needed to forget that his lips felt like heaven upon hers. She absolutely needed to stop thinking endlessly upon the possibility of more kisses.

"We've arranged our rooms upstairs," she said instead. "Bethany will be moving into a child's bed now." Shrugging, she didn't know what else to say. "I see that the pantry and larder have been supplied. Thank you."

He nodded at this, thoughtful for a moment. Then a strange grin lifted his mouth and made him appear near boyish. "I hate to ask, Emma, but do you even know how to cook?"

She stared, dumbstruck. Her lips moved to answer but no words came forth right away until a bare, "Well, no," finally did. She would learn. Eventually, she guessed. But with Mrs. Smythe soon to be here, she hadn't thought to worry about her own present inadequacies. She didn't know if or what she might tell him about the coming of the Smythes and Langdon. Would he disapprove? Refuse them? Could he?

He chuckled outright at her response.

Emma smiled herself. "It cannot be very hard... can it? A lot of cutting and chopping and—and," she wavered and then glanced at the vegetables in the baskets, "and a boiling of things."

Zachary nodded helpfully. "Sounds not difficult at all." His carefully held façade burst then and he erupted in outright laughter just as Emma did herself. Bethany chimed in, having no idea what they conspired in laughter over, but happy to participate all the same.

"I don't suppose you would be any help to me," Emma accused when their laughter had begun to fade, but there was a hopeful element to her tone.

The earl looked mildly affronted. "Me? No. Even when I served with Wellington, I had staff to cook for me." He set Bethany down then as she was wiggling to be free and take up again with the stool. "But you might be right—it shouldn't be that hard. 'Get the food hot' seems to be the basic premise of cooking."

"Exactly," Emma agreed, clinging to this tenet as something on which she could build. "I can light a fire," she told him proudly. She thought for a second then guessed, with less surety, "Bread might be more difficult a task."

"Mmm," he agreed with a nod. "And puddings, likely, take some greater amount of knowledge."

Emma grimaced. "And gravies and pies and porridge and stews—I suppose they might all be rather tricky." Thank heavens that the Smythes *were* coming. Soon, she hoped.

"Beginning to sound like a problem," Zach decided in an even tone.

"Hmm, yes." She chewed her lip determinedly. "But nothing that cannot be remedied, I imagine. We certainly won't starve in the meantime."

"No?"

Emma frowned at him.

"I mean, no, of course not," he amended with a grin.

At this, she laughed again. Aside from his constant affability with Bethany, she'd seen not so much more of his personality than his rude and overbearing person. This was a pleasant, wholly unexpected side of him. Instantly, she was wary; she desired his kisses when he'd been a less than desirable character, and if he turned charming on her now, what more might she crave?

"'Tis a good thing I arrived when I did," he said into that small span of silence. "I suggest we head immediately for Perry Green and see what sustenance they have to offer."

Her mind screamed an abrupt, *No!*, but as he was smiling so handsomely at her, and as he'd showed a boyish charm with his wonderful laughter, she acquiesced.

Perry Green was a small but thriving market town in eastern Hertfordshire, though presently it boasted only one main thoroughfare, High Street. Aside from this, there were two rear access roads, Back Lane and Weir Lane, which allowed vendors to place their wares inside the mostly Georgian-styled buildings. As Hertfordshire was conveniently close to the English capital; much of the area was owned by the nobility[1] and thus the local economy of Perry Green was regularly boosted by this wealth.

This would be Emma's first good view of Perry Green, and she truly hoped it was all she'd promised it to be to the Smythes and Langdon.

On High Street sat the Crown Inn, a coaching inn which served mostly nobility on their passage from London to their country homes. While Emma had always thought the King's Arms a respectable and well-tended inn, she'd not much to compare it to, her visitation of other inns limited indeed. Thus, she was pleasantly surprised to find the Crown Inn so well-appointed and filled with so elite a crowd. In the next instant, however, surveying the large victuals barroom with its open fireplace, and all the grand people sitting about, she felt uncomfortably like the very poor and non-elite person that she was.

The earl apparently sensed or felt this not at all and steered her to a table near the windows, requesting of the steward a higher chair for Bethany. His very elegant appearance and the obvious air of nobility made things happen rather quickly and very shortly then Bethany was set into a chair which fit perfectly against the table, the seat and arms small enough that she was held snugly within.

Perhaps the earl perceived Emma's discomfort then—she felt his eyes once again watching her keenly—because he didn't allow her to have to make decisions but expressed himself to the steward, ordering their meals and beverages. This time, Emma was rather glad for his sometimes high-handedness. It occurred to her suddenly that she had never once sat at this side of the service trade. She felt conspicuous and ill at ease and so, rather without thinking, blurted, "I daresay I might rather learn to cook."

Zachary Benedict laughed outright at this, a loudness above the general din of the room, though he seemed not to care. "They are no different from you or I," he said, having correctly interrupted her timid expression.

"They are no different than you," Emma clarified, "but I remain situated well below you."

The earl leaned forward across the table. "My mother taught me from a very young age that we all put on our pants the same, one leg at a time."

This caught Emma off guard, and she fastened her bright eyes onto the earl. "Your father subscribed to that truism as well."

"Ah, then mother's work paid off at last," Zachary remarked.

A woman appeared at the table then, dressed finer than any server at the King's Arms had ever been, and set before them a mug of lemonade for Emma and one of ale for Zachary. She announced her name quite boldly as Molly and trained her eyes appreciatively upon the earl. "If you have any other need, my lord, please ask for me," she offered before sashaying away from the table.

"What if I were in need of something?" Emma asked, before she thought better of it, a quirky grin teasing her face.

Zach's shoulders shook as he chuckled at this bit of nonsense. "Then I would imagine you could ask any gentleman present and likely they would jump to do your bidding." There was only the slightest hint of reproach in this remark. He sipped briefly of his ale and then surprised Emma by taking up her mug of lemonade to offer it to Bethany, helping her sip easily of the fruity brew.

They were then amused by Bethany for quite a while, as she had taken a serious liking to the drink and was persistent in her efforts to have more of it. Soon, however, their meals were delivered, a mutton stew for Emma and roasted duck for Zach, Emma vocally lamenting the fact that she might never cook like this.

Something he'd said just a bit ago played in her mind. She thought to tell him, "You probably know this already, and first-hand as well, but I always liked how your father talked of your mother. He cherished her, didn't he?"

She'd surprised him, she gathered from his next expression, a light frown. He looked at her thoughtfully for a moment.

"He spoke to you of the countess?"

Emma nodded, unsure how she should—or *if* she should—proceed.

"He spoke of you, as well, always with boundless pride."

Zachary seemed still thoughtful. After a moment, having only stared at Bethany in that time, he lifted his dark eyes to Emma. "I wish I had spent more time with him these last few years. I miss him."

"I do, too." She thought it must seem odd to him, to hear her say that. "I know you haven't any siblings," Emma continued, "But you do have family, very dear cousins, if I remember....Your father told me of his sister, Augusta, and her charming children—Edith and Giles?" She thought she recalled correctly, and knew she had when Zachary rolled his eyes at the mention of their names. "Hmm, not so charming?" She teased, and then sympathized with him, "How awful to have grown up with such disreputable cousins! And always blaming you for the troubles they gotten themselves into!"

Zachary's head tilted curiously at this last statement. "Father knew?"

"That it was rarely—if ever—your fault? Yes, he said it was a favor to you to have you punished instead of them. First, by sending you off as punishment, it took you away from your cousins, which is what you wanted anyway. And too, he thought you strong enough to handle the censure of any family or staff who might have witnessed your reprimand. Made you a better man, he said," she delivered this last part slowly, the words sinking in to her just now. When Michael had ever talked of his son, she'd been able to truly put no face to him, and the anecdotes and tales had lesser meaning. Now, knowing his son, all Michael's stories took on new significance. Her lips tilted upward, rather thoughtfully, thinking of this insight she was afforded, even as it contradicted so much of what the earl had shown to her, today's delightfulness aside.

After a moment she lifted her eyes to Zachary to find him watching her attentively.

"I'm looking forward to hearing more stories Father may have shared with you," he said, his brow knitted slightly. He wiped a napkin rather distractedly across his mouth and returned the linen to his lap.

Emma lowered her head, pretending a notable interest in her food, having no idea how to interpret so negligent a remark. It hinted at future meetings between them, causing her to wonder how much of his attention was merely him keeping a fair eye on her as the recipient of his father's boon. Or was keeping company with her merely a by-product of visiting with Bethany, whom Emma was quite sure he still believed might be his half-sister?

Whatever the case, whatever the reasons behind his suddenly affable attention, Emma knew it would behoove her to keep their relationship on a neutral, unthreatening level. He was, after all, a man, and as Mama Smythe had reminded her on many occasions throughout her life, some men just thought the entire world and everything in it was theirs for the taking. Lady Marston's speech to her had lent credence to Mrs. Smythes words. The earl's kisses offered further proof that there was some merit to the caution issued by both women.

With this in mind, she searched for a suitable and impersonal topic of discussion, and thought to ask him about the current session in parliament over the last week, but he surprised her by asking instead, "What was your sister like?"

A very personal topic indeed, but one that Emma was happy to talk about.

She smiled prettily. "She was wonderful. Honest to goodness, you'd have thought she swallowed sunshine, she was so cheery. We looked nothing alike, Gretchen being this willowy and perfect blonde-haired beauty. She was just so...brave. Nothing frightened her." She fed several more spoonfuls of stew to Bethany, and thought aloud, "She wasn't overly alarmed by her predicament, being unwed, and already responsible for me. We played games to help her decide upon a name. She spent her free time knitting and making little baby clothes. And it slowed her down not at all—she worked just as hard right up until...this little darling arrived." A bittersweet smile came, watching Bethany chew her stew while using her chubby little forefinger to touch the buttons on the earl's coat sleeve.

Her eyes moved from Bethany's tiny hand to his, over his long fingers, over that sparse showing of dark hair at the top of his wrist before the sleeve showed no more of his arm. She let her gaze wander further, up his forearm and along the line of his bicep, the size of it pronounced by the sleeve of his perfectly fitted jacket, and across one wide shoulder to his face, to find his dark eyes upon her. Her perusal had been slow, and as he had apparently been watching her, Emma blushed and attended the stew once again.

"How is your duck?" She wondered, after a moment, and when the silence only seemed awkward because she knew his gaze was still settled upon her. She lifted expressive eyes, raising a brow for his response.

And found his gaze now attentively set upon her lips.

"Delicious," he said.

Emma blinked.

Thankfully, the kitchen girl returned to break the spell and dismiss whatever Emma might have made of his possibly nuanced reply. The server inquired of the earl if everything was too his liking. He assured her it was so, and she departed, inciting a bewildered laugh from Emma, as the lovely Molly had not bothered to ask if her meal, too, was acceptable.

Possibly grasping Emma's response, the earl granted, "She's working the purse holder, I imagine." But even he grinned at the girl's very obvious conduct.

"And quite adeptly, I should say."

Henry arrived rather early the next morning with his gig and began to give Emma quite a history of Perry Green, which Emma politely listened to, until she feared she must interrupt to mention that they needed to change direction, as the local village was actually not her destination today.

"Henry, I really haven't any need in Perry Green just today," she interjected while he drew breath. "Would it be a terrible imposition to ask you to take me over to Little Hadham? I have friends there and it is imperative that I reach them immediately," she pleaded. "I know it's a bit further away...."

Henry looked about as surprised as she imagined Henry could look, in regard to the change of plans. His surprise amounted to his brow—just one—rising almost but not quite to where his hat sat on his head.

But Henry was agreeable and soon had the gig headed west.

In Little Hadham, she found only Mrs. Smythe at their borrowed home.

"Alice is gone, my dear," the old woman said sadly. "She wouldn't listen to any of us, that she should stay with us. Met a fella, I'm guessing, hasn't been 'round in a week. I'll be hoping she'll be all right, 'tis all I can do."

Mrs. Smythe told her that her husband and Langdon were "about town" attempting to find an inexpensive gig or wagon, to bring them all to Emma when she was ready to receive them.

"Oh, you needn't worry about that. I'll send for you. That's why I'm here—it's all ready!" Emma said excitedly.

"So soon?" Mrs. Smythe looked bewildered.

"Shall I send the carriage 'round tomorrow, or do you need an extra day or two?" Emma asked, but couldn't imagine what might delay them, as they had no possessions to speak of.

"Oh, no, dear," Mrs. Smythe said, covering her heart with her hand. "We cannot be coming until the end of the month, when the house's lady returns. We promised we'd keep the house for her whilst she were gone. That was our deal."

"Oh, I see," Emma sad, a bit dejected, But not for long. "'Tis all right, Mistress, that's only a few weeks away." She shared the information on the Daisies Cottage and advised Mrs. Smythe to send a missive when they were ready, and Emma would send a carriage for their short trip. At a later date, she would give worry to what, exactly, she would tell the earl about her plans for her family and the cottage, and also, how exactly she might conspire to have Benedict House's fine carriage sent 'round to retrieve the Smythes and Langdon.

Chapter Fourteen

Emma and Bethany settled into a regular routine over the next few days. Their mornings began early, as they had ever been up at dawn, either because of Emma's work, or Bethany's sleep schedule. They'd begun to walk into Perry Green as the weather was mild and allowed these excursions. The walk itself proved to be a bit tiring for Bethany and Emma usually found herself carrying the child more than half the way, but once in town, Bethany was enlivened by the goings-on and busyness of the quaint little village.

They made friends with the butcher, who kindly answered Emma's questions about what cuts of meat to buy for stews and such, and even took the time to give her a basic start on the actual cooking of the meat. She'd decided that even with Mrs. Smythe's eventual coming, she should herself learn to cook. Emma also found a fine seamstress, three doors down from the butcher, her prices reasonable for a few more gowns for Bethany, though Emma advised that she would have to purchase these one at a time. The woman, of French descent, inquired boldly of Emma what her status in life was. Rather hesitantly, Emma explained vaguely that she received a small monthly income.

"From a man, no doubt," the woman said, her accent thick, her brows raised provocatively. She tilted her head a bit towards Bethany.

Emma's spine straightened a bit. "Not exactly," she said, her tone indicating that was all she would say on the subject.

Curiously, the woman offered her a job. She told Emma that her regular cleaning woman, who came three days a week, after hours, had died only recently, and offered Emma the position in exchange for one outfit, either for herself or Bethany, every other week, in addition to a very modest wage. Emma excitedly accepted this proposition, for it seemed quite reasonable, and promised to start the following week. Madame Carriere gave a small mew when asked if Bethany might accompany Emma, until Emma made it clear that this would only be for the first few weeks, until Mrs. Smythe arrived to take charge of the little girl.

However, she despaired a bit over the time schedule. She wasn't required until after seven in the evening, and she imagined the work—cleaning the two story modiste—might take several hours, and so she worried about having Bethany out so late and then walking home in the dark. But she figured she could at least try the job and see how it actually worked, and she kept in mind that it was only for a few weeks perhaps until the Smythes arrived and would likely help with Bethany.

Walking back to her new home once again, Emma gave some thought to the French woman's question. How was she to explain her circumstance to her neighbors, or in this town? Bethany had been calling her 'mama' since the day Michael had insisted it was indeed acceptable. People would assume she was... like her sister. Or worse. She chewed the inside of her cheek, her frown thick while she thought upon this. She almost missed the sounds of a jotting horse and harnesses and wheels turning.

Just as a horse and cart was nearly upon her, Emma realized its' presence and took up Bethany in her arms, keeping to the side of the road.

Emma turned as the cart slowed, shielding her eyes from the early afternoon sun while she considered the man driving the rig.

"Good morning," he called, his smile friendly and handsome. "You must be Miss Emma," he guessed as he stopped completely, while Emma stood just in the fringe of weeds along the dirt road. "I'm Callum MacKenzie, your nearest neighbor." There must have been a question in her gaze, for he said then, "Henry told us all about you and your little girl." And he wiggled his fingers in hello to Bethany, who only stared curiously at him.

"Very nice to meet you, Mr. MacKenzie," Emma intoned.

"Can I give you a lift?" He asked, raising a thick and dark brow.

She liked his deep voice. "Oh, you're very kind, but no, thank you."

"Not puttin' me out, miss. I'll be passing yer place to get to my own." He moved over on the bench seat. "Don't be shy now, miss."

"Well, all right, if you're sure," Emma agreed, thinking the offer would make it easier on Bethany. She lifted Bethany up onto the wagon, and Mr. MacKenzie steadied her while Emma hiked up her skirt and stepped up and into the vehicle herself. Once seated, she pulled Bethany onto her lap and thanked Mr. MacKenzie for the ride.

"Now, we're neighbors, miss, so you'd be calling me Callum. None of this formal stuff, this ain't the city." And he smiled, glancing sideways at her and Emma liked him immediately. He was handsome, it was true, with broad shoulders and thick, light brown hair, and a curious dent right in the middle of his chin. His eyes were grayish blue and his smile the friendliest thing she'd seen in many a moon. "See over there, you can just make out the line of your place," he said then, pointing much further ahead. Emma's eyes followed and indeed, there was just the top of the thatched roof of the Daisies Cottage. "Now," Callum continued, "I'm down the lane, about a half mile or so, so that makes me your closest neighbor. Winn Klein, at the edge of the hill, is closer on the north side. But you come to me if you need anything that ol' Henry can't help you with, miss."

"That is very kind of you, Mr. Mac—Callum," Emma responded with a smile of her own, while Bethany made a fuss about being able to so clearly see the horses of his rig.

"Just neighborly, miss, that's all. And what takes you into Perry Green today?"

"If I'm to call you Callum, I insist you call me Emma. Please," she added when he looked as if he'd refuse. "Bethany and I only look to learn about our little town, I guess. Nothing specific to bring me to Perry Green, though it's a good excuse to get out of the cottage a bit."

Her neighbor nodded at this. "When old Mrs. Finch lived there—just before you—she'd tie a bright ribbon on the front porch when she needed something from town, or to get there herself. That way, I'd see it as I got close and either pick her up or run some errands for her."

"I would hate to be a bother," Emma demurred. "As it is, I do have family coming in a few weeks." She smiled prettily at her neighbor.

He appeared rather disappointed by this last news. "Wouldn't be no bother at all, miss."

Once in front of the Daisies short drive, Callum deposited Emma and Bethany near the petite gate and inquired whether or not she knew if she'd like a ride the next day.

"You're very kind, Callum. I haven't any plans as of yet, and I'm guessing the walking to and fro might aid in my efforts to get this little one to nap."

He nodded in understanding and tipped his head in farewell before flicking the reins to move the cart again. Emma watched for a moment as he guided the rig further down the narrow road, hoping all her neighbors were as pleasant as Callum MacKenzie.

The very next time Emma saw Callum MacKenzie, it was at the Daisies. She and Bethany were trying to make some semblance of the vegetable garden, or what remained of it. Henry had offered, if she desired, to tackle the project himself, but Emma had declined his intent, claiming that it would give her and Bethany something worthwhile to occupy their time. This had been actually a bit of an understatement, as Emma found herself quite engrossed in the work. The immediate rear yard was conveniently contained by tall hedgerows which aided in keeping Bethany within close proximity. Sadly, her daughter hadn't much interest in weeding and pruning as Emma might have hoped.

Presently, Emma glanced up, pushing her wide-brimmed hat up off her forehead, and saw that Bethany was safely occupied chasing a small yellow butterfly around the yard. Emma removed one of her heavy cotton gloves, provided by Henry for this task, and wiped at the small beads of sweat beginning to form on her brow. She considered her work as of yet—there remained at least two-thirds of the small tract yet to tackle—and thought it might take many more days to get the garden ready for planting. Apparently, this had been neglected for quite some time.

"Hullo, neighbor," came a call then from around the side of the cottage.

"Hullo!" Emma called back, recognizing the voice of Callum MacKenzie. He appeared at the gate at the corner of the yard, peeking over the wooden slats before entering. Emma stood to greet him, giving her back a good stretch to work out the small kink from bending for such a length of time.

"Good day, Callum," she greeted her neighbor, wondering suddenly about his family and farm. Surely a man as handsome and pleasant as Callum MacKenzie, who appeared to be in his thirties, at least, was well-married with children by now.

"Miss Emma," he said and removed his hat, working it round in his hands. "I'm headed into Perry Green, if you have a need of anything."

"How very kind of you, Callum," Emma said, smiling at his thoughtfulness. "I haven't any pressing need, thank you" she said with a shrug, but then she thought of something her neighbor might be able to help her with. "Callum, I was wondering if you might be able to help me with a small dilemma I have."

"Anything you need, Miss Emma," he said, moving his hands with an indicative gesture of openness.

"Well, I've taken a job in Perry Green," she told him. "Next week, I'll start cleaning Madam Carriere's modiste after hours. Bethany and I can walk into Perry Green after dinner, but I was worried that my return trip might be too late for both her and me. Is it too much to ask you to fetch us in the evening?" While he did not at all look as if he might refuse, she was quick to explain, "It would only be for a few weeks, at most. Just until...my family arrives. I completely understand if you cannot," she rushed on, "seems terribly forward of me to presume upon you so soon after meeting." She rather grimaced at him, awaiting his reply then.

Callum's gray-blue eyes crinkled a bit at the corners. "You're not much used to asking people for help, are you, miss?" He watched her shake her head. "I can pick you up in the evening. It's no problem at all."

"You are very kind, Callum. It's only two nights a week, and I think I'd not be later than nine o'clock or so—your wife or family won't mind?"

"No, Miss. I'm a loner over there. No wife to speak of," he told her with a lowering of his head and a shuffling of his feet. Emma could almost swear at that moment a blush crept up into his sun-tanned cheeks.

"I can pay you for the transport." She thought she might be able to, anyhow.

"I'd not take your money, Miss Emma. That'd not be very neighborly."

A scream from Bethany turned both their heads towards the rear of the yard, just in time to see the little girl fall from the hedges she'd been trying to climb. Emma ran immediately to her, picking up the now crying child, checking for scrapes or cuts. "She's all right, I think," Emma told Callum, who hovered at their side. "Just scared herself, that's all. Didn't you, darling?" And she snuggled Bethany to her chest and stood again, while Bethany settled her head on Emma's shoulder.

"She's a nice girl, your daughter," Callum said. "She's got your eyes."

Emma blushed at this. It was always, she guessed, going to be difficult to explain Bethany's parentage to people she met. Michael had insisted that she needn't have bothered, and Emma began to think he'd been right. Bethany was her daughter, in her heart, and in her mind.

"Yes, she does," she agreed after a thoughtful moment, her voice quiet. Then, with more candor, "But I've yet to figure out where she gets her daring from."

Callum laughed at this and they began walking toward the cottage. "Well, I'll be off now, Miss Emma. And remember, I'm happy to help you and will see you next week."

"Thank you, Callum," Emma replied. "Thank you for everything."

She watched Callum let himself out of the gate and went toward the back door. It was time for Bethany's nap, and truth be told, she was very excited as she planned to make her first meal—today, she was going to attempt a stew. All thoughts and enthusiasm about this endeavor fled as she lifted her eyes to the back door.

The Earl of Lindsey was here.

Zachary Benedict stood in the open doorway. He looked, while not quite angry, at least cross about something. There was definitely a storminess about him now.

Emma, for just a moment when she saw him, felt her stomach flip a little at the very picture he made. He was entirely too handsome for her peace of mind, and she recalled—immediately and thoroughly, while she wished to the heavens that she did not—the feel of his mouth on hers. "Good day, my lord." She greeted him and he stepped aside to let her enter the back hall to the kitchen.

"Who was that man?" He asked pointedly, not bothering with a greeting.

Ah, she thought with an irritated grimace, therein lie the crux of today's agitation. "That was Callum MacKenzie. He is my neighbor. Will you excuse me while I put Bethany down for her nap?"

He nodded curtly, and Emma left the kitchen, aware that he had begun to remove his riding jacket, wondering how long he planned to stay.

She returned fifteen minutes later, the fresh air having aided her efforts to get Bethany to sleep. In the kitchen, she found Zachary seated on the lone stool at the cutting table and grinned nervously at him as he watched her. She washed her hands in a basin full of now tepid water and used a cloth to dry her hands and quickly wipe her face.

Finally, she turned to face the earl. "What brings you out to the Daisies today, my lord?" He looked so casual, in his fawn colored breeches with his tall riding boots, his lawn shirt open at the neck, one booted foot propped on a lower rung of the stool. He was smiling at her as she neared the table and her heart turned over yet again. Without warning, he reached across the narrow table and took the towel she twisted now in her hands from her. He beckoned her nearer with a wave of his hand. Bemused, Emma leaned a bit over the table, wondering what he was about, until he wiped at her cheek, where possibly there remained smudges of dirt from her work in the yard.

She staunchly refused to be affected by the touch of his other hand holding her chin, while he used the cloth much as she might to Bethany probably thirty times a day. From so close a distance, their eyes met, the cloth lowered now, though he still held her chin. He stared intently at her, his eyes seeming to bore into her very soul. Finally, just as her cheeks began to redden under his mesmerizing perusal, he released her.

"And what has this MacKenzie fellow promised to help you with next week?" He now wanted to know, his voice just slightly less than disagreeable.

Emma shrugged, having not the slightest clue why she should be nervous to tell him of the position she'd taken at Madam Carriere's.

"I've a job which begins next week," she rushed out then, turning away from his probing eyes to pretend great interest in the vegetables she'd planned to use for dinner. She faced the window which overlooked the back yard. "The hours are in the evening—just a few days a week—and so Callum has agreed to come and fetch me so Bethany and I haven't to walk home in the dark." She didn't need to turn around to gauge his reaction. She could just *feel* his disapproval, shooting off him like sparks from a fire.

It was almost a full minute before he spoke, in which time Emma was able to do nothing more than nervously rearrange the carrots and potatoes and onions in front of her.

"I don't even know where to begin," he said from behind her, his voice now edged with disbelief and anger. "Number one, you will not take a job. Number two, you certainly will not take a position that keeps you out late at night. Number three, you don't even know this man—you've only been here a short time—and you'll not trust him to drive you or Bethany anywhere." As he continued, his voice grew louder and angrier still. "And number four, are you going to actually do something with those vegetables or are you content to have your dinner be nothing more than a finely displayed *picture* of what you might have cooked?"

Infuriated at his high-handedness—once again—Emma turned to confront him, startled to find that he'd moved from the stool and now was directly in front of her. She jumped in reaction to his closeness, and words she'd intended to throw at him scrambled in her head. "I'll have you —you have no right.... who do you think...? If I want to have a job, you are not anyone who can—"

"Emma, think." This, given sharply, his brow showing a matching annoyance. "You are provided with enough moneys to see you comfortably through each month—why on earth would you think you need to take a job? And if you had need of a job, why would you accept one that offers such dreadful hours for you?"

"But I have the Daisies now," she stammered. "There mustn't be very much left. And I am still uncomfortable taking money from your father, which is now essentially yours."

He sighed in frustration. "We've been over this. Why not take what is available to you?"

She fumed at his frustration, angered that he thought her a simpleton—his tone said as much. "I balk at accepting the money for just this reason," she spat out. "Because you think you have rights—or that you have some say over my life and my decisions."

"I am just trying to help—"

"You are not trying to help me! You are trying to control me!"

It appeared to Emma at that moment that the earl made a visible effort to lessen his anger. Coolly, he said, "You've never had to completely take care of yourself before now, have you?"

When she hesitantly shook her head, he went on, "I just don't want you to make mistakes or get into a situation that might cause you harm."

Emma said sadly, "It's just... I feel I haven't earned it. I've no right to it."

The earl nodded. In agreement? She wondered.

"My father obviously thought you had," he finally said. "Listen, Emma, what's done is done. It's already yours. That is what I am trying to tell you. You've an account in Perry Green. That is another reason for my visit today, I wanted to give you the records for that and tell you how to go about getting pin money and such."

Emma rolled her eyes and threw up her hands. "How can I possibly have pin money left when this place surely took more than what your father wanted me to have?"

He laughed briefly. "You obviously have no idea how great the amount was that my father put aside for you, Emma. There is plenty, trust me. So you needn't work to have spending money, it's all waiting there for you. You also have an account at the general merchant shop in town. You can set up more if you like."

Emma slumped against the counter behind her. "I–I'm just so uncomfortable with this entire arrangement. Why did he do this for me? I told him repeatedly that I..." she let it trail off, hating then that a lone tear spilled onto her cheek.

Zachary shrugged, a flash of displeasure in his dark eyes. "It's done." When Emma said nothing else just then, Zachary said, "Let's talk no more of money and jobs you'll not have to procure. And you can tell this MacKenzie fellow that he needn't be sniffing around, that his help won't be required."

"That is unnecessarily rude," Emma accused. "Callum has been nothing but kind to me and you make it sound as if... as if he's a dog, looking for a meal!"

"Exactly!" Zachary hissed at her.

Emma moved away from him, stalking around the prep table, until she faced him again from the other side. "And what does that make you, my lord?"

"Touché, my dear. But your argument is unsound," he said in an oily, unattractive voice. "I believe that was you, responding so agreeably to my kiss for quite a few moments."

Her bottom lip sagged in mortification at this reminder. She lied pitifully, "I did not...want you to kiss me."

"I beg to differ," he countered evenly.

All right, so she was not going to win this argument, she determined with a huff. "I think you should leave now." And she took up the well-arranged bowl of vegetables and began chopping them ferociously upon the cutting table, pretending—hopelessly—that he was, indeed, already gone.

And in the next minute, he truly was. Emma heard the quiet closing of the kitchen door and she breathed again, dropping both hands upon the table in front of her to steady herself.

On a good day, having a clue what she was about making a stew, she might have been successful in this endeavor. Today, with that ugly scene playing in her head over and over—and still being without a true knowledge of what she was about in regard to stew-making—Emma was quite sure she was doing nothing more than wasting fine vegetables and a good cut of meat in an effort to keep her mind off what truly troubled her. She didn't think they had successfully settled any matter between them and was not so naïve to think that these issues would not arise again.

Within a half hour, however, she did have what she guessed was a good beginning to her dinner coming to a boil in the huge pot hung over the open hearth. She wiped her hands upon the apron she'd donned—when she'd remembered to do so after he had left—and happened to glance out the window into the back yard.

She blinked twice, shock rooting her to the spot in the kitchen while she watched the Earl of Lindsey work in her barely tilled garden. Unmoving, she saw that he had found a larger shovel than the small handheld one she'd struggled with earlier, and that he was turning the earth over with much greater ease and speed than she had. As ever, Emma was captivated by the sheer beauty of the man and his form. He struck the hardened dirt with the shovel and then used great force to push it further into the ground before turning it over, and all the while the muscles of his upper body were clearly visible through the white lawn of his shirt. He withdrew the tool from the earth and repeated the process time and again, until the entire plot of land, perhaps being a ten by twelve piece, had been worked to reveal dark, fresh dirt, ready for planting.

When he was done, he leaned one forearm upon the top of the shovel, now struck firmly into the ground, and used the other forearm to wipe the sweat from his brow. His head then lifted, his eyes squinting into the late afternoon sun, charting the flight of a blackbird across the sky above.

Many thoughts flitted through Emma's mind as she stared at Zachary Benedict, and she was surprised that at this moment not one of these ponderings were of a censorious nature. But there was, however, one troubling thought that crept into her mind.

She wouldn't let it complete itself, but the foundation of it was there. If only....

Zachary returned the shovel to where he'd found it on the side of the house, where Henry obviously stored many of the yard's necessities. It was then that he noticed, over the top of the hedgerows, that many of the trees within the pear and apple orchard outside the hedges seemed to be in need of some attention. He considered the stack of tools and such at the side of the cottage and selected several different pruners and a saw and ventured out into the orchard to see what might be done for the poorly maintained grove.

Counting fourteen trees, two of which he could not identify, Zachary began trimming away at the closest pear tree, thinning the canopy as efficiently as he could without causing too much loss to the healthy branches and late spring flowers. Menial, physical tasks such as this were exactly what he needed to keep his mind off the fact that he wanted—indeed, had thought of little else for most of this day—to kiss Emma again. His mind and body seemed not to care that mostly they just annoyed each other, that often they were at odds. She spoke and railed and fumed, and while he did hear her words, he focused much of his energy upon her lips. Their softness was already met and well-proven, and likely there wasn't a man who'd tasted those lips and then was able to think of much else when in her presence, and even when not, he imagined.

Naturally, this thought—another man kissing her—darkened his already unsettled mood. Here was an avenue he thought best not to travel. He recognized, although unhappily, that she had a past just as he did. Swiftly, shaking his head while his jaw tightened, he put an end to these unruly thoughts just as he spied Emma walking toward him.

She approached, if not stiffly, at least shyly, sticking out her hand, offering him a glass of cool lemonade. Zach ducked out from under the branches, watching her eyes, which watched anything *but* his eyes, and took the proffered glass with a low, "Thank you."

"You needn't do this, you know," she said, arms once again crossed over her chest—her protective or defensive stance—as she glanced around her orchard. "I'll tackle these chores... day by day, I suppose."

"I needed to work off some steam," he said, only half-teasing.

At this, she turned her enchanting eyes upon him, gauging his seriousness. A half-smile teased her lips. Zachary, as ever, was instantly captivated. She could ask that the proverbial back forty be tilled and he'd likely trudge out that way. Never, in all his life, amidst all the women he'd known, had he ever been led so easily—yet by one who remained so unknowing. Inside, he cursed himself a fool but heard himself say, "I'm guessing you finally did something with all those vegetables. I hope it had something to do with a big black pot and some fine cut of meat, and—as you say—a 'boiling of things.'"

She rewarded his small humor with a full smile now. Actually, she responded rather pertly, in good fun, "I'll have you know that I have successfully put together a beautiful looking stew."

"Congratulations."

Hesitantly then, so endearing to Zach, she added, "Would...would you care to stay for supper?" She seemed then to hold her breath.

"Are you asking me because you would like my company? Or," he said, unable to resist coaxing her into a smile again, "are you inviting me merely as your back-up plan, should dinner go awry?"

She responded as he'd hoped, grinning beautifully as she pronounced saucily, "I said dinner *looked* beautiful; I haven't a clue how it might actually taste. It might be necessary to have you around should the need arise for a late trip into Perry Green."

That's my girl, he wanted to say. He liked that so much about her. She truly was often angry and riled by him, some of it deserved, he allowed, but she was never of an unchangeable nature, and her mood seemed genuinely to be rather blessed by easiness. "I'll be in shortly to clean up."

She nodded, shy again and turned to retreat into the cottage.

It was easy then to imagine that she was his and that this was theirs. So satisfyingly easy.

Zach wrenched his gaze away from her and gave his attention to the suckers growing out near the base of the tree, not reading anything into her willingness to have him here.

Dinner was then, for obvious reasons, a very informal affair, with the earl even helping to set the table, while Bethany, done with her nap, trailed after him wherever he went. Emma had changed from her working frock into a simple gown of pale blue. She'd cleaned herself up, and even dabbed a bit of vanilla from the pantry at her wrists and neck, not even bothering to dissect why she might want to do this. She hadn't time to fuss overly with her hair and so only clipped up the sides at the back of her head and left the mass of it to fall down across her back.

All within the sturdy black pot looked good, and Emma only hoped it tasted as good at its appearance promised. She thought the earl might like a glass of wine with dinner but hadn't any to offer, and then felt embarrassed for this lack, saying as much to him. He was polite and insisted that he was more interested in her stew. Emma laughed and told him that was exactly what she was afraid of.

Carefully, she ladled two large plates full of the stew, having thickened the broth just as the butcher had instructed her earlier in the week. She spooned out a smaller portion onto a tiny plate for Bethany and carried these three dishes into the dining room, while the earl held the door for her. Emma set the plates down, putting the earl at the head of the table, though she didn't know why, but guessed years of servitude had dictated this move.

They sat as one, Bethany climbing up into her usual chair at the middle of the small table while Emma sat at the end near the kitchen. She saw the earl looking eagerly at his full plate and watched him settle his napkin—another courtesy of the previous owner—into his lap. He looked down at Emma and her heart twisted when he raised his glass of lemonade up to offer a toast.

"To your first home-cooked meal at the Daisies," he said simply.

"Cheers," Emma answered, raising her own glass.

"Chairs!" Bethany cried, but her small cup was raised directly to her lips.

Zach and Emma laughed at this and both picked up their forks, yet Emma hesitated, pretending to urge Bethany to eat, though her daughter certainly never needed coaxing in this regard, while she anxiously awaited Zach's reaction. He speared a carrot and piece of beef onto his fork and put this to his mouth, already considering his next forkful as he looked again to his plate. Emma might have wished for the floor to open up and consume her then when he seemed to struggle with the chewing and actually grimaced as he finally swallowed.

"Oh, dear Lord in heaven," she murmured, which brought his eyes to hers. His pained expression—he had to sip largely from his glass to work the piece down his throat—was erased instantly when he found her watching him.

"A little tough," he acknowledged—there was no lie he could have told to explain the contortion of his features as he'd swallowed. "It happens. This one will be better," he said and gamely stabbed another piece of beef onto his fork, along with a chunk of potato, and plopped it into his mouth.

Emma watched him, narrowing her eyes suspiciously as he made quite a show to chew and swallow with ease this time, even holding up his hands as if to say, "Voila!"

Unsure if he did this only to avoid hurting her feelings, Emma looked down onto her own plate and tried for herself a bit of the beef. It was not tender, not the way Mama Smythe could have made it, but it wasn't too tough. Perhaps he'd truly just had a rogue piece of meat. Aside from that, the flavor was good, the butcher having been right about the marjoram and the onions. Convinced then that she'd made at least a decent meal, Emma began to worry—as any hostess might—about the lack of conversation. Aside from Bethany's near constant babbling between bites, it was silent here at this table.

"My lord, are you—"

"I wondered if you—"

They'd both spoken at once. They smiled, suddenly awkward, as if this need in both of them to fill the silence was a testament to the true unease that suddenly filled the room. Emma made a show of wiping her mouth delicately with her napkin, allowing him to speak.

"I only wondered what you had planned for the garden," he said.

"I hadn't given it much thought, to be honest. Clearing away the debris seemed an obvious chore, but I guess I might like some herbs and perhaps only a few vegetables." She lifted her glass of lemonade but did not drink immediately from it. "I remember—vaguely, mind you—that my mother had a garden, much grander than anything to which I might aspire."

The earl tilted his head at this, his frown curious. "Do you mind me asking what happened to your parents?"

Emma shook her head and answered, "I mind not at all. 'Tis no great story. They married young and had a little farm a bit north of here, I cannot recall where. My father died in a hunting accident when I was four and my mother from pneumonia when I was nine. We'd already moved to the King's Arms after Daddy had died, and my sister was already working alongside my mother. The Smythes took pity on us and allowed my sister and me to stay." She paused, unprepared for the mistiness that stole into her eyes, but it had been a while since she'd spoken of this. Wistfully, she told him, "Gretchen was beautiful and vivacious... everyone loved her. Perhaps because I depended so much on her, because

I'd had her longest, I grieve most for her—and for Bethany, too, for she'll never know her true mother."

"I didn't mean to upset you, Emma," he said in a deep and low voice from the other end of the table.

"You haven't, really," she assured him, meeting his tender gaze. "Grieving is good, you know, it helps the heart to heal," she pronounced with a false smile, thinking to lighten things up a bit. "Now, I wish I could offer you some treat of a dessert, but my knowledge is decidedly limited, and apparently even this needs work."

The earl chuckled somewhat at this. "You do yourself an injustice, Emma. You put out a fine meal—"

"And you are a fine liar, but I thank you all the same."

Zachary suggested, "You will need to have some staff here, I imagine. Apologies that I hadn't thought on this yet."

Oh, but that was the perfect opening she needed, she decided. "That may not be necessary, my lord," she began, her eyes bright. "I wanted to tell you that I found the Smythes—" at his blank look, she explained, "who owned the King's Arms Inn? Yes, well I found them in Little Hadham—and Langdon and Alice are there as well!" She said excitedly. "They are all together, my lord, but in poor circumstance. Oh, it was so lovely to find them—even Alice, though she may have since left them for greener pastures, I believe. They seemed very surprised to see me, indeed. I have told you that as they have always taken care of me, I thought to return the kindness. So they'll be arriving hopefully at the end of the month. Well, not arriving, I daresay, as I need your larger carriage to pick them up." She rushed all that out in just about a single breath. And waited. Her hands around the napkin in her lap. Why, oh, why did he unnerve her so?

He seemed then to chew upon this, not with so much effort as he had upon that first bite of her stew, but several long seconds passed before he spoke.

"There are your servants then, I suspect," he said. "A butler, housekeeper, and footman—"

"My lord," she interrupted, "you seem to be seeking to ascribe some greater worth unto me than the circumstance of my birth necessitates. I am of the working class, same as the Smythes and Langdon. I am not above them, regardless of the boon provided so kindly by your father. They are my family. We will work together, in this house, and likely with occupations outside of the house—"

He held up his hand and Emma stopped speaking.

"Emma, I only meant that employing the Smythe's and Langdon is a logical decision. You *will* have servants here," he insisted. And just as she opened her mouth to refute this, thinking of the expense, he added, "Again, the bequest of my father will easily cover their employ. Why would you want all of you traipsing about the villages, seeking jobs, when good and clean and manageable positions are all within the home. The Smythes and Langdon will receive a salary and you your monthly benefit."

"But what need do I have of a butler or a footman?"

Zachary shrugged. "What need do I have of a hundred servants across three properties? The estate can afford it and it offers employment to those who might struggle otherwise. It's just how it's done."

"But what would they actually *do* all day?"

"Whatever you tell them to. Whatever you wish them to do," this last, with a rather meaningful glance, which Emma determined to mean the positions were more a formality to offer them an income and her, some complacence and company.

"Oh, I see."

"The boy, Langdon, can split time between here and Benedict House, if you want. Plenty of work up in the stables there."

"He would enjoy that."

Emma rose then to clear the table, taking Bethany out of her chair and into the kitchen to clean her up. She felt the earl enter the kitchen as well, bringing dishes with him. He set the dishes down near the deep sink and pump, very close to Emma. His arm brushed hers as she tended to Bethany. The contact, light though it was, caused them both to stiffen. The earl stilled after his fingers had released the plates. Emma stood motionless, closing her eyes until he moved away.

His proximity, even with Bethany so near, was as always, a very treacherous thing. She couldn't do this, she realized. She couldn't have him here like this, pretending all was well, pretending she didn't desire his kisses or yearn for one of his smiles—not when he hadn't any idea what his very presence did to her heart.

He won't marry you.

He was an earl and she, nothing more than a chambermaid, even if she no longer held that position. There wasn't anything else for him to desire of her but the obvious. And Emma knew she'd have no part in that. Her heart—indeed, her very soul—could not survive that.

She turned to him with this dreaded look about her that must have presented itself well to him, for he considered her only a moment before thanking her for the meal and announcing his intention to leave. Even then, it was in her to beg him to stay. But she did not.

Chapter Fifteen

It was Emma's unfortunate luck that had the earl repeat his visit to the Daisies on several occasions when Callum MacKenzie was either already there, or just about to leave. Callum did stop by rather regularly, always solicitous of Emma's needs, several times taking Emma and Bethany into Perry Green in the early morning. She considered this unfortunate because there seemed to be something about the simple presence of her neighbor that brought out the beast in Zachary.

He could apparently forget all his good breeding at the snap of a finger, for the introduction of the two men was thick with something Emma could not name, but she felt it in the air; and two encounters after that had the earl nearly growling, all but curling his lip as he only nodded a greeting to Callum. While Callum seemed not immune to Zachary's unmistakable displeasure at finding him again and again at the Daisies, he seemed, on the whole, unperturbed by the earl's aloofness.

It was in Emma to inquire of the earl exactly what his intent was—if he visited solely to harass her and her neighbor with his foul mood, she did not then, desire his company.

On the first day of the next week, when Emma was set to begin her job at the modiste's shop, the earl arrived as was becoming his habit shortly after the noon hour. Emma herself was just arriving home as Callum had driven her and Bethany into Perry Green to visit the butcher. She stepped out of Callum's wagon and lifted Bethany down as well, reaching up to Callum to accept her purchases from him just as the earl's fancy carriage pulled into the small drive in front of the daisies. Emma nearly groaned aloud at this untimely occurrence.

She gave no thought to the sleek vehicle and fine horses of the earl sitting next to the well-used cart and work team of Callum's, but did forgo her thought to invite Callum in to luncheon as she'd thought to do, in appreciation of all the assistance he gave her. She only bid Callum yet another 'thank you' and 'good day' and then rolled her eyes as she watched the two men all but square off, skinnying their eyes at each other before Callum pulled his wagon from the yard and headed down the lane.

The earl set the brake on the carriage and jumped down fluidly to stand before Emma, taking up Bethany in his arms as she was ever happy to see him.

"Really, my lord, you must refrain from scaring my company away," she said as they moved toward the door, waving to Henry, who was out in the orchard, though he appeared to have no tool in hand, and seemed to be about no vocation.

The earl held the front door open for Emma and followed her inside, to the kitchen. "I don't like him," was all he said.

Pertly, Emma replied, "I don't care. Callum is a very good friend and he is very kind to us. And correct me if I am wrong, my lord, but I thought I was my own person, who made her own decisions."

Having set the meat down, Emma was surprised to find herself spun around by the earl, his huge hand tight around her wrist. He still held Bethany in his arms but spared her not the frustration in his voice.

"Emma, what the hell are you doing? Are you wanting him or me?"

"What are you talking about?" Her growing frown matched his.

"Emma, you cannot go about being courted by two men. Eventually, you've got to cut one loose."

"Courted? Who said anything about courting?"

"What, in the name of all that is holy, do you think I'm doing?"

"You are courting me?" Her tone alone conveyed appropriately the extent of her shock. She stammered and stalled and hadn't a clue how to answer that, and was peripherally, yet vaguely aware that Bethany was watching them, wide-eyed. Finally she said, "I—I thought you were just trying to...." she didn't know the polite term for what she'd really thought.

Zachary lifted his brow, waiting. "What?"

While her heart flipped and flopped inside her chest, she stalled him by saying lamely, "Well, you have to admit, your technique leaves a bit to be desired. If your idea of courting involves being bossy and controlling and grumpy, then I guess I should have known."

"And kissing," he added. "Don't forget the kissing."

As if she could!

Something occurred to Emma just then. Perhaps what he called courting—and its ultimate goal—and what she knew courting to be—and her idea of the desired end result—were two different things. Now, this made more sense. Now she understood. Oh, she didn't doubt that he wanted her. She was not blind to his watchful and appreciative glances, nor a stone to be unaffected by his kisses, but she felt deep inside her that his desires were to be a short-lived thing, and immediately an image of her sister came to mind. Men such as the earl only embarked on relationships with girls like her for one reason. And, as they so often did, Lady M's cautionary words haunted her just now.

She met his eyes, her own filled with sorrow. "I'm sorry, my lord. I...I have no desire to be courted by you."

His expression did not change. She could well sense that he was trying to read her, while his eyes remained maddeningly inscrutable. A vein in his neck bulged and faded, and then repeated the motion, so that Emma was sure he wrestled internally with something, perhaps holding back words inside his clenched teeth.

She didn't have to feign mournfulness, only attempted to project it on to him, and not at herself. "I may have given you the wrong impression," she lied, "that I...desired or enjoyed...your kiss. I have only my inexperience to blame, and I hope you'll pardon my lapse in judgment, and certainly anything else I may have done to give you the idea that I would want to be...courted." Dear Lord! As thrilled as she was to have been able to utter those remarks with some conviction, she was sure no words have ever tasted more grotesquely false coming from her lips.

He continued to stare at her. Glare, really. He was glaring at her.

After several moments, when she'd become very afraid that holding her breath so frantically as she was might prove deadly, the earl stepped forward and passed Bethany over to her. Surprised, Emma received her daughter, and then felt immediately a modicum of peace, that the child created a bit of a barrier, to which she clung.

The earl strode to the door, his steps measured and stark. He turned and said to her, "Of course, you are lying to me," which shattered any peace she might have gained. "But I'll give you time to get used to it. Cut MacKenzie loose, Emma. You are mine."

It wasn't right that a man could do that—woo you with promises he hoped you'd believe, and all in an effort to effect your own demise, in the end. She would not be a party to her own downfall.

At six-thirty in the evening, Emma and Bethany set out on foot for Perry Green, Emma having dressed Bethany in her nightclothes, assuming the child would fall asleep before they returned home. They had barely started down the lane when Callum MacKenzie pulled up alongside them.

He didn't bother to pretend that he was here for any other reason but to drive Emma to her job. She smiled happily at him—he truly was a fine gentleman. "Honestly, Callum, you are too good to me," she protested as he lifted Bethany up onto the seat next to him. "I don't expect you to cart me around everywhere." She climbed up as well, and Callum gave a "Git on," to his team and they were off.

"I don't like the idea of you walking into Perry Green even at this hour, Miss Emma."

Emma laughed, holding her hat in place as it was a bit windy tonight. "Callum, when are you going to drop the 'miss' and just call me Emma?"

If she didn't know better, she'd swear the big man sitting on the other side of Bethany actually blushed before he answered, turning his sheepish smile upon her. "That depends on you, I guess."

"On me? I've already given you leave to do so."

"It'd not be any of my business, Miss Emma, but exactly what is the fancy earl to you?"

Emma removed her eyes from him, just the smallest hint of guilt coloring her own cheeks. "He is nothing to me," she said and knew, even as she spoke the words, that they were false. "Absolutely nothing."

"Methinks she doth protest too much," Callum said gently. "Frankly, Miss Emma, if you were mine, I'd call you Emma. But I've a feeling your heart lies elsewhere."

She suspected as much as well, dreadful as the very idea was to her. She cast her misting eyes to Callum, who watched her carefully with a wan smile, and could do nothing more than shrug, that one motion expressing a wealth of turmoil and sadness.

They pulled up in front of the modiste just then and even before Emma could move, she felt his hand upon hers in her lap. "I'll be here at ten," he said.

Emma shook her head. "You needn't be. I don't want you to think—"

He squeezed her hand. "You're still my friend. True, I'd wish more, but I can see that your affections are otherwise engaged."

Sadly, Emma nodded, "And that, *I* wish otherwise."

"Can't tell the heart whom to love," he said sagely and let go of her hand.

Emma entered the shop on High Street just before Madam Carriere might have locked up for the night. The little French woman was coming down the stairs of the beautifully appointed shop, a tape measure thrown around her neck, and a plump pin cushion cinched at her wrist. She stopped, near to the bottom of the stairs, staring at Emma with a confused expression on her face.

Emma smiled and greeted the woman, who slowly descended the remainder of the stairs. "I'm here to start working for you," Emma said, when the woman seemed to not understand why she might be here.

"Non, *ma petite*," Madam Carriere said. "The big man—the earl—he was here to see me. He said you wouldn't be taking the job after all," she went on in heavily accented English. "I've hired a girl—even now, she is upstairs, scrubbing."

Emma's jaw gaped. How dare he! So absorbed was she in her fury, she paid no attention to Bethany, who was beginning to climb all over the modiste's fine furniture. Madam Carriere's widening eyes, trained on the child, alerted Emma of trouble. She scooped Bethany up and apologized hastily to Madam Carriere, making a quick exit before her tears ran fully down her cheeks.

Seething, she glanced up and down High Street, wondering if Callum were still about, but he was not. Walking so briskly, Bethany had to skip to keep up with her, Emma began to head home, her anger at this moment greater than any she could ever remember. He had no right! He didn't own her!

When she realized what she was doing to poor Bethany, she slowed her pace straight away and kept her fury to the activity in her mind. And when the sky above, roiling with clouds for most of the day, opened up upon them when they were not halfway home, her tears became sobs and she and Bethany were quickly soaked through. She picked up Bethany and began to run, a difficult task when the road was now slick with mud and her gown waylaid her efforts and Bethany was just getting too big to be carried for any great distances.

Thankfulness flooded her when she spied the Daisies coming into view nearly half an hour later. Emma winced then, thinking she might as well keep going—she would have to tell Callum that she didn't need to be retrieved. She kept on in the rain, cursing Zachary Benedict with every step she took and trudged up to Callum's front door, pounding heavily to have her raps heard above the rain. There wasn't even an overhang to offer them protection here, and no one was answering the door. Bethany had begun to cry, miserable in her wet clothing, and Emma continued to cry, sure as she was that the earl was the dastardliest man she'd ever met.

She gave up in this endeavor to notify Callum, as glancing around showed neither he nor his cart anywhere, and began to walk again, back up the hill toward the Daisies. She met Callum about halfway home. She knew when he spotted her for his gig picked up speed and pulled up sharply beside her. She wasted no time with pleasantries but handed Bethany up to him and followed quickly herself, crying to him that she hadn't a job after all.

Her very kind neighbor beat himself up over this as he turned the wagon around to bear her home. "I should've waited to make sure you were well settled—"

"No, Callum," she called back over the rain, "this is not your fault and please don't ask me to explain. I just want to go home and have a good, long bath."

Callum was ever a gentleman and so did not ask questions but sped up the team again and within a very few minutes they were pulling up to the Daisies. She thanked him profusely once more and cursed again the Earl of Lindsey.

An hour later, Emma had bathed Bethany and warmed her by a fire in the parlor before putting her down to bed. The storm still raged outside, seeming to grow worse by the minute. She'd removed her own wet clothes when they'd return but had yet to rid herself of the chill of the rain. Bucket by bucket, she emptied the shallow bath she'd prepared for Bethany and then refilled the copper tub with the steaming water she'd set to boil over the hearth. It was probably unwise, but it made sense for Emma and Bethany to have their baths in the kitchen, as it kept Emma from having to trudge up the stairs with many kettles of water.

In the dim light of late evening, the kitchen aglow with only the small flames of the hearth's fire, Emma discarded her heavy night rail and stepped into the knee-high tub. She'd stopped crying quite a while ago but there still remained a sniffle or two. Exhausted now, drained as well, she laid her head against the higher back of the tub and closed her eyes.

She woke—she didn't know how much later, though the water was only lukewarm now—to the sound of her name being called. Eyes widening in alarm, recognizing the voice of the earl, she scrambled to stand and reached for her night rail, just as the swinging door to the kitchen opened to present the man.

Emma squeaked, aware of her disastrous state of nudity and clutched the cloth of her robe tightly to her.

Zachary Benedict stopped in mid-stride, his eyes riveted to her wet and naked form, as startled as she. Instantly, Emma was aware that a change came over him. She didn't know his intention upon coming to her home, but she saw a purposeful glint enter his dark eyes as he studied her unabashedly.

"Get out!" She tried to scream, but it emerged as only a croak.

His eyes met hers, she only half aware of the ticking of a muscle at his jaw. Trying to keep the night rail covering the majority of her bare skin, she stepped from the disadvantageous position of the bath and ordered again that he leave. But being then nearer to him seemed to spark some greater force in him and he strode resolutely toward her, his eyes not leaving hers. He ignored her apparent outrage and the wetness of her skin and gathered her into his arms, having come at her without stopping at all. His lips found hers, his need urgent, devouring her at once, giving her no time to adjust to this intrusion, or gather the wherewithal to resist him. His desire enveloped her now like a warm blanket, Emma being completely conscious of exactly where his bare hands touched and burned her naked flesh.

Zachary's tongue traced the softness of her full lips, then pushed within, tasting the recesses of her mouth, while his hands began to caress her in places that only she had ever touched.

She wasn't entirely aware of when her robe was dropped but knew soon the full heat of him from head to toe. There wasn't a thought in her head but a recognition of the feel and taste and scent of him, and too, her own body's response to him. She shivered in reaction to his coaxing kisses and thrilled at the feel of his hands upon her skin, moaning when his hand closed around her naked breast.

He'd taken his mouth from hers, showering kisses down her neck and over her shoulder before settling those lips devastatingly on her nipple, tightening the peak to marble hardness. A delicious shudder racked her body. The sight of his dark head lowered over her breast enlivened her, and she dug her slim fingers into his thick crop of hair, holding him to her nipple, reveling in the insane swirling inside of her. But he lifted his head, came back to her lips, scooping her up in his arms in one fluid motion, not having to remove his mouth from hers as he strode through the door and down the hall and up the stairs.

"Which one?" He asked raggedly, still so close to her lips.

Emma, imbued with desire, had to glance around to get her bearings. She pointed vaguely toward her bedroom door and he proceeded easily enough through it. Inside, he kicked the door closed with the heel of his boot and gently lowered Emma onto the bed.

He paused now, ever so slowly unbuttoning his shirt as he gazed upon her. She knew instinctively that this pace was not set to entice her, but was necessary while he looked his fill, the hunger in his eyes a fierce thing to behold. She had all she could do to not cover any part of herself from his ravenous gaze. Only the bare light of the room, provided stingily by the moon, and filtered through the barely-covered windows, kept her still. Holding her breath, she watched him pull his shirt away from his impressive form, then made quick work of his boots and the rest of his clothes until he was as naked as she. And he paused no more, but having stood at the foot of the bed, now crawled up toward Emma, pressing kisses onto her ankle and her shin, and further, upon her knee and then her thigh.

When his hot mouth touched the triangle of hair at the juncture of her thighs, Emma nearly jumped off the bed. "Easy, love," he murmured, his voice deep with passion, husky and bearing its own bit of titillation. Hands settling upon her hips soothed and stilled her momentarily until his tongue touched her *there*. Her hips rose off the mattress, her embarrassment as large as she could ever recall.

"Shh," he purred against her and continued his tormenting assault. Soon she lifted her hips, not to stop this tantalizing madness, but seeking more. Zachary did not disappoint, sliding one arm under her bottom while the other hand attached again to her nipple, just as his tongue flicked against her once again. His touch was smooth, just the slightest pressure over her nub, back and forth, over and around, until Emma was moving rhythmically up against his mouth, her hands finding again his hair, threading her fingers through it, her supplication.

Inside her, waves rose higher and came faster with each thrust of his tongue. Emma began to moan aloud, the sound deepening with the furtherance of her desire. When he slipped one long finger inside the very core of her, she purred for him, craving something unknown, somehow knowing he would give it to her.

And then he was gone, and Emma cried out for the loss of him, but he had only moved, coming fully atop her, settling between her legs, his lips again finding hers. She gloried in the hot length of his flesh press so intimately against her, felt the hardness of him pushing between her legs, and excitedly caressed the hard muscles of his chest, while he held himself still for only a moment before he began to enter her.

"God, you are passionate," he breathed into her face, his gaze, even in the darkness, seen to be worshipful.

She looked away at that moment, kissing his shoulder to hide her sudden and searing doubts. But then it was too late as he was rooted inside her. Emma had not expected the pain and cried out against him just as he stiffened.

He seemed equally surprised, his voice emerging not without some hint of sorrow when he said, "I'm sorry, Emma. I—"

Rather than say more, he kissed her again, kissed her rather decadently, and began to move in and then out, slowly, again and again. The sensation of him inside her had not been imagined, could not have been imagined. Intimate, thrilling, fascinating. Her heart hammered in her ears. Every inch of her body was on fire with the feel of him.

The pain receded quickly enough and just the smallest shift of her hips to better accommodate the size of him reignited those burning coils of heat throughout her. Her breasts tingled with each scrape of his chest against them. Experimentally, Emma moved with him, and there it was, that building fire. She matched his rhythm, even as it increased, until this thing rose to such a degree that she wordlessly begged for release. And it came, cresting and slamming upon her, opening her eyes with the wonder of it, tightening her thighs around him, pushing her beyond reason or reality.

Zach slipped one hand again under her bottom, shifting her, pressing his long fingers into her burning flesh. He moved faster and faster while she could barely recall her own name. Emma felt him shudder several moments later, and heard his cry given into her hair before he slumped against her.

When their breathing had returned to relative normalcy, Zachary lifted his head and looked down upon her. Gently, he kissed her lips, and her eyes, caught the tears at her cheeks. Her hands lazily traced patterns over his back, even as she struggled to keep at bay the threatening shame and remorse.

Another tremor racked her, though she could not say if it were lingering passion or a sob thwarted. Under him, she closed her eyes. They'd adjusted well enough to the darkness that she dared not look into his eyes to note his emotion just now.

Thankfully, Zach withdrew from her and rolled away. He lay on his back, an arm flung over his head, the other scratching idly at his chest. He said nothing. Not for the longest time. And he did not look at her.

Fearing that a great weeping was imminent, for everything that was wrong about what they had just done, Emma turned away from him, onto her side, facing the wall and the pretty and dainty flowers that covered it. A long, long time seemed to pass before he said anything.

His voice was husky yet, the words were slow, reflective. "That wasn't really the plan."

She hadn't any idea of what he spoke and made to lie as still as she could.

"But now you are mine, love," he said tenderly, his breath tickling at her ear as he shifted onto his side behind her, pressing himself warmly against her.

Emma closed her eyes at this, the full complexity of this enormous mistake crashing into her with all the force of a damaging storm. "Oh, God," she moaned, "what have I done?"

She felt him stiffen behind her, felt it upon the entire length of her body.

His words, when he spoke next, came cautiously. "You have, I hope, been struggling with the same desires as I, which led to this."

She shook her head miserably against the pillow. No. No. No! This was all wrong, and Emma began to cry. It was not an outright sob, but a soft keening noise she made while inside she railed at herself for having let this happen. He has won, she thought. She was no longer her own person. She didn't know herself anymore. "Please leave," she implored on a ragged indrawn breath. When he moved not at all, save to rub his hand up and down her arm, she wriggled away from his touch and shrieked at him, "Just leave me be!"

"Emma—"

"Get out!" She raged.

And he did. Slowly, with careful movements, he left the bed. She heard him gather up his clothes, donning a few before letting himself out of her bedroom.

Emma pressed her face into her soft pillow and sobbed as she never had, for her own loss of innocence, for her foolishness in all things regarding the earl, for having learned nothing from her dear sister's own heartbreak. She cried mostly for the very truth that she loved him too much to simply be his mistress, even though she'd just unmistakably aided and abetted him, and she was, if only for this moment, just that.

Zach closed the door, staring for several seconds at the barrier between them. He acknowledged that more than a door separated him from her, it seemed. Sighing, while the taste and feel of Emma still enveloped him, he angrily jabbed his arms into his shirt and threw it over his head as he descended the back stairs.

He stalked around the darkened first floor, unable to return his boots to his feet as he'd left them in her room. He seethed and stormed, exactly as the night did the same outside. Thrusting his hands onto his hips, he paced up and down the hall.

Having no experience whatsoever with virgins, he could only wonder if this were normal. Supposing the loss of innocence, something never to be recovered, was an emotionally raw wound, was this then a natural aftermath?

But shouldn't he be with her, if that were so?

Good God, or had she been telling the truth when she'd insisted that she had no desire to be courted by him?

Zach swiped his hand across his face, over his stubbly chin. "Christ," he groaned, at a complete loss. His pacing had brought him again to the front of the house. Glancing up the stairs, he considered his options just now, but every question seemed only to be answered by, *you cannot leave her*.

Purposefully, he pivoted and took the stairs three at a time, though his bare feet were quiet upon them, and slipped silently into Emma's bedroom. She cried still, was the first thing he noticed, though she'd turned onto her stomach and now had her face hidden in her pillow. She'd pulled the bedcovers over her naked body. She did not lift her head and rage at him, so was likely yet unaware of his return.

Grimly, Zach approached the bed, on the side in which she lay and sat beside her, his hip butting against hers. She jerked and jumped, quickly scrambling onto her knees, wiping clumsily at her tears.

"I want you gone."

Quite possibly, she'd only exhausted herself, but not yet her venom, that had her demand sounded only weary and pitiful but not at all as desperate as her initial edict.

"I cannot leave you." He reached up his hand.

She smacked it away, scrambled from the bed and fussed dramatically inside her wardrobe, withdrawing some heavy wrapper in which she covered herself, tying the sash with such virulence as to send the edges flapping smartly.

"Emma, that's enough," he said, standing as well, moving to the end of the bed. He tried to imbue a bit of calm, unnerved by her harsh words and tortured expression. "Let's talk and—"

She strode right up to him, across the darkened room, and slapped him across the face. "Talking should have come first! How dare you! You want to talk? Should we discuss your overbearing and imperious self, taking away my job? Shall we speak of your constant disfavor with my neighbor? Let's talk about your control of me! Or, pray tell, would you rather discuss the fact that I specifically said I don't want your attention—"

He shook his head. She wasn't allowed to use that argument, after all. Not when she'd answered every single touch and kiss and sigh with her own.

"Don't shake your head."

"I will shake my head," he informed her curtly. "Rant and rave at me for the things I've done wrong, but do not lie to me. You did want my attention, and your own response not so long ago right there—" he jabbed a finger at the bed, his voice thundering, "—proves that you lied!"

"I don't *want* to want you! Why can't you understand that? And...and it doesn't matter now. That's done," she said, her voice breaking on a renewed sob. "I blame myself, for being weak, for being in—" She stopped suddenly, her gaze frantic, fingers covering her mouth while she silenced another sob. Seeming to both mentally and physically gather herself, she took a step backward and presented squared shoulders and a lifted chin. "You had no right to take away my job. You don't get to say who my friends might be. You have no right to me, no claim to me. None at all."

Zach's eyes widened at the coolness of her tone.

"This was a mistake, but it was my own," she continued. "Yet it means nothing, do you hear? You do not own me. And I want you gone."

He lifted his hand in supplication, an imposing mournfulness overwhelming his anger. When he opened his mouth, while he stared, frankly alarmed at such wild hostility from her, as he'd never seen before, he said what he supposed might have been true for some time now, "Emma, I am in love with you."

A breathless and disbelieving cry was her response. Her lips moved for several seconds before words came. "No," she said in a weak voice. She began to shake her head now. "You are not. You cannot be."

"You're going to tell me how I feel?" He stepped closer.

Emma held up her hand, which stopped him from reaching her. "I'm telling you I do not—would never, actually—believe it. And let us focus on the matter at hand—"

"The matter at hand?" He returned sharply, incredulously. "The matter at hand? Is it not this?" Again, he indicated the bed, "What we've just done? Are you supposing I coerced, or—or forced you? Is that why you're upset?"

Emma jabbed her own finger at the bed, and shouted at him, "I've told you it means nothing! The issue here is your high-handedness, and me having reached the end of my rope in all regards to it. I was forced—Bethany and I were forced—to trudge home, the entire two miles, in the dark and in the rain, because you thought you had some right—" she broke off, and turned her head toward the side door. Her lips parted while she listened.

Zach's gaze followed hers, and he, too, heard the soft whimper of Bethany's cry. Throwing him an accusing glare, Emma rushed into the next room, where he heard her cooing tenderly and consolingly.

Frustrated beyond words, he ran his hands through his hair, and stared at the floor. He understood her anger to some degree. He shouldn't have acted with such disregard for her desire for that position at Madame Carriere's. But he'd told her it was a bad idea. He'd made clear all the reasons it would not suit. Whatever his methods, he had only her best interest at heart.

After what they had just shared, how could her rage still be so enormous? Zach was at a loss. For the amazing step forward he'd taken with her tonight, he also knew he'd suffered an impossible setback, taking many huge steps in reverse. It did not completely make sense to him. Not that he'd purposefully used it as a means to hopefully lessen her anger over his part in the loss of the damn job, but it seemed to him that their lovemaking should have softened her wrath a bit. She couldn't possibly and actually mean what she'd said, that what they'd just done meant nothing to her.

He turned, lifted his own weary gaze to her when she reappeared, clutching Bethany to her. He supposed this, now, meant their discussion was at an end. Likely to Emma's chagrin, Bethany realized his presence and reached her chubby little hands out to him, whimpering still as she called his name. Zach walked toward the pair, intent on soothing her daughter, but Emma shook her head.

"No, darling," she said, her voice gentled for Bethany, "the earl was just leaving. Say goodbye to him."

Not *goodnight*.

Bethany accepted this, and turned her head, laying it upon Emma's shoulders, mumbling something, which he guessed was his farewell.

Ignoring Emma's still wrathful mien, he did approach, and pressed a kiss onto Bethany's head. "Goodnight, moppet." Pivoting, his movements angry and brusque, he scooped up his boots and jacket and strode to the door. There, he turned and faced Emma again. "I'll be gone to London for a while. We'll talk when I return."

"There is no need."

"Nevertheless, we shall," he said. With his hand on the door handle, he added, "I meant what I said, Emma." He was keenly aware of the dejected exasperation saturating his tone.

Chapter Sixteen

Three days later, rains having kept Emma and Bethany rather trapped inside the cottage, she was very surprised by a knock at the front door. She stared, rather dumbstruck, at the door, the first time she felt vulnerable, living alone. There was no window close enough to the door to see who might be standing upon the stoop so then she hadn't any choice but to open the door, if she wished to know who came.

Pulling the door open showed only a young man, his shirt and breeches travel worn, carrying a large leather satchel, strapped over one shoulder and leaning against the opposite hip. He lifted his hand and presented an envelope to her. "From the post, ma'am."

"A letter?" She said, further compelled to wonder, "For me?"

"If you're her," the boy said, pointing to the script on the envelope.

Indeed, her name, *Miss Emma Ainsley*, was scrawled across the paper, along with her direction.

"I am." She smiled at him, bemused by this circumstance. She had never received a letter, or anything at all, from the post.

The lad tipped his cap to Emma and left, climbing up onto the nag waiting just outside her little gate.

Closing the door, Emma considered the bold script, and the very happy occurrence of receiving a letter. It dawned on her suddenly that this must be from the Smythes; perhaps they were ready ahead of schedule. She stepped into the front parlor while she carefully slid her finger between the fold of the envelope, loosening the wax seal. Sitting upon a wooden armed side chair, whose upholstered seat had frankly seen better days, she pulled several folded pages from within, and flipped these open.

The same bold script of the envelope was found inside, the strokes sure and neat.

Miss Ainsley,

I'm not quite sure how familiar you are with the politics and procedures of parliament, but I thought it prudent to remind you that I will remain in London for the time being as the session is heating up, as it normally does before it closes for the year. Sadly, our day does not begin in chambers until late afternoon, and often we find ourselves still upon the benches into the wee hours of the morning. I tell you this, and ask that you make my excuses to Bethany, as I had promised that we would ride regularly, and that will not, cannot, be the case until parliament closes for the season.

Lest you think I am enjoying myself, I will correct you with the news that yesterday I listened to one man speak for more than an hour and a half. He did not speak specifically to the bill to be brought before the House, but only that we should be having discussion about bringing the bill before the House. Thus is my status here, annoyed, impatient, and wanting to be away from London.

You might reply to this correspondence with news from Hertfordshire, if you have any, and of the Daisies, to keep me entertained and somehow connected to you and true reality.

Lindsey

Her bottom lip had fallen, remained lagging while she read the entire missive. And then read it again. The Earl of Lindsey had written her a letter.

Was this an olive branch? Did she want one?

She'd managed, over the past several days, to put the entire sordid encounter into perspective. She'd made a huge mistake, one she'd not like to repeat. He had felt guilty, for his role in losing her the position at the modiste's and perhaps even for having taken her virginity, and hence, his unbelievable declaration of love.

She gave no quarter to how that bit of news had been presented, how he seemed equally as shocked as she by the words, the way his voice had hesitated as she was positive the earl's never had before. *I meant what I said, Emma.*

In hindsight, she was embarrassed by her behavior, many aspects of it. She shouldn't have done what she had with him. She certainly should not have liked it as much as she had, nor given it the amount of attention and recollection as she had over the last few days. She shouldn't have overreacted, screaming at him as if she were naught but some bat from hell. She could not properly justify either behavior.

Likely, she was half in love with him, but she thought she should not be. Truthfully, aside from a simmering gaze that weakened her knees and his infinite affection for Bethany, what part of him was worthy of her love? His clever political mind and his drugging kiss? The fact that he was certainly the most handsome man she'd ever known? That little boy in him who wanted only to tend bees all his days? The man who ate her not-even-close-to-perfect stew and pretended he hadn't almost choked, just to spare her feelings?

Rubbish, all of it. Above and beyond all that, he was over-bearing and dictatorial and apparently intent only on causing her grief.

I meant what I said, Emma.

Emma tightened her lip and took his letter upstairs. She tucked it into the small desk in her chambers, after she read it through one more time, running her fingers over the dried black ink of his precise script.

The rains stopped, and the post boy found Emma and Bethany just returning from Perry Green, their conveyance courtesy of the always amiable Mr. MacKenzie. With a slight blush to her features, Emma accepted the letter, already familiar with the bold scrawl across the front. She bid a good day to Callum, and then wasn't quite sure how she managed to wait to open the envelope until Bethany was settled for her nap, but she did.

Miss Ainsley,

I begin to believe your George Fiske might have had the right of it: putting thoughts to pen is both cathartic and engaging. Yet I am no George Fiske, of the fanciful words and earnest declarations, so I shall spare you an attempt to charm you with any such thing.

I enjoyed dinner yesterday, before our session, with Lady Marston, who inquires of your well-being. Curiously, after I'd explained your connection to Hadlee, she became rather animated, or as captivated by any subject as Lady Marston might be. Even

*more peculiar, her attention seemed to hover and waver between
excitement and trepidation as I answered whatever queries I could
in regard to your new—and, according to my godmother, her
old—friend.*

*I had wanted to mention to you, as we'd discussed about your
lad, Langdon, that he should be presented to Mr. Talley, the stablemaster at Benedict House, when the time comes. I know very little
of the boy, but Talley might serve nicely as a fine mentor. I daresay
he'll learn more and better in only weeks what he might have accumulated over the years.*

Signing off now, heading back to the Palace.
Lindsey

Two days after that, the post boy gave her what she deemed an
annoyed scrunching up of his youthful face, until Emma passed
him two farthings, to which he lost his frown and tipped his cap
to her.

Miss Ainsley,

*Thurman has mentioned that you've asked for the carriage for
Friday, this week. This pleases me, as it never sat easily with me that
you and Bethany were on your own there at the Daisies.*

*Still taunting me with the promise of his support, Lord Kings-
ley insisted I take dinner with him, even as our session ended well
after midnight. Dinner was reserved and informal, and while I
continue to express my gratitude for your assistance in warding off*

that aforementioned and addressed Hindrance, your absence has now rekindled her enthusiasm, and the quiet planned interlude of Lord Kingsley and myself was interrupted not once, not twice, but three times by nonsense and the woman who brought it. Thus, prepare yourself, Miss Ainsley. I may soon and again request your company.

Scattered thoughts here, but do you think Bethany might like to come to London? I imagined taking her to Bartholomew Fair, which comes 'round at the beginning of September. Kindly advise of your thoughts on this.

Lindsey

Biting her lip, Emma re-read this latest letter three times. Several things came to mind as a result. First, she had to acknowledge that the Earl of Lindsey, whatever the status of their so often antagonistic relationship, was likely to be in her life for a very long time, if only vicariously through his affection for her daughter. Next, she pushed aside the not entirely unpleasant thrill that rattled her belly at his supposing he might send for her to assist him once again in his efforts to frustrate the Hindrance. Lastly, Emma's shoulders fell, realizing that as he had asked a particular question, she felt rather bound to reply to his letter. Perhaps there was no harm in it; it was only words on paper. She might more easily ignore his missives if they were indeed written in the same vein as had been George Fiske's, with efforts to woo her and beguile her with his words. But he did not; these were safe letters, ones to which she could foresee no harm in replying, although her response was forestalled by several days with the preparations for, and the coming of, her family.

By the time she did sit down to write the earl, Emma was quite intrigued by the burgeoning idea which had come to her, that *she* might dictate where next their relationship ventured. She could write to him as friends, not with the seething animosity that accompanied so many of their meetings and, obviously, not with any mention or hint of what she was now referring to as *The Second, But Far Greater Most Inglorious Blunder*. She would speak to him in the letters as if she wrote only to Mrs. Smythe or any dear friend that she might have. It would set the tone for how they might go on, Emma unable to imagine that she could successfully cleave him from her life completely. She thought that an impossibility, because of his grand affection for Bethany and for the very fact that he now possessed the entire estate from which came her present income.

Dear Lord Lindsey,

Be forewarned—and politely at the very beginning of this missive—that I've never written a letter to anyone before in my life. Isn't that amazing?

As it is, I will operate completely on instinct, though additionally I have it on good authority (courtesy of Mrs. Smythe) that casual correspondence is meant primarily as a way to keep persons informed, in their absence. As you've done just that, so I shall endeavor to return the favor.

First, to answer your question, I cannot imagine a child, or any person, who might not enjoy a fair. Though, truth be told, I'm not entirely sure all that a fair might encompass. However, I would trust Bethany in your care for such an outing.

As you have been apprised, the Smythes and Langdon have indeed come to the Daisies. We are all quite over the moon to be reunited finally. They are, as I feared, quite dismayed to learn they haven't really any profession within my household, save to keep me company and assist with the small upkeep. But as the weather is fine, and the summer fully upon us, we've been spending an inordinate amount of time out of doors. Langdon has already been several times up to Benedict House. He returned once, very happily, with a new nag and cart for our use, courtesy of your Mr. Talley. Assuming the instruction for this came from you, I thank you for the loan of the vehicle. And please be advised that Langdon was quite sincere in his vow to take very good care of both animal and cart to please the stablemaster.

Yesterday, the Smythes and I and Bethany, too, drove into Perry Green. I introduced the Smythes to the butcher and Mrs. Carriere, the modiste, and then to Mr. Crandall at the mercantile.

Bethany has picked up a new word this week. I wish she hadn't. It's horrible. That's the word, horrible. She has employed this as her response to any and all questions or comments, which makes even the very mundane, 'Did you have fun reading your book with Mama Smythe?' an exercise in futility. It really is horrible. Perhaps when you return, you might teach her a new word, as our efforts thus far have proven unsuccessful.

Cordially,
Emma Ainsley

Several days later, with news to impart, Emma did not await a reply, but sent off another letter to the earl.

Dear Lord Lindsey,

Writing quickly (and pardon my poor penmanship, as I've so little occasion to use it over the years) to get this sealed before we head into town, where I can drop it off at the post, without waiting for the boy. Saves me tipping him as well, which is awkward for me, as I was forever on the other end of gratuities.

Oh, but I must tell you! As agreed, while we stayed in London, George Fiske visited me yesterday. Lord Hadlee and I had a charming tea in the drawing room. Officially, he is my first guest to the Daisies, and I was quite excited to have tried out my tiny learned hostess skills, but I fear they may have been wasted on the poor man. He was interested and consumed only by those letters, for which I had run up to Benedict House and collected from Mrs. Conklin, and which I have dutifully returned to the sad man. I think he is lonely and considers me a connection to something he lost and mourns still. True, the connection is nebulous, but I feel he understood how deeply those letters had affected me and stayed with me. He promises to visit again in the next month or two.

In other news, Mr. Smythe is appreciative of your efforts within the orchard and has found a new love, I dare say. He spends countless hours there, in that wicker chair when not pruning and growing and watering. And not two days ago, he was gone for three hours to Perry Green by himself and returned, flushed of face, and still excited for the lengthy conversation he'd had with the grocer, who apparently manages his own orchard rather successfully, so that Mr. Smythe promises more apples and pears than we'll know what to do with. (I see pies and cakes and tarts in my future.)

Honestly, this letter writing is fairly easy. I find the words just spill out on the paper. (Do you care for this stationery? Mrs. Smythe and I found it in town, while Mr. Smythe wondered what was wrong with plain white vellum.)

Cordially,

Emma Ainsley

Postscript. The scribbling on the next page is from Bethany, who is just now learning what letters are all about. I'm sure you can imagine that her fingers were stained with more ink than the page. And that, my lord, is all that I am bound to pen just now, as I'm hoping to make the stationery last as long as you are in London.

Emma received another letter from the earl not two days later. Privately, she wrestled with the thrill that accompanied the arrival of his correspondence, though she was sure it had more to do with the letter itself and attached no particular significance to the sender. However, knowing he was likely busy in parliament for as many as ten or twelve hours a day, she felt a certain fluttering in her belly that he'd taken even just a few moments to send a missive her way. Today her delight was only heightened by the small parcel that accompanied the letter, delivered by a different post boy than Emma was accustomed to, that she wondered if the earl had employed a private messenger. This raised Emma's brow, as the messenger must have cost more than the extravagant pennies she laid out to send each letter.

Emma tore at the wax seal and perused the earl's words.

Miss Ainsley,

I might suggest, as my stay inside the city might surely be of an extended duration, that we employ your lad Langdon to carry notes back and forth. He can make use of a different mount each trip—good exercise for the horses—come and go as his other chores necessitate, and you needn't then worry about the tuppence put out for each letter sent.

Yesterday was frightfully long and tortuous. At one point, Sir Lionel of the Tories spoke non-stop for over six hours. I understand how important some of these measures and debates are, but still I was hard-pressed not to cry out that he could have managed his entire argument in four sentences. A more harried, pointless, and overdone speech, I vow I have never sat through.

I hope the parcel found its way to you as well. Do not, for my sake, scrimp on the words to save the paper. I look forward very much to your exceedingly entertaining news from the Daisies. (Honestly, I neither chose nor approved the parcel-ed item, only gave direction as to what was necessary to keep my sanity while ensconced and enslaved in the city.)

Shall I send down ink as well? New pens?

Until next time.

L

Less curious, and more convinced that she knew what the package might contain, Emma tore through the brown paper and found as she'd suspected, as his words had hinted—a box of stationery paper, in the softest shade of blue imaginable. She hugged the package to her chest, though wasn't sure why she should be so excited over a box of paper.

Dear Lord Lindsey,

 I thank you, genuinely, for the gift of the stationery and, as you see, have set aside the old to make good use of these fabulous sheets. Is it me, or does the ink flow more easily over this paper?

 When I was very young, when my mother lived, she read to my sister and me quite often. But honestly, since mother has been gone, I cannot remember that I've read a book in all those years. But I have, just yesterday. Bethany was napping, and the Smythes had gone to Benedict House to visit with Mrs. Conklin, as she'd invited them to make use of the dairy next to your fine kitchens for butter making. So there I was, all alone, and had already written a letter to you, that I hadn't anything to occupy me. And then I considered the books, offered so prettily upon the shelves of the study. Oh, and what a wonderful way to spend a rainy summer day, tucked into the parlor, and with a cup of hot tea to chase the chill, and with a book called Robinson Crusoe. What a fabulous hero! What a wonderful adventure!

 Do you enjoy reading, My Lord? For pleasure? If you were trapped in an empty house, no work to be done, might you find yourself digging your brain and your time into some dusty old tome? It seems to me you are not the sort to be idle, though I shouldn't think exercising your brain with words is truly useless. But then I do not know you very well at all, do I?

 Emma Ainsley

Emma,

 I do enjoy reading. When I have the time.

What else would you like to know?

Apologies for my brevity. Busy morning and back in session now.

L

My Lord Lindsey,

Seems more like cheating, if I only ask things I might wonder about, and you answer promptly and succinctly. Some things might be nice to discover, slowly, over time, much the same as I learn something new about my darling Bethany almost every day. She will be two and a half next week. I cannot believe either that I've been blessed for so long with her in my life or, sadly, that my sister has been gone for that long. Yet, there are times that it seems only yesterday Gretchen was braiding my hair and telling me tales of my father that I was too young too recall.

We had a fine dinner last eve. Nothing at all like that pitiful stew I once tried to feed you. Perhaps you'll allow me another attempt, as Mrs. Smythe has now given me regular and perfect instruction, that suddenly pies and pastries and gravies seem not so inaccessible after all. Our neighbor, Mr. MacKenzie joined us, and Langdon had returned from London, that we had a fine full table and used the formal dining room for the first time. You will likely scold me for sitting to dine with what you assume are the Daisies staff, but you may not. I will not allow it (penned with no animosity, my lord, but only as a reminder) as the Smythes and Langdon, and now Mr. MacKenzie, are my friends.

Closing here as Mrs. Conklin has come now to begin to teach Mrs. Smythe and myself some needlework that hasn't anything to do with mending. I'm picturing embroidered table linens when next we have company.

Emma

Emma,

Young Langdon surprised me, arriving earlier than expected, and now the poor lad must sit and wait. Ah, but something is afoot, I begin to imagine, as the boy runs straight to the kitchen, even when no scent of cakes or scones can be detected, so that I think he's quite taken with one of the Lindsey maids in the house. Hence, his early arrival and never seeming to mind the hours he sometimes must idle away awaiting my return post. Perhaps he is not idling, but working his...charm? That word doesn't seem to fit the boy, though I can find no fault at all with his occupation and temperament.

As it stands, we've still a week or more to go inside the present session. Currently, it will please you to know that my yesterday was plagued by eleven hours of dubious discussion of the Protest Against the Silver Coinage. Scintillating, I assure you. Lord save me, for having heard the word 'metallic' spewed and sputtered no less than one hundred times then.

Should we think about employing a nurse for Bethany? Lady Marston assures me it is too soon for a governess.

Yours,

L

My Lord Lindsey,

Scintillating, indeed, as I saw your argument, type-set in the Times that came today with Langdon. 'Lord Lindsey assisted the protest, reminding his fellow and fine MPs that "the bill endorsed a plan for the future regulation of the metallic currency for this country, yet was founded on erroneous views."' Is that, then, one hundred and one instances of the word metallic? (Now 102? Dear Lord.)

Just this morning, Bethany quite out of the blue, asked where you were, and when you might visit again. Of course, I feel completely inept, and the words seem useless to a child of not-quite-three, telling her you are very busy with important (dare I say, scintillating?) work. Nevertheless, I offer that to remind you that you have an admirer, less so a hindrance, I should hope. But no, I see no reason to employ a nurse, as I am happy to care for her myself. And we have years yet, until we need to consider her schooling and what that might entail.

That is very fine news to hear about Langdon, though he has made no mention of any sweetheart up at your London house. And just yesterday, we spent several hours together, walking to and from Perry Green, and yet he mentioned no London love at all. Regardless, I had wondered if the nearly everyday trips might be too taxing for him, even as he'd assured me that in traveling at not quite a full gallop had him in one direction in less than an hour. Hmm, even as I write now, he has come to collect this letter, seeming quite anxious to be on his way. I wonder that he can stand to wait all the time it will take for the ink to dry.

Emma

Sometimes, she re-read his letters, even the very briefly penned ones, not quite sure what she was looking for, yet imbued with a sense that indeed she did search for something in his words. Which then had her questioning what she might be wanting from the Earl of Lindsey. And then one day, when he'd been gone for nearly a month, and they had by now exchanged at least a dozen letters, telling only of trivial and daily amusements, Langdon came to the Daisies just in time for dinner, and handed a small envelope to Emma, who hurriedly wiped her hands on her apron and snapped the wax seal and read the very few scrawled words. Few indeed, though their impact was huge.

Emma,

Are you, as I am, ever plagued, tortured, or otherwise accosted (often most happily) by memories of our shared kisses?

L

Emma gasped, not quite noiselessly. Mrs. Smythe jerked around from the kettle over the fire, her cheeks flushed, her concern swift. "Aught amiss, my dear?"

Emma shook her head, covered her mouth with her hand, and used the other to press the paper to her chest.

"Oh, but you've gone as white as a ghost, Emma," Mrs. Smythe persisted, leaving the wooden spoon inside the boiling pot and coming to Emma's side.

"Oh, it's fine," Emma blathered, smiling awkwardly. "Un-expected news, that is all," she added, when Mrs. Smythe re-mained skeptical and alarmed. "If you'll excuse me just for a mo-ment...?" She saw that Langdon had sat down at the kitchen table with Bethany, where Emma had been perched while she and her daughter trimmed beans for dinner.

She ran up the stairs, went into her bedroom, and locked herself within. Leaning against the door, she held the letter very close to her face, using two shaking hands, and read the words again. *Are you, as I am, ever plagued, tortured, or otherwise accosted (often most happily) by memories of our shared kisses?*

Oh.

Oh, my. Lowering one hand, she settled it against her belly to calm the butterflies that had taken flight.

She did not answer his question for three full days.

Lord Lindsey,
*   Maybe. Sometimes.*
*   E*

Emma,
*   I rather think about it, and them, and us all the time.*
*   L*

Lord Lindsey,
*   Is that wise?*
*   E*

Dear Emma,

Possibly no. Unless I were to know it was to be repeated.
I might dwell upon it then. With greater effect and time than even now.
L

Lord Lindsey
Repeated? To what end?
E

My Dear Emma,
There is so much more I want to show you, to know with you.
L

Lord Lindsey,
As you have important work to be about in these last days of parliament's session, we must needs retire the preceding discussion.
Hopefully, we might return to our very dear former manner of corresponding, which had seen you grousing with growing annoyance for the behavior of your esteemed peers of the realm, while I surely bored you to tears with tedious anecdotes of my little country life.
(Nevertheless, I shall continue.) Dear Langdon has begun, or is trying, to teach me how to ride one of your fine mares. I cannot say I am unafraid, or truth be known, even very interested, yet the Smythes and Langdon have convinced me it might serve as a useful skill to have. The whole side-saddle arrangement makes me feel

firstly, very small and precarious upon the large beast, and then, in a constant state of fright that I will topple straight off the horse. Oh, what a long way down that would be.

Perhaps it is best that Bethany receive her introduction and instruction at such a young age, that she grows up with no fear, but only ease whenever near the beautiful animals. Assuming you might continue this time with her upon your eventual return, I thank you for your assistance in this regard.

There was a fire in Perry Green just yesterday. The sawmill at the edge of town went up in smoke, which was visible to us even two miles away. We all—the Smythes and Langdon, and Bethany and Mr. MacKenzie and myself—headed into town to see what the rising black plume of smoke was about, and if we might have been of any help. We were not, though it took many hours for any control of the blaze to be gained. Sadly, the entire building and contents were lost. There was a group taking up donations to help out the Prescott family, who have owned the mill and contributed to the community for many generations. I gave willingly, as not two weeks ago, old Mr. Prescott, whom we regularly passed on our way in or out of town, offered a whittled horse figure to Bethany when we'd stopped to chat with him.

You needn't fear that that my donation should have me begging an increase from you, as I have budgeted the remainder of the month quite cleverly to do without the humble sum I could afford to give. I have your father to thank for that, for my ability to help out another person. I was so pleased to be able to do so, and mayhap I finally understand your father's constant wish to aid and assist me. It simply feels good.

Closing now, to attempt to put Bethany down for a nap. Of late, she resists more and more, and I've had to employ new and different tactics almost every day.

Emma

My Dear Emma,

Apologies to you, for my rudeness.

I skimmed over your most recent missive, looking only for some hint, some response to the robust clue of my desire to repeat our kiss and more.

I'll read your letter properly when tonight's session is done.

Yours,

L

Of course, there would be no more letters from London, as Zach expected tonight at the earliest, and tomorrow night at the latest, for this session to be finished finally. He stared at her words once again, in her last correspondence. Indeed, he thought her neat little curly script as darling as the letter writer herself and was only mildly disheartened that she'd not truly answered his initial revealing query about their kisses.

In other regards, her letters truly had been a blessing, Zach having committed so many of her words to memory. Her sometimes mention of that bounder, Mr. MacKenzie, had startled and angered him at first, until she'd at least answered that she *sometimes* thought of their kisses. With those words, he'd known, she was his still.

Her words, to which he eagerly looked forward each day, admittedly being disappointed if he received no visit from Langdon, had truly served to keep him grounded and sane, this particular session having worn on him so much more than in recent years.

Leaning back in his desk chair, he lifted the letter and perused it casually once again. If he hadn't already been in love with her, he would have been easily wooed by the tales of her life down there at the Daisies and the very clever way she treated a letter much as she would a conversation. She was engaging, didn't take herself too seriously, and showed so much of her true self, which he'd previously suspected their fragile affiliation might have scared away. There hadn't been a day, not since he'd left her, that he hadn't thought of making love to her, as they had, and as they would. He was beyond anxious to return to her, and finally, satisfyingly, straighten out this mess between them.

Chapter Seventeen

"But my dear," said Mrs. Conklin, giving Emma that familiar frown that tipped her head downward, highlighting her disagreement, "you *must* glass the fruit if you care to preserve it properly."

"But I haven't enough glass jars, Mrs. Conklin, and the Smythes and I wondered what other vessel might be employed."

The housekeeper was shaking her head even before Emma had finished her statement. "'Tis no other that will do. Now we've spares, to be sure. But you'd be needing to return on the morrow, as I couldn't put my hands on them right at this moment."

"You are very kind, Mrs. Conklin," Emma assured her, "but I cannot continue to forage and gather right here at Benedict House. Yet Perry Green doesn't seem to stock or sell them that I can find. I only wondered what else might substitute."

"You fret too much, my dear," said Mrs. Conklin. "We've plenty to share and when you do eventually locate some for purchase, you'll return the borrowed ones."

"You are too good to me." Emma kissed the old woman's cheek and said she must be on her way. "But you won't forget about dinner Sunday, will you, Mrs. Conklin? We're very excited to have you and Mr. Thurman as our guests. Mama Smythe will dazzle you with her pike with the pudding in the belly."

The housekeeper's eyes lit up. "Oh, we'll be there. Looking forward to an evening of ease and fine company."

Emma waved and left the kitchens, trotting up the steps to the main floor, coming into the foyer just as Thurman was pulling open the door.

Lady Marston was welcomed into Benedict House, which saw Emma frozen just near the grand staircase, so stunned was she by the woman's presence. Emma would not have said the woman showed an equal surprise to find her here.

"Just the person I was looking for," Lady M intoned, removing her gloves and flapping the pair into Thurman's hands. "We'll take tea, for two, in the drawing room, if you please, Thurman."

Recovering, Emma gave a quick and mediocre curtsy. "Pardon me, my lady, but I'm not dressed for tea, and must get back to the—"

"Nonsense. I just sat uncomfortably in an ancient carriage for more than an hour. You can spare twenty minutes."

Ignoring then both Emma and the butler, who lifted his brows to Emma, though showed no exact emotion, Lady M mounted the stairs, using both the cane and the bannister to see her further up the steps.

Her shoulders fell, but she could not refuse, and so Emma followed the lady and joined her in Benedict House's impressive drawing room. She glanced down at the thick Aubusson carpet, where the earl had entertained Bethany. Or had it been the other way around?

Lady M sat nearly at the edge of one of the more-prettythan-comfortable side chairs and Emma took the other. Hoping she wouldn't be delayed too long, she swept the hat from her head, laying the pretty, wide-brimmed article on the arm of her chair.

"I cannot imagine why you should have sought me out," Emma said, when the lady only stared at her with that familiar, not entirely enjoyed, pinched look about her lips.

Lady M did not squander any more words than necessary. "I hear you've met, on more than one occasion, with Hadlee."

"I have," Emma answered, exhibiting some hesitation. Was this woman, like her godson, about to tell her whom she may or may not befriend?

"About some confounded letters, I am to understand."

"Yes." As Lady M's tone was indicative of her mood, and her tone was prickly, Emma would leave off giving more than asked, having no idea why the subject should concern her.

The Lady's thinning brows bent further over her sharp eyes, possibly unappreciative of Emma's short replies.

"Did he mention me?"

This confounded Emma yet more, certainly as the query was attended by so hesitant a voice, something Emma was sure not many could claim to have heard. "Um, he said only that you were acquainted with Caralyn Withers, but...but that you hadn't any idea where she might have gone."

"So, it's true?" She said, stamping her cane onto the floor. "They were love letters."

Still unaware of why this should bother the lady, Emma could only nod. She wasn't comfortable sharing George Fiske's story with Lady M.

"And that's all he ever said about me?"

Emma nodded. "I don't' understand—pardon me, my lady, but I'm not sure what you're looking for, or why George Fiske's letters to Caralyn should be of interest to you?" Even as she believed she'd recognized some affection for George Fiske from

Lady M when she'd observed their brief encounter at the ball, she couldn't imagine why the woman had driven an hour to put these vague questions to her.

Drawing a deep breath, which lifted both her shoulders and her chin, Lady M announced, "I was in love with him myself." She set her cane aside, leaning it on the side of the chair, and retrieved a handkerchief from some unseen pockets in her voluminous gray skirts.

Emma admitted, "I gathered as much," which returned the frown to the matron's face, prompting Emma to explain, "I saw your reaction to him at the ball."

"You are very clever, indeed."

"But...but what do you want to know?" Emma persisted.

"I wondered if he truly did love her."

"He did," this, without hesitation, having read those letters, having borne witness to George Fiske's grief over the loss of his Caralyn. "This still doesn't answer why—"

Lady M cut her off, her voice thin as she murmured, "I won't take it to my grave. I cannot. It has eaten me alive for forty years."

It was a calamitous prelude, uttered with such anguish as to beg from Emma, "What did you do?"

The gray crepe of the veil that hung down over her hat swayed on her drooped shoulders. "I told her—Caralyn—that he loved me. I told her we'd been...intimate, that she was only a toy to him—"

"That was not true!" Emma argued, instantly outraged.

Lady M tossed her head back, worrying the handkerchief in her hands. "No," she fairly hissed, "it was not." And then her black eyes misted, and her chin quivered. "I was right there," she whispered brokenly, right in front of his eyes. He never saw me. And I was so in love with him."

"But you had taken up with Lord Marston."

The hankie waved in front of her face. "I did that to make him jealous, when I thought I was losing him to her. My God, he never noticed. He couldn't care less. He saw only her." And then, with some disgust, "She was naught but a servant."

Emma sat back, gaping at the old, suddenly very frail woman. It was indefensible, what she had done. Emma could feel no sympathy for her.

Seemingly of a need to exorcise the entire circumstance from her memory, Lady M continued, "I told Caralyn he'd been only amusing himself, that she and Marston meant nothing, was just a little game we played before we settled down. She was... distraught. Lindsey's mother, believing my lies as well though I think later she might have suspected, helped me find Caralyn a position with some family—Baron Grantham, if I recall. He was the ambassador to Spain. We sent her there. I—I never heard from her again, not until just a few years ago, when I happened upon news of her death. She'd stayed in Spain, had married I believe. Lived there for thirty years."

Emma's lips twisted while her hands fisted. She felt a rage engulf her, for what this selfish woman had done. It occurred to her that mayhap the woman had come today seeking a certain acquittal of her crimes. "I'm glad to hear it has given you no rest. I hope it never does."

Lady M glanced sharply at Emma, but then quickly melted with renewed weakness. "You are right. I don't deserve it."

"If this were my house, I would kick you out," Emma said, her voice tight. "As it is—"

"Miss Ainsley!"

Emma jumped and turned to face the door, finding the earl standing there.

She squared her shoulders against his clearly displeased expression.

Her breath caught, two calamitous events in one day nearly unraveling her—the matron's unforgiveable folly and now the return of Zachary. If she'd questioned at all if she'd missed him, if she'd wondered if she might have become starved for only a glimpse of him, if she'd forgotten how impossibly handsome he was, all these things were resolved just now, at the sight of him. The air was thick with outrage and sorrow, but Emma found herself irrationally, inopportunely pondering if any circumstance in their lives would see her running to him, throwing herself happily in his arms after so long an absence.

He strode across the room, stood beside Lady M, his brow furrowed in such a way that at one time would have alarmed her.

"Apologize at once, Miss Ainsley. We cannot have Lady Marston believing you to be—"

Emma gave Lady M a humorless smirk. "I do not care what she thinks of me. And as I cannot have her removed, I shall take my leave." She swiped her hat off the floor, where it had fallen, and left the room.

"Miss Ainsley!" The earl called after her. "Emma!"

Emma left the drawing room and ran down the stairs, sailing through the door that Thurman pulled open for her.

A fine day for a walk, she decided, with little other choice, and marched across the drive and onto the lane. She plopped the hat upon her head and tied the strings under her chin.

She'd not thought he'd have chased after her. She thought he'd not leave Lady M unattended. But he did. She heard him call her name, heard his boots tearing up the gravel of the drive.

"Emma!"

She continued walking.

He yanked on her arm from behind, spinning her around.

"What has gotten into you? Whatever would possess you to alienate and infuriate Lady—"

Emma shoved at his chest, used both hands to push him back, bringing him to a jaw-gaping standstill.

"What has gotten into me? Me? I'll tell you what has gotten into me. The bloody nobility! In your fine homes with your fine manners and your rules about everything, and not one of you have any idea how to practice a little human decency, or—do you know what that woman did?"

At his blank stare, she informed him, "She is the reason George Fiske and Caralyn Withers are not together. She lied, to both of them, had Caralyn sent away, because she, herself, was in love with George and couldn't imagine that he could possibly be in love with a servant."

"But that was years ago—"

"She ruined the lives of two people!" Emma raged. "Who cares if it were yesterday or a hundred years ago? She's awful, looking down her nose at me, telling me that you would never lower yourself to marry a chambermaid. Give me ten chambermaids, I'll bet they're each and every one of them a better human being than her."

"Emma, calm yourself. Let's put this into perspective."

Emma stared at him. He didn't get it, either. "Oh, you're a fine one to talk. You're as bad as she! Running around, thinking everything rightfully belongs to you, having no care for all those left weeping in your wake when you're done with them. But you'll wind up alone and lonely, just like George Fiske. At least he tried. He didn't let so absurd a notion as class distinctions imperil his heart. But for her—" she thrust her hand back toward Benedict House, "—he would have been happy rather than miserable, all these years." A wave of grief overtook her, the complete impact of Leticia Marston's vindictive betrayal crashing around her. That poor man, believing all these years that Caralyn had never loved him, having married another whom he could never love, having born that idiot of a son. All because Lady M wanted it her way, thought she was more deserving than a lowly servant. Emma began to sob. How could that woman live with herself? "She's so rotten," she murmured through her tears.

Zachary reached out a hand, mayhap meant to be soothing.

Emma slapped it away. Anger overran her tears. "Get away from me." She began walking again, stomping actually, swiping angrily at her tears.

He caught up with her once more. Perhaps fearful any touch might be rebuffed harshly again, he came around in front of her, and stopped suddenly. Emma was forced then to stop as well, lest she crash into him. She stepped left, and he did, too. Giving him a warning look, her lips curled with the height of her anger, she delivered through clenched teeth, "Let me pass."

"Marry me."

Emma went completely still, her startled gaze fixed on his face, seeing nothing but her own amazement. She ignored him, and whatever that was meant to be, and tried again to move around him. He shifted accordingly.

"Let me by," she ground out slower, with more force.

"Marry me," he demanded again, his own tenor rising.

Planting her hands on her hips, she faced him, squinting up at him, "Why? So you can prove you are above your lot, that you are a better person than you actually are? Show the poor, pitiful Miss Ainsley that you're just a regular bloke so she'll let you...plow her again?" The most disbelieving jolt overtook his features. She had never seen his eyes so huge. Her use of *plow* might have been the cause, she supposed. She ignored this, keeping her anger close. "Pardon my disbelief, my sincere doubtfulness. Now, move."

"Marry me," he insisted again, recovering himself. "Because I love you. Because I want you. Because you belong to me."

Admittedly, this weakened her. Weren't they just the words every girl dreamed of hearing one day from the man they loved? Certainly in that tone. Truly, he must practice this often to hit that very sincere note so adeptly.

"Because I don't want to be George Fiske," he continued, "pining away for forty years. I can't...not love you."

Luckily, the mention of George Fiske compelled further resentment.

"Very pretty, my lord."

"You are in love with me as well," he accused with a growl. "I know you are. I know you wouldn't have *made love* with me, if you were not."

Emma ignored the emphasis attached to his words. She ignored the fact that he was right; she was insanely and irrationally in love with him. Yet, she staunchly refused to consider even the possibility that he might be genuine.

He was just like Lady M. They only wanted their way. They expected it, with little regard to the consequences. He would only break her heart. He *wasn't* sincere. He just couldn't be.

He'll say he will, or would, wed with you, of course; that's part of the game.

"You are afraid, and I get it. Your sister, Caralyn Withers, George Fiske, your very own heart. But Emma, I promise you, I—"

"Good day, my lord." She finally stepped around him, fairly concerned the pain in her chest might be fatal.

He allowed her to walk away from him.

It was incredibly difficult that evening to pretend nothing at all troubled her. Yet, she had no choice, seated at the dining room table, surrounded by all her friends, their usual merriment in stark contrast to the hollowness of her heart. But she smiled, even if she did not participate so freely in the conversation, her mind overtaken still with the events of the day. Naturally, her altercation with the earl led the charge across her mind. She certainly hadn't dismissed Lady M's confession, but to some degree, the earl had been right: it was years ago, too late to fix it now. She could do naught but write to George Fiske, at least give him this news, finally cure his heart of the pain of unrequited love. She only prayed that anger, which most certainly must accompany the receipt of such bitter news, would not then prey upon him.

But the earl....

"You're frightfully quiet this evening, miss."

Emma glanced up, instinctively widening her false smile as she looked to her left at Callum MacKenzie.

"Apologies, Callum," she said, laying her hand over his, but only briefly. She glanced next to him, where sat his new love, Miss Fiona Gall, who, ironically, had recently found employment at Madam Carriere's, and who had quite obviously stolen Callum's big heart. "And to you, Fiona. We are thrilled to have you join us, do not let my wandering mind tell you otherwise."

"Been quiet since she returned from the big house," said Mr. Smythe, at the head of the table. He lifted a worried brow to her. He was so much softer and lovelier since he'd come to the Daisies. She absolutely adored him.

Shaking off her melancholy, which had proved debilitating for most of the afternoon, she said, "Mrs. Conklin insists we can only use glass jars, and when I told her we were unable to find any in Perry Green, she said of course that I must return tomorrow and collect whatever spares she might find by then."

"Then we'll start the picking right away," Mr. Smythe decided, enlivened.

"But what do you think about the grocer's notion of adding cinnamon to the apples?" Mrs. Smythe, seated next to her husband, wondered.

"My mum doesn't do aught with her apples, but with cinnamon," Fiona mentioned, her heavy Irish accent the prettiest thing Emma was sure she'd ever heard. Her lovely green eyes and how clearly besotted she was with Callum only added to her beauty.

"I don't think I've ever had cinnamon," Langdon admitted, taking peas off his plate—the ones Bethany had deposited there—and returning them to the child's plate. This was a nightly occurrence, for which darling Langdon showed infinite patience. No one, not one person, could cajole Bethany to eat her vegetables as Langdon eventually did, every night.

"I say we try it, maybe in half the stock?" Emma suggested.

The room went silent. Emma followed the direction of their unnerved gazes, and found Zachary Benedict standing at the door to the dining room. She wouldn't have said his expression brimmed with disfavor, perhaps only showed a bafflement to match the faces of her friends.

Bethany broke the prolonged silence with a shrill but happy cry of, "Zach'ry!"

"Hello, moppet," he said, and a smile came readily to him then.

With his words, everyone at the table, as one, jumped to their feet. Save for Emma, who drew a weary breath before she stood as well. While the men bowed their heads to the earl and the women bobbed brief and nervous curtsies, Emma faced the earl, showing him no such deference.

"My lord, I wasn't expecting you. You have caught us in the middle of dinner, *en famille*," she said, with some emphasis, lest he think to instruct her on how she should go about managing her own home.

She was surprised by Bethany, who must have scooted from her chair, dashing between them to throw herself at Zachary. His smile grew, scooping Bethany into his arms. She could think whatever she liked about the earl, but she could not deny his sublime pleasure at seeing Bethany again. He hugged her tight and kissed her rosy cheeks several times. "I've missed you, Bethany."

"Missed you," Bethany parroted.

"Oh, but you must join us, milord," cooed Mrs. Smythe, likely swayed by the earl's unmistakable fondness for one of her favorite persons.

It was inconceivable, of course, to think that the earl would accept, more baffling indeed, than Mrs. Smythe's inexplicable invitation.

Apparently, this was to be a day chock full of surprising turns.

"Would it be too much trouble?" The earl asked, while Emma stared now with steadfast concentration at Bethany, and not at him.

Mrs. Smythe tittered happily and dashed into the kitchen.

Zachary stepped around Emma and returned Bethany to her seat, taking a moment to marvel over the smaller seat upon the dining room chair, which Langdon had fashioned so that she needn't sit upon stacks of books.

Emma turned back to the table, stood near her own chair.

"That's some fine craftsmanship," the earl was saying, before moving Bethany's chair forward a bit.

He shook Langdon's hand and then further shocked Emma by reaching his hand across the table to Callum. "Good to see you again, Mr. MacKenzie." If Callum were surprised by this, he gave no indication, stretching his hand under the chandelier to meet with the earl's.

"Likewise," he said evenly, and then recalled, "This is Fiona. Fiona, this is Lord Lindsey."

"Oh, gracious," squeaked Fiona, and then giggled as she curtsied again.

Mrs. Smythe returned to the dining room, setting a place beside Langdon, and near her husband at the end of the table. The earl moved to where she set him up and struck his hand at the old innkeep. "Mr. Smythe, Emma tells me you're making great progress out in the orchard."

Not many things surprised old Mr. Smythe, but this clearly did. His eyes lit up, and then came a rare merriment about his face, shown so beautifully in his jowly grin. He slapped his hand into the earl's, pumping enthusiastically, before proclaiming, "I am indeed. Emma said I've you to thank for the fine beginning. Oh, but you've got to see the fruit that's come!" Emma had never seen the man so animated in all the years she'd known him.

"I should like that," said the earl.

Soon, everyone was seated again, save for Mrs. Smythe, who still scurried around, adding glassware, and another utensil and finally a steaming plate of her lamb stew to the setting before the earl.

And all was quiet, the housemates and regular guests seemingly struck dumb by the earl's presence. He appeared unperturbed, or pretended ignorance of this, lifting his gaze, scanning the table, inquiring of Fiona if that linen covered basket contained bread.

Fiona, having no history with the man, this being her first dinner at the Daisies as well, nodded eagerly and passed the basket to him.

Zachary lifted the linen, his brows rising happily at the steam that rushed out, and said to Langdon, "Do you have formal training as a carpenter? Those seams are well-joined and the entire chair itself, so smooth."

The lad blushed a bit at this fine praise. "No, milord. My da worked wood before he died, is all I know. Guess I recall a few things he might have taught me."

These few words put the table, and the dinner, back to rights. Mr. Smythe joined in that discussion with the earl and the lad. Mrs. Smythe engaged Fiona, next to her, with some question about a frock she had seen in the window at the modiste's, while Callum said in a low voice to Emma, who had quite a time of it trying to keep her gaze off Zachary, "You said, not one week ago, how pleased you were that all your favorite people were gathered 'round your table. Would it be true still if you said those words now?"

Emma turned sharply to her friend, showing him a pathetic unease. No part of her imagined that his Fiona had anything to do with his very pointed query. To Callum, it was easy to give the truth. She nodded, silent, willing to give up nothing else.

"Shame then, that you look so outrageously miserable." Callum made a face, wrinkling his brow and twisting his lips, all without harshness. "If I were you, I wouldn't want ever to regret that I hadn't at least tried."

She didn't bother to pretend that she knew not of what he spoke. "I am frightened," she whispered, thinking she might not have admitted as much to many other people.

"But that man is sitting here, rather without fear. It's not too his liking, but he'll do it, probably a hundred times more if you ask, for you."

Primly, she said, still keeping her voice low, "It's all for show, I'm sure."

"Might be, but the point is, he's doing it. You think an earl wants to dine with us? He don't, trust me."

Emma felt compelled to confess, "I think it's beyond repair at this point."

Callum shook his head. "He's here, so that cannot be true. But let's find out." He straightened, pulling away from Emma, and called across the table, "Hey Lindsey, you ever get to fishing in that big lake of yours?"

The earl did not even blink at Callum's nearly rude address, only shrugged his broad shoulders and answered, "Not as often as I'd like. But I've been assured there's good brown trout, and plenty of eels. Feel free to test it out."

"I might, at that. Care to join me?" Callum persisted.

"Sure. Let me know when. I'm home for the remainder of the year."

Callum smiled, first at the earl, and then at Emma. When Mr. Smythe brought Zachary back to their conversation about the orchard, Callum said to Emma, "There, now you know. I've got a bloody fishing date with an earl, but at least you've got your answer."

Emma swallowed, digesting this, everything. She didn't think he'd come specifically to sit down to dinner with persons so far below him in class to prove a point to her. He couldn't have known he'd have found them here. She'd been an absolute harridan on the last two occasions that they'd met, and yet here he was. He had, by now, said that he loved her and that he desired to marry her. She'd be a fool to at least not investigate the possibility that he might be telling the truth.

He won't marry you. He cannot marry you.

But as she learned so depressingly today, Lady M liked to tell lies when she deemed a certain part of a pair unacceptable.

With her hands flat on the table, one on each side of her plate, she closed her eyes. She felt as if her mind could not yet sort and analyze and assess everything that she did know to be true.

Emma lifted her gaze, found the earl watching her, even as conversation continued around them. His gray eyes, made golden by the candles burning overhead, warmed her with the serenity of his gaze.

Mayhap, the only thing that was important was that she loved him.

"I don't want to be Caralyn Withers."

The table fell silent.

Emma's attention was fixed with such constancy on Zach, that she didn't think she misread the ever-so-slight quirk of his lips.

"What's that, dear?" Inquired Mrs. Smythe.

Fiona, bless her and curse her, offered, "She said she doesn't want to be someone named Caralyn Withers."

"Is that the miss who sells the oysters on High Street?" Asked Mr. Smythe, with a furrowed brow while he tried to place the name.

"No, that's Mary Mac-something or other," recalled Mrs. Smythe. "Remember the grocer told us about the accident she'd had, something to do with a saw and rowboat? Made no sense to me, but there she is, limping along the lane to the lake."

Zachary grinned at Emma. She wasn't there yet, could not respond in kind.

"Do you want to take this somewhere private?"

Emma shook her head, panicked. She could not be alone with him, not for so weighty and decisive a conversation. She didn't trust herself. My God, if he kissed her, even touched her at all, she might find herself upon her knees, begging him to just keep pretending that he loved her, that she could live with that.

"I apologize for my most recent unseemly behavior," she said to him, from one end of the table to the far corner of the other. "On the last two occasions that we'd met."

The quality of her expression and tone, both being rather severe, might have been what quieted everyone else.

"After some consideration," the earl returned, his voice level and sure, while all eyes turned toward him, "your reaction this afternoon seems to have been warranted, the cause of it so damnably intolerable. Regarding the first incident of which you speak, I will allow that the circumstances were unprecedented, neither of us having been in that exact position ever, not once, in all our lives."

Five sets of eyes swiveled toward Emma. Bethany was picking the remaining potatoes out of the stew with her fingers and putting the pieces on Zachary's plate.

It took Emma a moment to understand, to deduce that he meant because it had been her introduction to sex, and his first declaration of love.

"I don't want to be Caralyn Withers," she repeated, and explained, "acting and reacting on the probably false words of another."

Here, his mouth did tighten marginally. "Might I inquire what probable falsehoods you were given?"

She summarized, "I was told that you only toyed with me, that your career would prohibit you from wedding me. Yet, I was informed that you would *say* that you would like to marry me, as that was part of the game you played."

The dinner guests turned their rapt gazes to the earl, awaiting his rebuttal.

"That sounds frightfully familiar to words I compelled from another earlier today, after you and I had parted, so I needn't ask from whom they came. Do you believe them still?"

"I don't...*want* to believe them."

In her periphery, Emma thought she saw Mr. Smythe lift a finger, as if he'd like to contribute to the discussion. Mayhap he had a question. Mrs. Smythe, saying not a word, covered his hand with hers and lowered both to the table.

"I didn't bring you to London only to be of assistance with the Hindrance, but because I wanted you there with me," the earl said, "because I didn't like the idea of being away from you. I wanted you to stay, even as I realized you were pining for Bethany. And I understood, even before I brought you to London, that I wanted to marry you. Lady M tried to dissuade me, it's true. And when I found you talking to Beckwith, yes, I reacted poorly. And when I kissed you at Clarendon's ball, I'll admit that was brutish and unpardonable."

Fiona made a sound; Emma couldn't say if it were a gasp or a sigh.

The earl went on, "I cancelled your employment with the modiste because I thought it too dangerous, and unnecessary. True I should have gone about it differently. Christ, this list is getting on to be shamefully long," he acknowledged with a twitch of his lips, to which Mr. Smythe and Callum nodded, with some commiseration.

Mr. Smythe interjected idly, "Makes a man wonder what you might have done right by the girl."

Several nods followed this speculation.

"Oh, surely, many things," Mrs. Smythe cooed. "Wrote her some lovely letters, he did, which she's likely read a hundred times by now, always grinning like a silly fool when Langdon came with the notes. Set her up nice in this house," she added, nodding to accent her words, "could've just tossed the money at her and sent her on her way."

Langdon inserted, "Didn't have to give me the fine work up at the big house, but mayhap only did so to please her, I always thought. Lent us the fine rig and nag. We'd probably, all of us, have to save for a year just to buy the horse."

Zach was grinning outright now, pleased by the unexpected support.

Emma remained expressionless, even as her breathing had quickened while her heart raced.

"But I meant what I said, then and now. I am in love with you."

This time Fiona, and Mrs. Smythe as well, clearly made sounds of blissful sighs.

She accepted all this with a thoughtful nod, absorbing it slowly. "Do you realize, or admit, that you are high-handed and autocratic, sometimes unreasonably so?"

"I do not like this spoon," Bethany said, to no one in particular. Langdon replaced it with his own, which Bethany then handed to Zachary.

The earl took the spoon and set it on the table. When Bethany then lifted her arms, Zach pushed his chair out a bit and took Bethany into his lap.

When his compelling gaze met Emma's again, she detected a hint of a smile therein.

"I do. Do you, likewise, admit that you are stubborn—at times purposefully and irrationally so—and unwilling to accept that in some areas I might actually know a thing or two more than you?"

"That may be true," she acknowledged. "Occasionally."

Callum snorted next to her, trying without success to control his chuckle over this.

"So now," said the earl, "I've several times told you that I am in love with you, and just today I asked you to marry me—"

This summarizing was interrupted by Langdon's hoot of surprise and Mr. Smythe's quietly given, "Well, I'll be damned." Mrs. Smythe and Fiona sighed again, the older woman clasping her hands to her bosom.

"—and you've yet to respond appropriately—certainly not favorably—to either of these," the earl finished.

"Oh, why not, dear?" Mrs. Smythe asked sadly, her hands falling away from her breast, listlessly onto her lap.

Emma only briefly considered other eyes, fixed on her with varying degrees of disbelief and question, before she met Zachary's tender and confident gaze. Emma realized that he knew he would triumph, even as she knew she must finish it properly.

She needed to tell him all, admit her foolishness. She was nervous still, likely wouldn't be cured of that until he took her in his arms.

"Of course, I have been in love with you for quite some time."

Fiona clapped her hands together, a faint whimper of joy escaping.

Biting her lip, Emma considered what else he should be told. "I am sorry that I believed not your words, but those of a nasty old woman. I was afraid, of course, as you so astutely guessed. And I should like to marry you, if you are still agreeable, even if it means that one day you will break my heart."

"Should've led with that negative, not finished with it, I'm thinking," Callum said, finally entering the dialogue. When Emma turned a good frown on him for his critique, he shrugged. "Just saying."

Zachary Benedict stood with Bethany in his arms, and said, "Here are many witnesses who can hold me accountable to this vow: I will never break your heart."

"He won't, I'm sure," concurred Mrs. Smythe.

"He better not," Callum cautioned.

Fiona turned to Callum and glowered with some aversion to his words. "Clearly, he will not."

"Mrs. Smythe, would you kindly hold Bethany," the earl said as he walked around the table, "while I take my future wife in my arms and seal this betrothal?" He handed Bethany off to the giggling, teary-eyed woman, and continued around the table until he stood beside Emma.

Zachary held out a hand to her.

She hesitated only a moment, more embarrassed than anything just now, and rose from her chair. Evidently of a mind that if she'd insisted her friends witnessed all they just had, that they might as well see it through to its finale, Zachary pulled her possessively into his arms and met her lips in a fierce and not-so-chaste kiss. Emma's knees failed her, but he held her firmly, and she knew the tightness in her chest was unbearable happiness, nothing more.

Cheers went up, laughter and joy sounded throughout the room, but they ignored them all. When finally he pulled his lips from hers, he said against her mouth, "Say it again, for me alone."

"I love you, Zachary," she whispered.

Another kiss followed, energizing the delighted watchers.

When he next looked into her eyes, shiny and wet with her elation, he said, "Tell me you always will. Tell me you won't doubt me. I'll love you forever and never give you cause to question it."

Emma nodded shakily. "I won't. I promise."

Chapter Eighteen

Zachary Benedict sat in his sumptuous study at Benedict House and glanced once again at the ormolu clock. Still a half an hour to go.

Impatiently, he drummed his fingers on the desktop, and then tugged anxiously at his cravat. In thirty minutes, he would recite vows with Emma. Never in all his life had he imagined that he might one day marry a chambermaid from a traveler's inn, or that she might come complete with a child.

A smile turned his mouth upward. The fingers stopped their tapping to smooth themselves in a fluid motion over the dark wood of the desk.

But then, never had he imagined that one day he would meet a woman who would turn his life upside-down in the most amazing manner.

I am the luckiest of men, he thought.

Further thoughts upon the exact extent of his luck and happiness were interrupted by the arrival of Thurman.

Zachary stood quickly, uncaring if the old butler read anything into his anxiousness. But Thurman was not here to call for his presence out on the terrace yet, where the nuptials were to be performed. He nodded precisely at Zachary and handed him a sealed letter from his silver tray.

"Delivered just now from your solicitor, my lord," he intoned.

When Zach had accepted this, Thurman set down a wrapped item and note on his desk. Frowning, and wondering what business his solicitor was about today—the man knew Zach was to wed—Zach hastily opened one envelope, only to find another within.

He sat down again, the breath knocked out of him as he recognized the broad scrawl of his father upon this second envelope.

"*To be opened upon the day of your wedding,*" was written on this envelope.

Curiously, Zach unsealed the wax and took out a folded piece of vellum.

My dear boy,

Congratulations and felicitations!

When I first met her, I was captivated—not in the sense you are, but spellbound, nonetheless. Isn't there just something about her that begs a man to love her? Have you ever met a girl so completely genuine and true as her? I thought not. I knew my bequest would confound and confuse you. But I was quite sure it would lead to this. I knew she was perfect. And meant for you.

I wish you joy and happiness—I know she'll bring you this.

You can thank me when next you see me.

Until then,

Always Proud,

Father

Stunned, Zach re-read the letter twice.

The old man knew! *My God, the old man knew.* Zach gave a short bark of laughter, even as his eyes misted. He stood and gazed at the portrait of his father behind his desk, painted with such devotion by his mother.

"You old devil," he breathed in wonder. Apparently, neither fate nor serendipity played any role in he and Emma finding one another, just the over-ambitious and hopeful will of his father.

Now, upon discovering this, and rather than feeling as if he'd been hoodwinked into his coming marriage, he only laughed yet more. He felt not deceived or tricked; he felt blessed. Just as it didn't matter that Emma and he had different standings, or came from different backgrounds, it didn't matter how it came to be. Zach was only thankful that it *had* come to be.

And yes, he would thank the old man when next he saw him.

It was several moments before he recalled that his butler had delivered two items. He scanned the words, penned in his bride's pretty script, upon the second envelope, which was attached to a small and flat, neatly wrapped package.

To be opened after vows are said. I love you. E

Epilogue

"Father! Father!"

Zachary Benedict heard the shrill cry of Bethany, coming from somewhere deeper in the house, as he strode down the stairs, carrying his youngest, sweet little Anna, fresh from her nap.

Bethany burst into the foyer from the first-floor parlor. "Father! Oh, there you are." She met him at the bottom of the stairs and turned her dazzling blue eyes to him. He saw an argument in his very near future. "Mother says I may not go to Amelia's house for the weekend. She thinks their country house party is no more than a shallow ruse to mislead some young man into dastardly behavior which might see a poor, unsuspecting girl wed not to the man of her dreams."

"Oh, dear," he said, and bit back a laugh. He consulted Anna's expression, to find his little blue-eyed sweetheart staring groggily at her sister. To Bethany, he mused, "She said all that, did she?"

He continued on, moving away from the stairs to find his wife, the one who was sometimes entirely too explicit with their children, even as it often worked to great effect.

"She did," Bethany griped, following beside him, clearly wanting to state so much of her case before they were in the presence of her mother once more. "I'm fourteen now, father. You said yourself I possess solid judgment and a principled breadth of reason. You said you trusted me to always behave appropriately, so why should she—"

Her words stopped abruptly as *she*, the countess, appeared at the doors to the parlor only seconds before Zach would have pushed it open.

"*She* also trusts your judgment and decision making capabilities," Emma said pointedly to her daughter, with a strict frown at her, "but she does not trust that of many young men, who are led not with their minds and hearts at this age."

Bethany groaned and tipped her head back, her expression displaying effectively her disagreement with her mother's statement.

Emma turned to Zach and Anna, her face dissolving instantly into first, motherly adoration, as she claimed her smiling baby from Zach's arms. She kissed Anna's soft and downy hair and fixed her gaze onto her husband of more than a decade, her smile now intimate and happy.

Zach's heart flipped.

Oh, but he was a lucky man.

He leaned in and met her lips, lingering longer than he should have, until he felt Emma's mouth curve with a smile at the length of this kiss, until he heard Bethany's, "Ugh," just before she stomped away from them, into the parlor.

"No house parties?" He asked, his voice low, as he knew the room behind was filled with little pictures with big ears—all their children.

"No. Not at fourteen years of age, and with you and I having previously decided that Amelia's parents are about as useless as guardians as would be a dressmaker's mannequin."

"Right," he agreed, vaguely recalling that conversation.

Emma was a loving, but ever-vigilant mother. Their children may not always like her answers or rules, but they could never doubt they were cherished so greatly.

They stepped into the drawing room, where the other children, Caralyn and Michael and Will, were gathered around Mrs. Smythe, who had served brilliantly as their nurse since Mr. Smythe had passed just before Emma had brought their eldest, Michael, into the world. The former innkeep's wife, who seemed not to have aged a day since he'd first met her, and who delighted in the Benedict children, had her gray head pressed against three light brown heads as they peered earnestly at some gadget Mrs. Smythe held.

"Will's dragon lost its wing again," Emma explained.

Zach squinted, seeing now that Mrs. Smythe indeed was trying to re-attach the moveable part into the socket of the toy dragon's body.

Emma sat on the floor as she often did, neatly spreading out her skirts while she gathered nearby toys with which to amuse Anna, who had just started sitting up on her own.

The four heads pressed together lifted all at once, with Mrs. Smythe proclaiming, "Aha!" while Will screeched in delight. Young Caralyn smiled happily for this successful endeavor and Michael watched his brother skitter away, flying the toy around the room.

Zach picked up two beekeeper helmets from the chair and set them on the table. He sighed, having repeatedly asked his boys to not leave them lying around. He sat down in the chair, close to Emma, close enough that his leg touched her. She scooched over, turning just enough to rest her arm upon his thigh.

Bethany sat next to Mrs. Smythe, in the spot Will had vacated. Mrs. Smythe had pulled to her feet the basket of their never-ending needlework. The house—the world!—did not need another doily or sampler or snippet of fine embroidery, Zach often thought. Yet he understood the inevitability of the chore, which allowed the ladies to practice not only their handicrafts, but also their patience, and vocation to polite chatter, of which there was plenty.

"Father," Bethany said, her voice beseeching, "Will you please talk to mother about this weekend?"

"I would, sweet," he granted, lifting her face, until he finished, "but I happen to agree with her." Her crestfallen expression was nearly enough to break him, until he proposed, "Perhaps you should consult with your mother about having a weekend house party *here* and inviting Amelia to spy upon the festivities with you at *your* home."

Bethany's eyes widened. She hugged her clenched hands to her chest while her face lit up, smiling happily at her father. And then to her mother, "Please. Can we?"

"We can certainly consider the idea," Emma allowed. "I suppose we might be due to entertain in grand fashion again."

Zach moved his hand, settled it upon Emma's shoulder. She turned her eyes to him, beaming at his clever solution. She shifted her gaze again, back to Bethany.

"It requires a lot of work," she cautioned.

"*Of which we are not afraid*," chimed three of their five children, as it was a statement Emma repeated often to them.

She grinned, her face in profile to Zach's hungry gaze.

God, how he adored her. Just absolutely loved everything about her.

"Why do you always look at mother that way?" Will asked, screwing up his face, his hand arrested mid-air, the carved wooden dragon paused mid-flight.

Zach wrenched his gaze from his wife. "Which way is that, son?"

"Like you're sore at her about something. Did Mother scold you as well today?"

"She did not," Zach answered, keeping a straight face. "Or, she hasn't as of yet. I like looking at your mother. I think she's the most beautiful woman on the face of this earth."

His wife turned to him, gave him his own smile, the one that made him want to kiss her in such a way that would require complete and prolonged privacy.

The children groaned and Mrs. Smythe chortled, and Zach calmed his expression, deciding his heated and greedy gaze ought to be tamed in front of his ever curious and incredibly observant children.

He sighed, a contented man. Content? No, he was not content. That was entirely too tame for the joy he'd known over the last decade and more, with Emma Elizabeth Ainsley as his wife.

Just this morning, he'd come across an old notecard he kept tucked away in his billfold. It was never removed more than a few inches from the leather pocket. Occasionally, he would unfold the faded and aged vellum of pale blue. He would read again her words to him on the day of their wedding, the little note having been attached to a small gift, a book on beekeeping. He'd since lost or misplaced the book, he wasn't sure; having shared it with his sons, it might be anywhere. But that little note was with him always.

Likely, after all these years, he'd read the words hundreds of times. Perhaps before he became only ashes in the ground, he'd have read them a thousand times more. He knew them by heart, heard them in his sleep, he was convinced. He strove every day to make sure he lived up to her words, her expectations, to the hard truth that he didn't deserve her, and must every day, earn her.

He closed his eyes and saw it again, the sentence set so prettily onto the paper in her delicate script.

I had a dream and it was you.

The End

Also by Rebecca Ruger

Regency Rogues; Redemption

When She Loved Me
If I Loved You
She Will Be Loved

Highlander Heroes

The Touch of Her Hand
The Memory of Her Kiss
The Shadow of Her Smile

Printed in Great Britain
by Amazon

49014782R00189